Taking Charge

Also by Ruth Cardello

Lone Star Burn

Taken, Not Spurred

Tycoon Takedown

Taken Home

The Legacy Collection

Maid for the Billionaire

For Love or Legacy

Bedding the Billionaire

Saving the Sheikh

Rise of the Billionaire

Breaching the Billionaire: Alethea's Redemption

The Andrades

Come Away with Me

Home to Me

Maximum Risk

Somewhere Along the Way

Loving Gigi

Recipe for Love (Holiday Novella)

A Corisi Christmas (Holiday Novella)

The Barrington Billionaires

Always Mine

Stolen Kisses

Trade It All

Trillionaires

Taken by a Trillionaire

Temptation Series

Twelve Days of Temptation

Be My Temptation

LONE STAR BURN

RUTH CARDELLO

Montlake
Romance

Published by Montlake Romance, Seattle

www.apub.com

Amazon, the Amazon logo, and Montlake Romance are trademarks of Amazon.com, Inc., or its affiliates.

ISBN-13: 9781503939615
ISBN-10: 1503939618

Cover design by Janet Perr

Printed in the United States of America

To my loving husband, who often jokes that I base all of my heroes on him. This time I did. Thank you for waiting for me, standing by me, laughing with me, and making every year better than the last. Nothing feels impossible with you at my side.

Prologue

Gorgeous men don't flock to a town like Mavis. They don't even drive through. I would have showered today if I'd known one finally would.

Lucy held the door handle of her ranch home in one hand while she brought the other up to smooth her hair down. It sprang back defiantly, wildly. *Probably because I didn't shower yesterday, either. What day is today? Thursday? Monday? God, I'm a mess.*

You'd think I'd be back to normal by now.

Does normal return?

Maybe not. It hasn't for Steven.

Her brother, wherever he was hiding that day, was no longer the man he'd been before their father had passed. Like Lucy, he'd always dreamed of more than the ranch they'd been born on. Her parents had blamed the Internet and television for why both of their children had spent more time planning how to leave than learning the business side of ranching. They'd both left, too, as soon as they were old enough. Lucy had gone to college in New England while Steven went west to California. She'd chosen a business path, and he'd studied how to create video games.

Lucy and Steven used to joke that they'd both been switched at birth. That in some far-off city there were parents who couldn't understand why their children dreamed of riding horses and raising cattle.

After their father died, Steven and Lucy, both worried about their mother, had come home, but Steven had been the one to take over running the family business. Lucy had done her best to help her mother through her grief, and, proud like their father, Steven hadn't asked for help with the ranch.

She'd never forget the day he told her how behind he was in the mortgage payments. She'd seen how deeply his pain ran when he'd explained how leaving had been his first mistake—at least in the eyes of their parents—but thinking he could step into his father's shoes had been his worst failure, according to the bank.

I shouldn't have accepted it every time he told me things were fine. I had wanted it to be true, but I should have known better. No matter what he said, I shouldn't have let him try to do everything himself.

Then he wouldn't be off in some bar today drinking himself to death the way Mom did. And I wouldn't be a shell of my old self, waiting for him to leave me as well.

Which brings me here, to answering the door of my home, unshowered and unable to remember how long it has even been since I bothered to.

The tall blond man standing in her doorway removed his Stetson and smiled at her kindly. He introduced himself, but Lucy didn't focus on his words. His deep voice felt far away, as if she were watching herself meet him. A part of her appreciated the wide, muscular expanse of his shoulders and the strength he exuded. He looked like a man who was not only used to manual labor but also comfortable in his own skin. The flicks of excitement that tickled through her surprised her. She hadn't felt anything but sadness and anger in so long, she'd forgotten what it was like to be excited about anything.

She clasped her hands together and watched the beautiful man continue to explain why he was there. Perhaps it was the number of nights she'd gone without sleep, but she fought back a punchy laugh. Her friends in Fort Mavis had sent this man, David Harmon, to help her save her ranch. Her old roommate from Rhode Island, Sarah Dery, was about to marry a local, world-famous horse trainer and was probably the happiest person in Texas. She also had a huge heart. It wasn't a surprise that she'd go this far to help Lucy. *How do I tell her that the ranch is fine now, but I'm falling apart?*

Lucy was broken.

Defeated.

The only reason she still had her ranch was the kindness a neighbor, Ted York, had shown. He'd given her a substantial loan when the bank would have evicted them. Steven had wanted to refuse his money. He'd suggested they both walk away from the ranch. Lucy hadn't been able to. Her promise to her mother was all she had left to hold on to, the last shred of anything that made sense.

She could hear her mother's voice in her head, asking her where her manners were and suggesting she invite the man inside or at least offer him a lemonade. Her mother had considered herself a Southern lady. Lucy doubted she'd ever looked or smelled the way her daughter presently did.

"Lucy Albright?" David asked, as if he wasn't sure.

She wished she could deny it. "Yes."

"You look like you're not feeling well. Do you need someone to run to the pharmacy for you?"

"No, I have medicine here." *Crap. I should have said yes. That would have given me time to shower.* Lucy looked down at her cutoff jeans and ratty college T-shirt she'd thrown on, seeking comfort. Sick sounded better than the reality. She coughed into a fisted hand, then lied while looking directly into his eyes. "It's probably best, though, that you don't come in. I could still be contagious." She tried unsuccessfully to once again tame a wild side of her hair.

My life is in shreds. Why do I care what he thinks?

Tired as it was, Lucy's body knew why. It wasn't simply that he was an attractive man; there was an instant sexual tension that invigorated her. She momentarily felt free from all that had happened until she caught a whiff of herself and reality slapped her in the face. "I could use ginger ale if you wouldn't mind making a trip to town. It's about fifteen minutes south of here." *Not that I will look much better, no matter how much soap I use.*

He replaced his hat and nodded. "Is there anything else you need?"

Lucy's stomach tightened pleasurably. Her mouth went dry. She held back another laugh as she pictured what he'd say if she told him what she was imagining they could do together. Then she shook her head in self-disgust. *Why am I torturing myself like this? Do I really think someone like that would want someone like me? He is probably scrambling to think of an excuse to drop off the ginger ale and run back to Fort Mavis. I should seal the deal and ask him to pick up tampons while he's there.*

She reached into a pocket of her shorts for the ten-dollar bill she remembered putting there earlier. When she pulled it out, a tear-soaked tissue clung to it for a moment, then floated to the floor. As if in slow motion, they both watched its agonizingly awkward descent. Their eyes met again while she held out the bill to him. "Please take some money for that."

"Uh—I've got this."

So that's how this plays out—we'll pretend things aren't as bad as they are. Just like when you're eating a salad and accidentally spit a leaf out on an acquaintance. You know they know where it came from. It's better for both of you to pretend it never happened, though, rather than lean over and try to brush it off their cheek. Some things only get more painful the more you acknowledge them.

Lucy closed the door after David left and sagged against it.

I have thirty minutes to shower. Clean clothes. Clean hair. She glanced at herself in the mirror in the hallway. *Makeup might hide the dark circles under my eyes. Might.*

Is it better to still look sick?

Lucy pushed herself off the door and raced up the stairway to her bedroom. *Nothing will change no matter how I look. Mascara or no mascara, I'll still be me when he returns.*

What a cruel twist to meet a man I could feel something for at a time when I'm too numb to feel anything.

Her body countered with a residual hum at the memory of David. *Besides that.*

Why can't I feel this way with Ted? She'd tried to tell herself that Ted had offered her a loan because he was a good friend, but she suspected he wanted more. Since she'd returned home, Ted had been a frequent visitor at the ranch. His friendship had made being home bearable. There had been a look of anticipation in his eyes when he'd offered to help her that made her feel guilty about accepting money from him.

He wanted more than friendship from her.

He'd taken her acceptance of money from him as a sign that she wanted more, also.

She was already feeling guilty that she felt nothing toward Ted.

David has to go.

Before I hate myself more than I already do.

If that's even possible.

A short time later, David returned with a bag of groceries. Lucy offered to take it from him, but he insisted that she sit and relax at the kitchen table while he put the soup, saltines, Popsicles, bread for toast, and ginger ale into the fridge and cabinets. He placed a bottle of ibuprofen on the counter along with a box of tissues and then said, "You look like you're feeling a little better." His eyes fell to the wound she'd inflicted on her leg while rushing to shave. Lucy glanced down and saw that it had started to bleed again. He handed the box of tissues to her. "Do you need me to pick up anything else for you?"

Just my pride from the floor. Lucy ripped the box open and held a tissue to her cut. "Thank you. I am feeling better. I appreciate you getting food for me."

"Sarah said you were going through a tough time." He looked at her with sympathy.

"Nothing I can't handle."

"You don't have to weather this alone. I've managed Carlton's ranch for a long time. If you need someone to help you look over your books or come up with a plan for how to repay the bank . . ."

Lucy's face burned at the humiliating idea of her situation being discussed by people who didn't even know her. "The bank is no longer an issue, but I appreciate your concern. I'm sorry you came all this way. I have everything under control now. I should have called Sarah and told her I'd found a solution, but I didn't know she'd send someone here." Lucy smiled sadly. "She's a good friend."

"Yes, she is. She speaks highly of you, too. She said you two met in college."

The mention of college brought back memories of happier times. "We did. Although that feels like a lifetime ago." Lucy pushed herself back to her feet. Part of her wanted him gone now, but she was also grateful that he'd driven all the way from Fort Mavis to check in on her. "It's a long drive home for you, isn't it?"

David shrugged. "I rented a room in town."

Of course you did. Sarah probably made you promise to stay until I'm okay. Go home, David. Lucy swallowed hard. "If I felt better, I'd show you Mavis."

"My schedule is open. I don't mind hanging around until you're back on your feet."

Lucy's breath caught in her throat, and she swayed. There was something heady about the idea of a man like David taking care of her. What would it feel like to rest her head on those broad shoulders? To have those strong arms close around her? Her gaze went to his lips. *To feel any part of him on any part of me.*

If I were actually sick, you could be my cure. Rub yourself all over my chest, like Vicks.

She pressed her lips together. *But I'm not sick. I'm fucked.*

And apparently delusional now.

"That's a kind offer, but, really, I'm fine."

There was a stubbornness in his beautiful blue eyes. "I told Sarah I'd make sure you're okay. I wouldn't feel right about leaving before I can say you are." He picked up a pen and a piece of paper from the counter. As he wrote, he said, "This is my phone number. Get some rest today, and I'll take you to lunch tomorrow. If you need anything before then, call me."

He handed the paper to Lucy. The brush of his hand against hers sent unwelcome shivers of desire through her. Passion lit his eyes, and everything else faded away. For a moment, she was just a woman who wanted a man. Sexy. Young. Alive.

And he wanted her with the same intensity.

I can't do this.

How would this make anything better?

All it would do is hurt Ted. Even if I don't feel this way about him, he has been kind to me. He deserves better. I'll find a way to pay him back and break it to him gently that I'll always care about him, but I don't want more than friendship.

"I probably won't feel much like eating tomorrow or seeing anyone, either." Lucy sighed. Nothing about where she was or what she was doing felt good.

His eyes held hers, and Lucy's heart began to pound wildly. "I'll call you. You might feel better in the morning."

Lucy couldn't imagine how she could, but she found herself agreeing. Really, when he stood there, looking down at her that way, she didn't have the strength to deny him much.

She paced the downstairs of her house for a long time after David left. She should have said no to him. She should have sent him back to Fort Mavis. Instead, she would likely spend the rest of the day thinking about him, anticipating his phone call, and hoping she hadn't found the only way to make her situation worse.

That morning, she'd woken up numb, as if she were slowly dying from the inside out. She'd yearned to feel something, anything.

She could have, however, done without the lonely ache that meeting David had left her with.

A week later, David sat at a table in a restaurant in Fort Mavis along with some of the men who worked for him on Tony Carlton's horse ranch. There was a time when they used to gather off property to discuss the business side of training and selling horses because the climate on the ranch had been hostile, but that had changed when Tony met his fiancée, Sarah Dery.

A good woman could do that to a man. She could change the way he saw everything. Until he'd met Lucy, David had thought his place was in Fort Mavis, but after spending a day with her, he wasn't so sure. She was all he could think about.

Lucy was a complicated woman who was going through a difficult time. David admitted to himself that she brought out a protective side of him. He'd never been one to walk away from someone in need, but Lucy's hold over him was much more than that.

Yes, she was beautiful. She had large dark-brown eyes a man could lose himself in. Her body was rounded in all the right places. And that hair—long, thick, and wild. He'd imagined it spread across his bed while he made love to her again and again.

That part of their relationship would come soon, he hoped. For now, it was enough that she was beginning to trust him. She said she wasn't ready to see him again yet. If the breathless way she answered his calls was anything to go by, whatever was holding her back wouldn't for much longer.

His fascination with her hit him on every level. He admired her for coming back to care for her mother after her father had died. She could have sold the family ranch and moved back to the city, but she'd stayed out of a sense of duty to family. The more he learned about her, the more he wanted to make her his. And not just for a night; although that would be a fine place to start.

He smiled down into his coffee. He and Lucy had gone to lunch at a restaurant similar to the one he was presently at. After a tense drive into town, and twenty minutes or so of awkward conversation, Lucy had finally relaxed around him.

They'd sat and talked long after finishing their meal. Two cups of coffee later, they were laughing and sharing childhood stories. It had been hard to reconcile the woman across the table from him with the one who'd answered the door the day before. He'd almost said as much, but stopped himself. He wasn't sure any woman would see the compliment in that observation.

He remembered how Lucy had played with the spoon beside her coffee cup. "I was a challenging child. My mother always said I would do the exact opposite of whatever she told me to. She called it stubbornness, but I like to think of myself as spirited. I used to be, anyway." Her expression had momentarily turned sad, but she forced a smile. "I bet you were easy to raise."

Not quite. "I wouldn't say that, but like a good whiskey, I've gotten better with age."

Lucy had blushed and looked away. "That's a healthy ego you're sporting."

That's not all I'm sporting. David had kept that thought to himself, too. He wasn't used to being so turned on simply by sitting next to a woman. He didn't believe in love at first sight, but he'd never experienced anything close to how Lucy made him feel. Every time she touched him, even if it was as innocent as resting her hand on his forearm, his blood pounded and his cock jumped to attention. The more she spoke, the more he wanted to hear her voice. There was a natural easiness about being with her, a feeling he'd known her longer than a day. It didn't make sense. It didn't need to. It simply was.

Leaving her that night had been one of the hardest things he'd ever done. He'd come close, so close, to kissing her, but something in her expression had stopped him. Even though he was certain she felt the same way he did, she was holding back. Not scared. Nothing as simple as that. There was a sadness in her eyes, and some confusion, too. When he'd asked her what was wrong, she pulled away.

She'd thanked him for coming up to see her as if they hadn't just spent the most incredible day together. She said she appreciated that he'd come all that way to offer her help, but that she didn't need it. When he tried to push for how she'd solved the situation, she withdrew from him again. It had been a confusing end to their time together, so David hadn't been happy when he left.

By the time he parked his truck in the driveway of the Double C in Fort Mavis, he'd rationalized her reaction. She was, indeed, going through a rough time. She'd lost both of her parents. She hadn't spoken much of how her brother was doing, but that was also telling. Sarah had said Steven wasn't doing well. With all of that on her plate, it was no wonder Lucy wasn't ready to jump into a relationship. She needed time to heal.

He called her that night and every night that week. She was a hard woman to get to know, but she was slowly opening up to him. David didn't ask to return yet. That would come in time. What they were building was just as important as how good he knew that first kiss would feel. Lucy needed a friend, and if that's where she wanted them to start, that's where he'd begin.

"That must be a mighty good coffee for you to smile at it like that," Lucas said. He was in his early twenties and had worked with David since the day after he'd left high school. At David's encouragement, he'd recently gotten a degree in animal husbandry.

David looked up, caught, but not embarrassed at Lucas's quick sense of humor. He didn't bother to try to hide his smile. For the first time in a long while, he was simply happy. "It is. It really is."

Austin, another ranch hand who had been around long enough to appreciate the way they joked, added, "He's been like this ever since he came back from Mavis."

Austin's brother, Gunner, shook his head in mock disgust. "Don't try to ask him something from eight o'clock until midnight. He has that phone glued to his head with that same stupid look on his face."

They froze as if anticipating a verbal smackdown from David, but he just smiled.

Lucas chuckled. "So, if you're all in love or whatever, what are you doing here and not there?"

David looked down at his coffee again and pictured Lucy's expression the last time he'd seen her. "Some things shouldn't be rushed."

The men around him scoffed. David raised his eyes, not minding their comments. He was their boss, but they were also a family of sorts. "Someday, when your testicles finally descend, you'll understand. This is the one. Don't ask me how I know; I just do. I'm going to marry Lucy Albright."

Chapter One

Six months later

It's all me now. I have to make this work.

Lucy piled the last of the delivered boxes in the corner of what had once been her father's home office. One of her hands lingered on the top of a box. *Things are about to change around here. Do I have what it takes to start a home business?*

Home. Not too much remained of the original furniture passed down through five generations of Albrights. It had taken the sale of every heirloom to hold off the bank before Ted had stepped forward with a loan.

They say cowgirls don't cry, but that's a lie. They don't cry in public. They don't post their woes on social networks or burden their friends, but that doesn't mean they don't sob into their pillows at night. A person could only cry so much, though, before it started to change them. Just like a horse that stayed down too long, a person could be down so long they forgot how to get up.

That won't be me.

No one has to teach me about hard work or surviving tough times. I can muck stalls from dawn until dusk without a break. I can shoot a rifle with deadly accuracy. I'm a survivor.

Six months of living on her own had changed her. She wasn't afraid anymore. She still had more bad days than good, but she was determined to change that.

I don't blame Steven for leaving. We should have told Mom we didn't want this place instead of promising we'd keep it for our children. We wanted to cheer her up. We thought there'd be time later to remind her of how completely ill-suited we were to take it over.

A person could only hurt so much before they looked for a way to make themselves feel better. Steven had turned to alcohol just like their mother had. Thankfully, he'd left Mavis before it could claim his life as well. Wherever he was, she hoped he was putting his life back together, just as Lucy was determined to.

She sat on a folding chair and propped her feet up on one of the large boxes that had been delivered that morning. *If only*—a person could waste their life away on "if onlys." *If only my father hadn't been too stubborn to go to the doctor, he might not have died in the living room while arguing with my mother about something that clearly didn't matter in the end.*

If only my mother hadn't turned to alcohol for comfort, she might not have crashed the night of the storm.

If only my brother had come to me earlier before things had become so bad I couldn't fix them alone.

If only I could stop thinking about a man who has most certainly forgotten about me. An image of David Harmon came back with painful vividness. Attending her friend Sarah's wedding had brought Lucy face-to-face with another regret. It was impossible not to think of David without wishing life were different. Tall, blond, and rugged, with eyes so blue it was near impossible to look into them and remember what one was saying. *If only we'd met before my whole life fell apart.*

I shouldn't be thinking about David like that while I'm engaged to another man.

Lucy rubbed her hands over her tired eyes. *Problem is, I shouldn't be engaged.*

Her cell phone rang. *Speak of the devil.* It was Ted York. Lucy placed her phone back in her jeans pocket. Her neighbor was in his late twenties and attractive enough—a good, church-going man who hadn't pressured Lucy for sex even though they'd been engaged for nearly six months.

But I don't love him. I tried to.

Ted had proposed when Lucy's brother had left, and Lucy had clung to his support. She'd hit rock bottom, and saying yes had felt like the only way she'd survive. She'd been honest with him about not loving him, but he said he cared for her enough that they could make it work. She'd wanted to please him and had almost convinced herself she did love him—until she saw David again at the wedding.

I've made so many mistakes. So many stupid, stupid mistakes.

I could have refused his help. I could have found a way to make the ranch profitable on my own.

What do I know about ranching?

Mom, if you'd known how it would all turn out, would you still have asked me to promise to hold on to this place? I'm the last person anyone should ask to save anything. I've done a bang-up job of making a mess of things.

Lucy wiped away one lone tear and laughed sadly. *Poor Ted. I need to tell him the truth. What do you say when you realize you don't love a man even though he stepped in when everyone else left?* Ted's help had gone beyond the loan to ensure the ranch's survival. He'd sent his own men to handle everything for her. In the past six months, she hadn't needed to be involved at all in the day-to-day running of the ranch. Ted had said he would take care of everything, and he had. *Can't hate a man like that.* Lucy blinked back more tears. *Why can't I love him?*

Lucy remembered the many times her parents had warned her that her dreams got in the way of seeing what was important in life. If her mother had been alive to ask, Lucy knew exactly what she'd say about Lucy's engagement to Ted. *It was the right thing to do.*

She could hear her mother's voice in her head: "Life is full of tempting, bad choices. You steer clear of those. You hear me, Lucy?"

Tempting, bad choices.

Like foolishly wanting a man she'd only met a handful of times. Letting David into her dreams at night made her feel worse instead of better. Memories of him tortured her, mocking her each time she tried to tell herself she could be happy with Ted.

Yes, David was handsome, but her mother had always said physical attraction was like a rainbow—beautiful but fleeting, and not something a person builds a life around.

Ted says he loves me. Shouldn't that mean something to me?

Declarations like that aren't supposed to make a person sad, are they? Lucy was filled with shame and regret each time he spoke of their future together. *I should have said no when he asked me to marry him. I'm not a person who takes the easy way out.*

At least, I never used to be.

Lucy clenched her hands and looked around the room. In her head, she directed her words at the only thing she had left—the house. *I promised I'd do whatever I needed to hold on to you, and I will, but I won't do it the way my mother would have approved of. I'll do it my way.*

And alone.

It's time I stopped thinking about what I don't have and take control of what I do. It's not too late. Thank you, Sarah, for waking me up to that.

She spoke with Sarah frequently. Never about David. Sometimes about Steven.

Often about Ted, but it was impossible not to feel desperate and trapped when talking to the oh-so-happy Sarah. The last time they'd spoken, Lucy had blurted that out—along with the rest of what she'd been holding in. She had finally shared with Sarah how she felt about Ted, how when he'd first stepped forward to help her, Lucy had told him she couldn't love anyone. She had admitted that Ted had said he loved her enough for both of them.

And I said yes, even though I knew it was the wrong choice.

A tempting, bad choice I regret.

"You can't marry a man you don't love," Sarah had exclaimed.

Lucy had answered, "I don't know what to do. After all he's done for me, the public embarrassment alone would be enough to make him hate me." *And I don't need another reason to feel worse about myself.*

"He'll get over it. Trust me, a man would rather be a little embarrassed than find himself married to a woman who doesn't love him."

Lucy had smiled. "You've got a lot to learn about Texan men, even though you're married to one. I swear the reason most of them settled here was they were too proud to turn their wagons around and go home."

Her joke hadn't lessened any of the tension in the conversation. "You have to tell him, Lucy."

Lucy had sighed. In that moment, she'd acknowledged the truth to herself. "I know."

I know.

There wasn't another person on the planet Lucy would have shared so much with, but once she had started, the rest poured out. "I owe Ted a lot of money. If he wants me to pay him back now, I'll lose everything. I can't run this ranch by myself, and I don't have any of the old ranch hands. Walking away from him will bring everything crashing back down. Am I making a mistake? Maybe I should be grateful I found a way to survive at all."

"Never ever settle for survival. Every problem has a solution. All you need is to find a way to bring in some income," Sarah had said, as if it were the simplest thing to do.

"I've tried." Waitressing wouldn't bring in the type of money she needed, and the town didn't have the kind of jobs she'd gone to school for. It was the lack of opportunity that had been the largest reason she'd left. Ironically, she now saw it as the reason why she might lose what she'd once walked away from.

"The world is online now," Sarah had said, "and you should be, too. What about a franchise business you can run from your home?"

And just like that the world had opened to Lucy again. Sarah had always believed anything was possible. She reminded Lucy of herself before her parents' deaths. So positive. So sure everything always worked out for the best.

Lucy stood and walked to the window of her father's office. *Never ever settle for surviving.*

So easy to say.

Still, Sarah's words had echoed through Lucy many times after that day. If the past year had taught Lucy anything, it was that surviving was just a slow way of dying.

With renewed determination, she spent the next week researching ways she could make money online. She found an online start-up business and used the last money in her bank account to invest in it. Outside of somehow making the franchise financially successful enough to pay Ted back and float the ranch, there was only one thing left to do.

Lucy took out her phone again and called Ted.

"Hello, sunshine," he said.

Simply calling me that proves how little he knows me, how very well I've hidden my desperation from him. "Ted, we need to talk. Could we meet somewhere?"

"Today isn't good. Too much going on here."

"It's important."

"You don't know what important is, Lucy. Whatever is bugging you, we'll talk about it this weekend when you come to dinner with my parents."

"It can't wait that long. It's about the wedding."

Ted sighed impatiently. "Are you still upset about my mother wanting you to wear her wedding dress? I won't discuss it again. Starting a marriage by offending my mother is not the ideal way to enter my family."

Yeah, about that. "I can't marry you, Ted."

Ted's voice rose. "What do you mean you can't?"

"I'm not ready to get married. Not to you. Not to anyone." *Lame, but all I have.*

He fell silent for a long moment. "If choosing your dress is that important to you, then I guess we can throw good money away on it."

Lucy covered her face with one hand. *God, I'm a coward to do this on the phone.* "I don't care about the dress, Ted. I don't want to get married."

There was another painfully long pause. "Is there someone else?"

Lucy refused to give the memory of David that kind of importance. "No. I feel awful, but I tried to tell you that I'm not myself right now. I don't have anything to give anyone."

"If you need more time . . ."

"Time won't change my mind."

With an angry snarl, Ted asked, "What changed? The idea of marrying me wasn't so awful when I was paying off your loan."

"That's not fair." *It's what I deserve to hear, I guess. Still, it's not how I want him to see it.* "You know I appreciate everything you've done."

"I don't want your damn appreciation, Lucy. I thought we were building something together. Hell, you're wearing my grandmother's diamond ring. Now you want to call the wedding off for no reason at all. I've been good to you, haven't I? My family has taken you in as one of their own. What is so wrong that you're willing to throw all that away?"

"I don't love you, Ted." *There, I said it. He'll thank me one day.*

The sound of his indrawn breath was a hiss.

Lucy rushed to say something, anything that would make him feel better. "I can't tell you how grateful I am to you for all you've done for me. I'll pay you back. I swear I will. I'll just need a little time."

Ted's voice was tight with emotion. "You still have your ranch because of me, Lucy. My men have been there as much as at my own place. If you walk away from me, you'd better be damn sure you're ready to stand on your own." He didn't sound like a man about to lose the woman he loved. He sounded like a businessman who realized a deal was going south.

Lucy told herself it was because she'd hurt him. "I am. I'm sorry, Ted."

In a steely voice, he warned, "If you do this, Lucy, I won't take you back."

Did I expect him to beg me to stay? Proclaim that he loves me enough to wait, no matter how long I need? Love *is just a word people say. It never means they'll stay.*

"I understand."

Anger entered his voice again. "I don't know what you learned in those years you spent up north, but around here we treat people better. I should be grateful to discover your lack of character now instead of after the wedding vows."

If he thinks this will make me feel worse, he has no idea how much I already hate myself. "I never meant to hurt you."

"I'll be fine," Ted said, with coldness in his tone. "You're the one I feel sorry for. That ranch is as good as gone now. You won't find anyone else willing to help you. No one besides me gives a shit about you. You and your brother always thought you were better than us. All either of you ever wanted was to leave. Well, here's your chance."

Long after he'd hung up, Lucy stood there shaking. *They say when you hit rock bottom, there is nowhere to go but up. So how do I keep sinking?*

There was very little left that Lucy recognized about herself. The strong independent woman she'd been was now near giving up and so alone, she ached.

She walked over to one of the boxes the postman had delivered and rested a hand on top of it. *Am I an idiot to think I can do this? Or that I should do this? My mother would say she raised me better.*

But she left me, too.

Sorry, Mom, you forfeited the right to lecture me.

She ripped one of the boxes open and took out the tablet that rested on top. After researching the profit margins of many online franchises, she'd come across a start-up that had been looking to partner with a woman willing to market their inventions. The opportunity had everything she was looking for. There was very little up-front investment required; it had substantial potential for large monthly earnings, depending on how well she marketed the items; and the orders would be filled directly from the company. She would be both a partner and a salesperson working on commission. The goal of the company was to be cutting-edge, revolutionizing the market, and to gain a strong following of female clients.

Lucy picked up a bra that had been fashioned to look like a remote control for a video game. Both sides hosted colorful controls that looked functional as well as decorative. She held it to her chest and tried to imagine not slapping a man's hands away if she actually wore it during sex. A laugh erupted from her, but more from nerves than humor.

I can call Ted and tell him my grief confused me. He'd probably take me back.

Or I can do this and prove to myself that I am the person I was back in New England.

I'm smart and I am not beaten yet.

Not by a long shot.

She replaced the bra and took out a set of glow-in-the-dark dildos. Assorted colors and sizes. She read the label. Three settings for light options: "Constant," "Flashing," and "Disco"?

Disco?

She shook her head and tossed the package back in the box. Then she picked up the tablet.

If I leave this ranch, it will be because I choose to, not because I don't have what it takes to hold on to it. You hear that, Mom and Dad? I might not have been the daughter you dreamed you'd have, but you always told me to get up when I fell down. Well, this is me getting up.

She turned the tablet on. An icon for Technically Anonymous Pleasure filled the screen. Lucy scrolled through the table of contents: Company History, Company Contacts, Tax Forms, Product Description.

She took a deep breath and pressed the link to the last section. *If I'm going to sell high-tech sex toys online, I'd better figure out what the heck people do with them.*

Lucy shook her head at her own thought.

Of course I know what they do with them; I just need to learn the particulars of how.

David led a quarter horse through the center aisle of a barn and handed him off to Lucas, who was trying to hide a smile but wasn't quite succeeding. "Lucas, an intelligent man knows when his thoughts are best kept to himself."

Revealing his youthful overconfidence, Lucas tipped his hat back and looked his boss in the eye. "Just not sure why we bother saddling horses when we know they won't be ridden."

David didn't answer the question because he didn't have a polite answer. He liked Lucas. Over the years, the young man had proved himself to be both reliable and good-natured. David's present situation, however, was too much for even those who respected him to contain their amusement. "I'll be in my office." David walked away, retreating into the small, hot barn office he now considered a haven of peace every Thursday.

Life had changed drastically on the Double C Ranch in Fort Mavis. In years past, the ranch had been closed to all outsiders. Tony Carlton, the man who owned the ranch, had purchased it as a place to hide and drink himself to death. After taking over as his ranch manager, David had talked him out of the second part of that plan, but it had taken a sweet Yankee to change Tony's stance on the first part. The pair had married and participated in a variety of high-profile fund-raising events that had opened the doors of the ranch to people of all walks of life. On paper, it sounded like it was for the best, but in practice it had put David into more uncomfortable situations than he cared to reflect on.

A few of the public events had involved Kimberly Staten's father. Regardless of how civil he was, there was nothing pleasant about looking into the eyes of a man who had once fired David for trying to protect his daughter from the horse that ultimately—even being trained by Tony—had killed her. Funny how life tended to circle back to something, no matter how much a person didn't want it to.

Facing Kimberly's father had felt a bit like the first time a reporter had asked him how he'd come to training horses as a career. David had given a vague answer that had satisfied the reporter temporarily, but the question had resurfaced within his circle of friends. He'd told them there was nothing to tell about his life before he'd taken the job with Evan Staten, and then he'd changed the subject. He preferred not to think about the past.

Evan Staten wasn't the reason David dreaded Thursdays, though. No, the fault for that lay squarely on the shoulders of Melanie, Tony's ex-housekeeper, and Sarah, Tony's wife. The two had taken it upon themselves to cure him of his bachelorhood, although they hadn't used those words exactly. They'd asked him if he would give riding lessons on Thursdays as a way of raising funds for the local children's hospital. A man would have to be mighty hard-hearted to refuse such a request, so David had agreed to do it. What he hadn't anticipated was that each Thursday his schedule would be full of women who had very little interest in the only kind of lesson he was offering.

It wasn't that David minded female companionship, but his heart wasn't into dating. The women who showed up each Thursday were looking for a husband. Some were brazen enough to say it. Sarah and Melanie had practically taken out an ad proclaiming him single and financially stable, and in some parts of Texas, that was enough to cause a stampede.

David didn't welcome the attention. Not on Thursdays and not through the fund-raising that was now a regular part of life on the ranch. He didn't want to be the face that was shown when the Double C promoted an event. He'd often accused Tony and Melanie of hiding out on the ranch, but truth be told, he'd withdrawn from the world himself. Life had been much more comfortable when everyone had kept out of each other's business.

David didn't know how much longer he could stay if something didn't change. Lately he'd been thinking it was time to move on. To where, though? Not knowing the answer to that question held him back. All he knew was he was no longer where he wanted to be. Something was missing.

"Knock knock," Sarah said cheerfully as she entered his office without pause.

David turned and tossed his Stetson on his desk. "Not one of the women who came for a riding lesson today was interested in getting on a horse."

Sarah shrugged and smiled. "They paid, though. Think of the good you're doing. Your lesson program brings in thousands every month."

"Thousands?" David arched an eyebrow. "How much do you charge the women to come here?"

With a shameless grin, Sarah said, "I keep raising the price, and they keep agreeing. Does it matter? It's for charity, after all."

David shook his head. "You're misleading them, Sarah. I'm not looking for a wife."

"I tell them that, but they all want a chance at being the one who changes your mind."

David ran a hand through his hair in frustration and sat on the wooden chair by his desk. "I'll never understand the female mind."

Sarah plopped onto the other wooden chair in the small room. "Speaking of women you don't understand, I spoke to Lucy today."

David kept his face deliberately blank. "How is she?"

"Single again. She said she called off her engagement to Ted."

David stood and frowned. *If that bastard did something to hurt her.* "What'd he do?"

"Nothing. She doesn't love him, David." Sarah tended to blurt things out as fast as she thought them. It was something David had become used to over time and *occasionally* appreciated. On a ranch where most people spent years avoiding talking about anything of significance, Sarah was a bubbling well of information—welcomed or not.

David walked to the door of his office and folded his arms across his chest. "Getting engaged to him suggests otherwise."

David took a deep breath. It was far too easy to give in to his memories of Lucy Albright. He remembered every accidental touch, every brush of her skin against his, the way she smelled like lavender and soap, the desire in her eyes when he'd almost kissed her. Seeing her at Sarah's wedding had been torture. They'd been forced to be in the same room often enough for him to be sure he was still powerfully attracted to her.

She'd said at the time they met she wasn't ready for anything more than friendship, but he'd thought he found the woman he'd spend the rest of his life with. He'd been so sure that he'd been careless when it came to concealing his enthusiasm. When news of her engagement to another man hit Fort Mavis, people couldn't help but jabber on about it. Soon everyone in town was convinced David was a jilted soul in need of a good woman to heal his broken heart.

But really, he was just a damn fool who'd imagined something where there'd been nothing.

Sarah walked up to stand beside David. "Lucy doesn't like to talk about her problems, but she has had some rough years lately. Remember how angry I was with her for changing her mind about wanting me to stay with her and her brother that summer? I wouldn't have been if I'd known what she was going through. It was bad enough to lose both her parents, but watching her brother drink and then leave her—that couldn't have been easy."

David didn't answer, but Sarah wasn't expecting him to. She was perfectly happy to keep the conversation going on her own.

"She was alone and scared. Ted was there, offering her a lifeline. Who could blame her for saying yes to him?"

David turned and retrieved his Stetson from his desk, placing it firmly on his head. "She doesn't owe me an explanation, nor do I want to hear any more about this."

He moved to walk out of the office, but Sarah raised a hand and blocked his exit. "You can tell yourself you don't care if she's single again. You can lie to everyone and say you're over her, but how sad would it be if your pride kept you from calling her, and you lost her again?"

Sarah lowered her arm and let David pass. He strode out of the office, out of the barn. He marched up the steps of the bunkhouse, yanked open the door, then slammed it closed behind him.

Only a fool reopens a wound after it's healed over.

Chapter Two

A few days later, Lucy closed the laptop on her father's old desk and stood. She'd gone to Dallas to lay the foundation of her new home business. She'd met with an accountant to create an LLC that would ensure her privacy, opened a bank account in that company's name, and was now in the process of purchasing everything online from domain names to staplers. No one needed to know the nature of her business, and if she was careful enough, no one ever would.

A loud knock on the front door made Lucy jump. She hastily hid a stack of paperwork in the top drawer of the desk and double-checked that the boxes were closed. She closed the office door securely behind her, then paused.

I'm a modern woman. There is nothing wrong with what I'm doing, even if selling it from my hometown makes it feel that way.

She gave herself a quick check in the large mirror in the hall. She'd always been on the curvy side and normally would have loved how the weight had been pouring off her since she'd been home, but there was no glow to the woman who looked back at her in the mirror. Her brown eyes looked tired. Her hair was thrown back in a ponytail instead of styled as she used to wear it in the city. The jeans, which had once clung to her, now hung loose. She'd never considered herself a nervous person, but even as she told herself she had everything under control, she could see how close she was to unraveling. *What if I can't do this alone? What if I fail just like my brother did?*

I'm not my brother, nor am I going to give up like my mother. I can do this.

One step at a time.

Answer the damn door and breathe.

She did and found her father's old foreman standing on her porch. He swiftly removed his hat to reveal his familiar face, toughened from many years of working outdoors. "I know I'm probably about the last person you want to see right now."

"That's not true, Wyatt." Lucy's hand tightened on the door handle. He'd left along with the rest of the ranch hands when Steven had announced he couldn't pay any of them the money he owed them. If she hadn't known Wyatt for most of her life, seeing him again would have been humiliating. Although Ted's loan had made it possible for Lucy to set that right, she hadn't asked the old ranch hands to return. They'd already found alternate employment, mostly via Ted. She'd never blamed any of them for leaving. They had families to feed, and Wyatt, already in his fifties, needed to hold on to whatever work he could get. "Come in." Lucy led the way to her living room. "Would you like a lemonade? Some water?"

"I'm fine, Miss Lucy." He wiped the sweat from his forehead with the side of one hand.

"Would you like to sit?"

"No, I'd rather stand."

"Okay." Lucy braced herself by placing a hand on the back of one chair. Had Ted sent him over with a message? He might be there to collect the engagement ring. That would be incredibly tacky, but perhaps not more so than breaking up with someone over the phone.

"Your parents were good people."

"I know."

"You heard any from your brother?"

Lucy shook her head. He wasn't the curious type. If he was asking, he was doing so because he cared. "He said he needed time to clear his head."

"What are you doing, Miss Lucy? I've known you since you were high as my knee. You never wanted to live here."

Lucy held his eyes steadily. "People change."

He looked her over with a critical eye. "You looked a whole lot happier when you lived in the city. Have you thought about selling?"

Only about a thousand times a day. "Why are you here, Wyatt?" *Please don't let it be with an offer to buy the land. I might just take it.*

Wyatt cleared his throat. "I was in town yesterday, and I heard Miles say his father is buying your herd."

"That's right," Lucy said cautiously. Selling the herd would provide her with enough cash to jump-start her new business as well as partially pay Ted back. It wasn't enough to free her, but she had to believe her business would do that.

"You'd get a better price for them in Abilene."

I would if the men here actually worked for me. They won't do anything on my say-so. They do what Ted tells them to, how he tells them, and when. They don't pay me any mind at all. "I don't have the hands to do it, Wyatt. I'm grateful I found a buyer at all."

Rolling his hat in his hand, Wyatt said, "I could gather some men, and we could haul your herd for you." He was a timeless country gentleman. His jeans, boots, and faded plaid shirt had all seen better days. He was a man who wasn't ashamed to work hard, get his hands dirty, or drop to his knees in gratitude for all he had. The sun had tanned and toughened his skin, making him look older than he was, but his eyes were sharp and bright. His humble strength reminded Lucy of her father. She blinked back a tear.

Wyatt wouldn't say it, but he was risking his job, and they both knew it. *Ted didn't send him.* "I couldn't ask you to do that."

"No asking necessary."

Lucy clasped her hands in front of her. Ted had a reputation for firing men with little provocation. He wouldn't be happy about this. "Wyatt, Ted and I broke up. I'm not his favorite person right now. I'd steer clear of anything to do with me for a little bit."

Wyatt rubbed his chin. "You know I have my son and his wife living with us now, along with my grandbabies."

"I heard they'd moved home," Lucy said in a calm voice, while her stomach continued to do nervous flips.

Wyatt slapped his hat against one thigh. "There's something about looking into the eyes of your offspring that makes you want to be the kind of person they think you are. And my grandbabies think I put the moon up in the sky."

"That's a beautiful thing, Wyatt."

A flash of frustration hardened his face. "Let me speak, Miss Lucy. What I got to say isn't easy."

"Okay."

"I'm relieved to hear you're not marrying Mr. York."

Lucy smiled sadly. *Me too.* "He has been very kind to me."

"You mean he was right quick to take advantage of your situation."

Lucy's eyebrows shot up. She opened her mouth to say something, then closed it as she processed what he'd said. She remembered how Ted had sounded when she'd told him she didn't love him. He had claimed to love her and she'd believed it, but there had been no passion between them. No reason to believe his claim to have always been sweet on her. *"I'll be fine," he'd said. "You're the one I feel sorry for. That ranch is as good as gone now. You won't find anyone else willing to help you. No one besides me gives a shit about you."*

Definitely not the words of a man who had loved her.

Had his proposal been just about her land and not about her at all? *Did I only see what I wanted to see?* "Ted's a good man, Wyatt," Lucy said, but she was no longer sure.

Wyatt held her gaze. "Lucy, I work for him. I know his character. Rumor is that one late payment from you and the ranch is his. Did you sign papers saying that?"

"I don't think so." Lucy moved to sit down in one of the chairs and covered her face. "At the time, I was grateful he was helping. I don't know what I signed." She blinked tears back. "Oh my God. Could I have been that stupid?"

Wyatt moved to sit across from her. He was quiet for a long moment. "It's not stupid to believe people want the best for you, but, sadly, that's not always the case. Your parents were the kind of people who would help someone and ask for nothing in return. They gave me a job when I wasn't the man I am today. Not too many people were willing to take a chance on me back then. My family owes yours a lot. I couldn't sit back and watch you lose this ranch without warning you. Mr. York wants this land, and I'm not comfortable with how far he's willing to go to get it."

"What are you saying, Wyatt? Do you know something?" *Please say no.*

"Just rumors and rumblings, but where there's smoke, there's usually fire. You shouldn't be out here alone. It's not safe."

Lucy straightened her shoulders. "I'm never alone. There's always someone working here."

"York's men. If you and he aren't getting married, why are his men still here?"

A chill went down Lucy's back. "Out of kindness?"

Wyatt let out a guffaw. "Or he already considers it his."

"You don't really believe that, do you?" Lucy hugged her arms across her waist.

"I've got one question, Miss Lucy. Why do you want this ranch? Are you holding on to it for the right reasons?"

Lucy stood and walked to the window. "My parents were married on this land. My family was born and have died here for generations."

"I'm not talking about your family, Miss Lucy. I'm talking about you. Before you go up against a man like Mr. York, you'd better be sure you want what you're fighting for."

Lucy looked out the window of the living room. "I spent most of my life dreaming of life somewhere else, but that changed when I came home. Before my mother died, she told me the only real comfort she had was knowing I had returned home. She said she knew I would do whatever it took to keep the land in our family. I swore to her I would. My parents sacrificed so Steven and I could have this land. Their parents did the same before them. If I walk away from it, everything they gave up was for nothing." Lucy was quiet a moment, then in almost a whisper she added, "I gave my word I'd keep it in the family. I've lost so much; if I lose this place, too, I feel like I might just lose myself. I'm not leaving, Wyatt. If Ted tries to take this land from me, he'll have one hell of a fight on his hands."

Wyatt stood beside her. "Don't know if you realize it or not, but you just sounded a lot like your daddy right then. He's looking down, and he's proud."

Lucy kept her eyes averted. "I'm not so sure of that, but I'm not beat yet. I'm starting a business online. If I do it right, I should be in a better financial place soon."

"What kind of business are you starting?"

Lucy blushed and kept looking out the window. "Just selling knick-knacks online. The company does well, and with my degree I'm hopeful I can, too."

"If it's a business you think you need help running, I imagine I'll soon be unemployed."

Lucy's head snapped around. "I won't tell anyone you were here."

"In a town this small, you won't have to, Lucy. You know that. I don't regret it, though. You needed to know."

"Oh, Wyatt. I wish I could afford to offer you a job right now."

Wyatt squinted while looking out the window. "If I take your herd to Abilene, you'll have money you weren't counting on."

Lucy chewed her bottom lip. Ted would probably fire Wyatt as soon as he heard Wyatt went behind his back to help her. She owed him whatever she could do, but she needed to be honest. "It won't go far. And I don't know how this business will do. I can let you have your old house, though. And you're welcome to stay there as long as you need it. I hate asking you to settle for that little, but it's all I can do right now."

Wyatt held out his work-roughened hand. "I'll take it."

Lucy shook his hand. She would have hugged him if she were the hugging type just for giving her one moment when she didn't feel completely alone. She gave him a small, grateful smile and walked with him to the door. "The house is unlocked. Move in when you want."

Wyatt nodded. "I'll be back tomorrow with some men. Remember what I said. Be careful, Lucy."

After he'd gone, Lucy slumped against the door and covered her face with her hands. It had been hard enough to break off her engagement to Ted, but the idea that he might hurt her to get the property sent a shudder of fear through her. She pushed off the wall, went to her father's gun cabinet, and unlocked it.

She closed her eyes briefly and prayed she was doing the right thing. *A sane person would leave.* She took out her cell phone and considered calling Steven again. He hadn't answered her in months. *I'll make things right, Steven. We haven't failed yet.*

She took out a rifle and placed it behind the coatrack near the door, exactly where her father had always kept it. *I don't need a man to protect me.*

I don't need anyone at all.

Her phone rang just then, and Lucy's hands shook so much, she almost dropped it. She checked the screen and didn't know what to say when she saw who the caller was.

David Harmon.

He'd told himself he wouldn't call her. He'd reminded himself that he barely knew her, and he wasn't the kind of man who chased a woman. But he kept remembering what Sarah had said, *"How sad would it be if your pride kept you from calling her, and you lost her again?"*

Lucy answered, and for a moment he was tongue-tied like some fool teenager trying to talk to his first crush. He cleared his throat. "Lucy, it's David."

When she finally answered, her voice was soft and hesitant. "I know. Caller ID."

He plowed forward. "How are you?"

She let out a shaky breath, then said, "Good. Everything is good. I have to go, David. Thanks for calling."

"Don't hang up. There's something I need to say."

"Oh my God, is it Sarah? Tell me she's okay. I don't know what I'd do if she isn't."

"Sarah's fine. Everyone here is fine." *Shit. I'm fucking this up.*

"Oh, good." Her relief sounded profound, and he felt like an ass for worrying her. For a moment, she sounded as if she were laughing and crying at the same time. "Sorry. I had a rough morning. I'm still a little all over the place."

David's gut twisted, and he pulled his truck over to the side of the road. "Is there anything I can do?"

"No," she answered sadly. "I can handle this on my own."

"You don't have to. You have people in Fort Mavis who care about you." *Me, for example.*

"I appreciate your concern, David, but it's not necessary. What was it you called to say?"

That no matter how hard I try, I can't forget you? You're all I think about before I go to bed at night, and I wake up wanting you. That I haven't been with a woman since I met you because none of them have your smile, your laugh, that perfectly rounded ass of yours. David rubbed a hand over his eyes and shook his head. "I want to see you."

"You can't come here, David. Not now."

"Sarah told me you broke off your engagement. Did you?"

"Yes, but it doesn't change anything."

"I'd say it changes everything."

"I wish I could explain, but I can't, David. It's complicated."

"So let's uncomplicate things. I haven't slept right since I saw you again. I can't stop thinking about how much I want to taste those sweet lips of yours. Tell me you feel the same."

Lucy's voice shook with emotion as if she were on the verge of breaking into tears. "How I feel doesn't matter right now. I can't risk making the situation here worse. I'm sorry."

Fuck. What am I thinking blurting it all out like that? I've been spending too much time with Sarah. "What situation? Talk to me, Lucy." His heart was thudding heavily in his chest. He knew then that whatever was wrong, he'd move heaven and earth to fix it.

"David, do yourself a favor and forget you met me. I'm not in a good place right now. Not in my head. Not in my life. Don't come here. It wouldn't be safe for you." She hung up without saying another word.

David sat in his truck, staring at the long empty road ahead of him. *Not safe? What the hell is she dealing with up there?* The idea of her being afraid of anyone or anything filled him with a protective fury that overrode his normally calm nature.

He called Tony and pulled back onto the road. "Hey, I'm heading out of town. Lucas can cover for me as far as working with the horses. Ask Sarah to cancel my Thursday lessons."

"How long will you be gone?" Tony asked in his usual gruff tone.

"As long as it takes."

"Where're you going?"

Tony's question surprised David. In the many years they'd known each other, they'd deliberately stayed out of each other's business. Tony's curiosity was a testament to how much Sarah had changed him. "Up to Mavis."

"'Bout time."

David couldn't argue that point. "Has Sarah mentioned any kind of trouble?"

"You mean besides Lucy calling off her engagement?"

"Yes. Is she behind with the bank again?"

"Not that I know of. Why?"

"Something is bothering her, and I intend to find out what it is."

"You could ask her," Tony suggested dryly. In any other situation, David would have appreciated Tony's new, less abrasive sense of humor.

"I did. She wouldn't tell me."

"One might take that as a sign of it not being your business."

"She sounded scared. I don't know what's going on up there, but something's not right."

"You want company for the trip?"

"I don't believe so, but I'll call you if I need you to come with a shovel."

Tony laughed even though they both knew David was only half kidding. "Don't go doing anything that gets me in trouble with Dean again. He says he's finally enjoying being a sheriff."

David chuckled at that. "So I shouldn't ask your brother to bring the lime?"

"Oh, he'd bring it; he'd just grumble about it so long you'd wish you brought it yourself. He takes the law real serious lately. If he was here, he'd be lecturing us on talking about this on the phone."

"Nothing wrong with discussing gardening."

Tony laughed again, but when he spoke, his tone was serious. "I'll ask Sarah if she knows anything more than she's said, and I'll call you if I hear anything."

"Sounds good. It's a day's drive, so I won't see Lucy until tomorrow."

"Does she know you're coming?"

"No. She told me it wouldn't be safe for me if I went there."

Tony didn't ask him if that's when he'd decided to go.

They both knew it was.

Chapter Three

The next day, Lucy took an extra-long shower in an attempt to wake herself up after a long sleepless night. No matter how she tried, she couldn't stop going over her conversation with David. Fate had a cruel sense of humor. David was coming back into her life, and she still couldn't do anything about it. If Ted really was dangerous, flaunting another man in front of him would send him over the edge.

Lucy dried her hair and tied it back in a loose ponytail. She donned her jeans and picked a T-shirt out of her closet without much care. Wyatt would be there soon to load up the herd. She didn't know how Ted's men would react when they realized what was going on, but they had no right to stop her. It was her herd, her ranch. There would be no reason for any of them to be on her property after that day. She'd considered telling Ted her plans, but she didn't know what she'd do if he tried to stop her.

She'd found and read over the contract she signed with him. It was just as Wyatt had said. A man in love wouldn't have added that clause, nor would he have swooped in while she was still reeling from her brother leaving. He probably thought she would be an easy mark.

Ted had been right about one thing. She didn't have a lot of friends in Mavis, and the ones she'd grown up with hadn't seen much of her since her return. *My fault, not theirs. When I left, I wanted to leave all this behind, and when I returned, I wasn't anyone I thought they'd want to be around. I'm done beating myself up over things I have no control over. I'm putting my energy into changing what I can—and that starts with me.*

I'm taking charge.

One step at a time. Sell the herd. Pay Ted as much as I can afford. Lay low and get the website up and running so I can pay him the rest.

Save the ranch.

Call Steven and tell him he can come home. Make him see that I understand why he left.

I'll have plenty of time later for hometown friends.

For now, I need to stick to the plan.

Lucy stepped out onto the large porch that wrapped around her house. Two of Ted's men were finishing feeding the cattle as if nothing had changed. They didn't so much as look up in greeting, even though she was pretty sure they'd seen her. Another person might have stormed over and ordered them off her land, even used her shotgun to make her demand heard, but Lucy was determined to win this time. What she lacked in physical strength, she would make up for in intelligence. She'd thought through every action she was about to take, weighed the possible consequences of each, and had carefully chosen her best path.

And it was working. Even if Ted's men had heard she was considering selling her herd, they didn't seem to believe it. By the time the call had come in that the local buyer was no longer interested in purchasing her herd, Lucy had already lined up a sale in Abilene via Wyatt. She had no proof, but she didn't doubt for a second that Ted had been involved in the first deal falling through. *He thinks I'm gullible, easily manipulated, and why shouldn't he? I trusted him when he swooped in and offered to help like some hero in a romance novel. But I see him for who he is now. He wants me to fail, expects me to.* His underestimation of her intelligence and determination was something she could use.

He doesn't think I have any fight left in me.

But I do.

A huge red truck drove up the long driveway, pulling a long stock trailer. Several more followed behind. They began unloading horses and ATVs almost immediately. Wyatt was barking out orders for the men to put up the temporary chutes that would funnel the herd into the trailers. Lucy squared her shoulders and walked across the dirt driveway to greet Wyatt.

She laid her hand on his forearm. "I don't know how I'll ever thank you enough for this, Wyatt. Tell the men I should have the money from the sale by tomorrow."

Wyatt nodded and adjusted his Stetson. "You don't have to thank a man for doing the right thing, Miss Lucy, and you don't have to pay them. Your daddy was a fine man, and he did a lot of good in this community. This is what grows from planting those kinds of seeds."

Lucy blinked back tears. "I haven't done much to deserve this."

Wyatt gave her shoulder a pat. "You've got time, Miss Lucy. You've got time."

One of Ted's men stood in the path of one of Wyatt's while the other was on his phone. Wyatt said, "Looks like I might have to explain to some men that they don't work here anymore."

Lucy turned and squared her shoulders. "I'll do it."

Wyatt stepped in front of her. "Some matters are best handled between men."

Lucy's chin rose. "Wyatt, I appreciate everything you're doing, but this is my ranch, and I need to start acting like it is."

Wyatt moved back to let her pass. "I don't like this one bit, but go on."

Lucy was on her way to do just that when a big red pickup pulled up the driveway and all attention turned to it. *Ted.*

Breathe. This is actually a good thing. He would have never tried to take the land from my father. It's time for him to see he is wasting his time trying to take it from me.

Ted headed right for Lucy. The expression on his face was sad, as if he were indeed a jilted suitor. "Can we speak—privately?"

Lucy looked around at the concerned faces on the men who had stalled their work as they waited for instructions. She nodded. She still had to return Ted's engagement ring, so was that what he was waiting for before admitting it was over between them? She'd spent the last few days vilifying him in her head, but he had saved her ranch when she would have lost it. He could have kept his men at her ranch because he knew she couldn't pay anyone yet. Yes, he'd been harsh when she'd called off their engagement, but he'd been understandably upset. Had it been that male Texan pride that made him lash out at her? She'd been busy chasing her dreams when she was younger and hadn't put aside much time for boyfriends. Sure, her college boyfriend had been all about having sex with her, but Ted was older. Had she confused respect for her with a lack of passion?

And the first sale falling through? It might have been a coincidence. *Which doesn't mean I want to marry him, but I don't have to hate him, either.* They walked into her home, past the shotgun concealed near the door, and Lucy thought, *Or fear him.*

Please let me be right this time.

Lucy picked up a small box she'd placed in the hallway days ago. She held it out to Ted, but he didn't make a move to accept it. "I've been meaning to give this back to you," she said softly.

Ted folded his arms across his chest. "I hoped you would have come to your senses by now. You don't want to end our engagement."

Lucy took a fortifying breath. *Give me the words to do this in a firm but kind way.* "I wish that was true, Ted. You don't know how much I do, but I can't marry you."

"I love you."

Lucy's hand tightened on the jewelry box. "You don't. You might think you do right now, but someday, when you meet the right person, you'll see that what you felt for me wasn't real."

His expression cooled. "Your mind is set?"

She nodded.

He took the ring box and pocketed it. "Give me the east side of your property, the five hundred acres in the valley, and I'll consider your debt to me paid in full."

And there it is, the reason he's here.

Not me.

The land.

The ugly greed in his eyes made Lucy shudder. How had she not seen it earlier? On the surface, he was an attractive-enough man, but it didn't take much to see who he really was.

In that moment of desperation, with her emotions in a tailspin, she considered his offer. Saying yes would free her from him, but it would also give him the water rights to the area. It would cripple any chance of the ranch ever being used for cattle in the future. It was also the place where her great-great-grandparents had built the first family home. There were memories on that land, even a small cemetery. It wasn't an easy yes.

It would be so easy to leave.

Admit that I don't belong here.

But who will I be then?

How far is that from becoming like Steven or my mother?

Lucy shook her head and said, "By tomorrow I'll be able to pay you most of what I owe you. I should have the rest within six months. I'm sorry, but my answer is no."

The calm man of a moment before fell away like a disguise, and his expression twisted in anger. "We could have done this amicably, but you're dead set to make it ugly. If you don't give that land to me, everything that happens after I walk out of here is on your head. You don't want to cross me."

"I'm not afraid of you, and you're not getting my land. Now kindly get out of my house."

Ted firmly placed his hat back on his head. "Oh, I will, but do you know how many of the men out there work for me? All of them. That is, they used to. I wonder how good you'll feel about sitting in your house while you watch them lose theirs."

"You wouldn't do that."

"Consider it done—unless you've changed your mind. No? You've never been very bright, Lucy. I wonder how you'll leave here when you lose—like your brother or like your mother?"

Lucy gasped at the ugliness of his words.

"I've heard enough," a male voice said in a deadly tone.

Lucy swung around. *David.*

He was standing in the doorway beside Wyatt. They both looked angry to the point of violence.

"Who are you?" Ted demanded.

"Someone who can buy and sell your pathetic ass ten times over." David took out a checkbook. "How much does she owe you? I know all about the contract she signed with you. I'm prepared to pay you what she owes right now. Then I'll give you exactly two minutes to get your sorry self and your men off this property."

"Or you'll do what?" Ted snarled.

Lucy stood in paralyzed silence as the scene unfolded. She kept shaking her head, but none of the men in the room were paying attention to her. *No. No. No.*

This isn't right.

If David pays off Ted, how has anything changed?
What have I proved about myself?
All I will have done is lose again.

David handed his phone to Wyatt. "I've never cared much for technology, but every phone now records video. Funny thing about the Internet. Once things get on there, they're impossible to make disappear. I started recording as soon as we walked in and guessed where this was headed. The way I see it, the next part of the video can either include you graciously accepting a check from me to cover what Lucy owes, or it can be what justifies the beating I give you when you refuse. Your choice."

"Two hundred fifty thousand," Ted said, as if that would change David's mind.

David wrote out a check and threw it at him. "Take it and get the hell out of here. Now."

Ted looked from Lucy to David. He wanted to say something else, that much was obvious, but he glanced over at Wyatt, who was still filming, and pocketed the check. With a smile at the camera, he said, "I have my money, and I didn't marry a cheating whore. In the end, I did win."

In a flash, David closed the short distance between them and punched him full in the face. Ted fell to the floor, then scrambled back to his feet and wiped blood from his nose. "I don't know who you are, but you'll regret this."

David shot Wyatt a signal to stop filming. Then he said, "Rule one of battle. Know your enemy and what they're capable of. If I see you around Lucy again, I will kill you with my bare hands, and there isn't a court in Texas that'll convict me. Think about that when you consider tangling with me."

"Fuck you. You can have her." Ted stormed out, and the room fell silent.

David turned to Lucy and walked over to ask her if she was okay.

All the emotion that had been building in Lucy burst forth, and she slapped him.

David's head snapped back, then he rubbed his cheek and shook his head in confusion. "What the hell was that for?"

Fighting back angry tears, Lucy said, "You had no right."

He was still puffed up with adrenaline and too much testosterone. "He was threatening you."

A part of Lucy acknowledged that, but fury was whipping through her. She hated herself for believing Ted again, even for a moment. She couldn't understand why she'd simply stood there letting them discuss her fate as if she were no more capable of thinking for herself than the steers outside.

Instead of feeling freed from her debt, she felt like she'd been bought. Again. This time by a man who was looking so proud of himself, she wanted to smack him again. *Even harder than before because part of her loved how he'd jumped to her defense. Maybe kick him once or twice for how gorgeous he looked as he did it, how she'd found herself both excited and furious with him at the same time.*

I should have yelled for them to stop.

I should have told David to keep his money.

No wonder men keep taking over my life—I let them.

That ends now.

"I told you not to come." Everything she should have told Ted she now said to David. "I don't want your money. I don't want to owe anyone anything. By tomorrow night you'll have a check for most of it. I don't know how, but I'll pay you back the rest. Every last penny."

"You don't have to rush, Lucy. I did it because I care—"

"Don't say it. Those are just words people throw around to try to control each other. I don't want anything from you. And stop looking like you think I should thank you. All you did was make me hate myself more. Get out of my house."

David looked across to Wyatt for support, but the older man walked over and said, "When a woman asks a gentleman to leave, he does. Come on." He guided a reluctant-looking David out of the house.

Only after the door closed behind them did Lucy allow her tears to fall. She sank to her knees and wept into her hands. Her tears were those of anger and regret. Of all the times she'd imagined how she would feel if she ever saw David again, she'd never imagined she could hate him.

Or is it just me I hate?

Lucy wiped away her tears and stood. She was shaking from head to toe, but she forced herself to calm down. *If I stay in here, it's my fault no one thinks I can do this. My daddy raised me to be stronger.*

She opened the door and stepped out onto her porch. Ted and his men were gone. Wyatt stood with the men he'd brought over, showing them David's video. David was standing off to one side as if he were uncomfortable with what Wyatt was doing.

At her appearance, David took a step toward Lucy, then stopped and waited. One by one, the men turned and looked toward the porch. It was a pivotal moment, and Lucy knew it. *They want to know what I'm made of. Am I victim or a fighter?*

She raised her voice and used a tone she'd often heard her daddy use. "Well, what are all y'all waiting for? We've got cattle to load."

And just like that the men went back to saddling up their horses and positioning the fencing.

Wyatt nodded his approval.

David held her gaze for a long, sad moment—long enough for Lucy to regret most of what she'd said to him, but that didn't stop her from feeling that she could never be with him until she was no longer in debt to him.

She looked away and walked over to join some men who were deciding which stock trailer to fill first. She asked what she could do to help, and was soon positioning the vehicles with precision. She might not know how to run the ranch, but she'd certainly done her share of work on it.

Wyatt came to stand beside the door of a truck she'd just parked. "Do you think you were a mite hard on your friend?"

Lucy's eyes scanned the area until she located David on horseback helping the men drive the cattle onto the rigs. "He's not my friend. I barely know him."

"He appears to have some strong feelings for you."

"Appearances are often deceiving."

Wyatt tipped his hat lower and looked in David's direction. "Making one man pay for another man's sins doesn't right any wrongs."

Lucy stepped out of the truck and sighed. "I want to feel bad about what I said to him, but I'm drowning in guilt already. I don't have room to feel bad about anything else."

Wyatt looked back at Lucy and looped his thumbs through his belt. "You would have had a nasty fight on your hands with Ted."

"I need to believe I would have won," Lucy said, just above a whisper. *Maybe I didn't lose today, but I didn't win either. David stole that opportunity from me, and I don't know if I can forgive him for it.*

The challenge of loading the stock trailers left little time for David to reflect much on Lucy's negative reaction to what he'd considered a grand gesture of his feelings for her. A man could easily get killed if he let his attention wander while convincing eight hundred head of cattle to do something they had no desire to do. It wasn't until the tractor-trailers were pulling out of the driveway that David turned his attention back to the reason he'd driven to Mavis.

Lucy Albright.

Will I ever understand that woman?

He dismounted the horse he'd borrowed from one of the men, returned it to him, then scanned the area for Lucy and frowned when he didn't see her. After Sarah's phone call the night before, David had prepared to step in and help Lucy. Sarah had told him all about the loan and how Lucy was trying to break free from York but was afraid she'd lose everything in the process.

David had never been one to walk away from someone he felt needed him. His only regrets in life were the times he'd let himself be convinced to. After speaking to Sarah, David had felt positive he belonged in Mavis, helping Lucy.

He knew she'd be skittish at first, same as when she'd avoided him at Sarah and Tony's wedding. That didn't worry him none. He'd been confident he could win her trust and she'd accept his help. He hadn't imagined it would take long for their attraction to each other to lead to more. And more was what he wanted with her. Now. In the future. It was something he'd tried to deny when he heard Lucy was engaged, but he'd come to accept that without her, his life would always feel as if it were missing something.

Lucy was the something that had kept him feeling restless.

David had never paid much mind to people who spoke about love at first sight, even though his own father claimed he'd known by the end of their first date that he would marry David's mother. It was an outdated, ridiculous idea, but dismissing it would be harder to do after today.

When he'd heard that asshole threaten Lucy, David had been filled with a rage like none he'd felt before. He'd joked with Tony about possibly having to kill someone to save Lucy, but there'd been nothing funny about how easily David would have done just that if York had lifted a hand to her. As it was, David had been hard-pressed to stop at one punch.

His fierce, almost primal protectiveness of Lucy was too real to deny. He wanted her—in his bed, in his life. She belonged with him.

In his mind, it wasn't a question of *if* they would be together, but of how soon.

He replayed the scene in her house as it had unfolded. He could see her standing there proudly, declaring how she wasn't afraid of York, her long brown mane of hair swinging back and forth each time she shook her head. She was thinner than he remembered, and the faint circles beneath her worried eyes had torn at his heartstrings.

He'd fantasized about what it would be like to spend a wild night in her arms, but when he'd seen how hard she was trying to look brave, he'd been filled with an equal desire to simply hold her. Hug her until his strength became hers.

She was a woman in need of protecting, and it was hard for David to understand how trying to do just that had gotten him thrown out of her house.

Wyatt came to stand beside him. They'd exchanged only a few words before they entered Lucy's house. That brief conversation had ended as soon as David had learned that York was inside, talking to Lucy. *Berating his woman.* Even though he had just met Wyatt, David had a sense of who he was. Integrity shone in the proud lines of his grizzled face. Wyatt was a man who looked a person right in the eye, spoke with a soft voice, but would likely kick the tar out of someone he felt needed the correction. "I'll be heading out to Abilene to complete the sale for Miss Lucy. She wanted to come, but I told her to stay here. Someone needs to watch this place and make sure York's men don't return."

David nodded. He wasn't going anywhere until he knew Lucy was safe.

Wyatt said, "One of the boys looked you up on his smartphone. Seems like you've done well for yourself over in Fort Mavis, what with your horse training and all."

"I do all right."

"Said you're in all sorts of commercials. Showed me one or two."

David shrugged and kicked the dirt. "It's for charity. They say my face sells tickets. I prefer working with horses. But I must have *sucker* written on my forehead, because somehow I keep ending up on TV."

Wyatt looked David over again, as if assessing his character. "Doing good ain't nothing to be ashamed of no matter how damn-fool ridiculous you look in those commercials."

David arched an eyebrow at that comment, and Wyatt cackled. "Thank you, I think."

"You ever think of relocating some of your business out here? This town needs a man like you—someone Ted York can't buy and sell. Times are tough. Jobs are hard to find in these parts. The six men who came to help today feel good about what they've done, but that won't put food on their tables come Monday."

True enough. "I've considered getting a place of my own, but relocating here would be a bit premature." He rubbed the cheek Lucy had smacked.

Wyatt nodded at the house. "Anything worthwhile is worth the trouble. She's in a rough place, and I'm not sure you made things better today. York wants her property, and he thought he had leverage to get it. He ain't above playing dirty to get what he wants, so paying off the loan won't stop him. I keep asking myself why. I don't know, but my gut tells me Miss Lucy ain't safe yet. Don't let her run you off."

Wyatt was preaching to the wrong choir. Lucy was the one who needed convincing. "She told me to leave."

Wyatt shrugged. "She hired me as her ranch manager, seeing how she needs someone to keep up the outbuildings and such. That's more work than one man can handle. I considered hiring someone to help me, but Lucy can't afford to pay anyone yet. It might be a bit of an unconventional setup, but you could stay in the ranch-hand house, ship over some of your horses to train, and possibly hire on a few men to help with those horses."

David looked at Wyatt to assess the seriousness of his suggestion. "Isn't that similar to the setup York had? I can't imagine Lucy going along with that."

Wyatt rubbed his chin and stared off across the field beside the house. "That's because you're not seein' the most important difference 'tween the situations."

"And that is?"

Wyatt smiled. "Miss Lucy never cared for York, not romantic-like, but she looks at you the same way my wife used to look at me when I was working up the nerve to ask her out. Women are complex creatures, but just like horses, if you watch 'em close enough, you can read them. I've known Lucy most of her life. She likes you. She hates you, too. If a man cared enough, he could work that through."

David couldn't believe he was considering Wyatt's idea, but a better one hadn't come to him. "So, which one of us gets the pleasure of telling Lucy I work here now?"

Wyatt gave David a pat on the shoulder. "I would, but I'm late already. I have to be in Abilene before four. Good luck to you. Hopefully you'll be here when I get back."

Chapter Four

From the window of her father's office, Lucy watched Wyatt and David talking. Part of her wanted to rush outside and apologize to David before he left. The mess she was in wasn't his fault. He wasn't Ted with a sinister agenda.

He had no way of knowing how much I needed to prove something to myself today.

I want to be grateful, to trust, but he handed over $250,000 to Ted. Why? Because he cares about me?

That's a lot of money to drop and not expect something in return.

He said he wants me. Did he think I was for sale? If he'd asked me, I would have turned the money down.

Wyatt climbed into his truck, and David waved good-bye, then turned to face the house. He caught her watching him, and their eyes locked. Lucy's cheeks warmed as desire licked through her. She tried to deny it, tried to look away, but she couldn't.

Please leave, David. Get in your truck and drive back to Fort Mavis. I'm not ready for how you make me feel.

David clearly didn't receive her silent plea, or he decided to ignore it. With a nod in her direction, he started walking toward her house. Lucy stepped away from the window and hurried out of the room, closing and locking the door behind her. *Just because I sell sex toys online doesn't mean I'm an easy mark.*

She imagined herself standing naked with David's arms around her while he bent to tease one of her excited nipples with his mouth. She hadn't even kissed him, but her body hummed with the pleasure it knew his hands and mouth could bring her.

Apparently, I should purchase some of those toys for myself. To take the edge off. Two years without sex can muddle the brain—makes me want to pounce on a man I hardly know.

Her cheeks warmed even more at the thought of masturbating while imagining herself with David. *Stop that. What is wrong with me?*

I've had an emotional day. That's why I feel out of control. I feel alone, and that's the only reason David is such a temptation.

Lucy opened the door before David could knock. His large, muscular frame filled the doorway. Even shadowed from the sun, his blue eyes were gorgeously brilliant. And his lips looked every bit as amazing as she'd imagined a moment before. It was all she could do to not lean forward and test if there was any possibility that his kiss would live up to her fantasy.

She needed to gain control of herself as well as the situation. She gripped the door handle tightly and stood, blocking his entrance. "Thank you for your help today. I'm sorry I hit you. I was still all wound up from talking to Ted." She paused and chewed her lip before saying, "I shouldn't have taken it out on you."

"No apology necessary." His smile was as warm as the sun shining behind him.

Lucy took a deep breath, then realized her mistake. He smelled as good as he looked. Masculine. A city woman might smell cattle or horse, but those familiar scents faded to the background for Lucy. David didn't need cologne; he was heady enough. He'd worked hard, and the light shine of sweat on him was a turn-on that had her biting her lip again. *I have to get him out of here before I bookend this day with bad choices.* "I'd offer you something to eat, but I'm sure you're anxious to get home, and it's a long drive. I should have a check for you tomorrow. I can mail it or have someone take it to you in Fort Mavis if you need it sooner. Whatever you prefer."

David removed his hat, and the sun brightened his thick blond hair, giving it an almost halo effect. "I'd rather you invite me in."

Lucy leaned on the door handle for support as her knees almost buckled. *I've watched too many vampire movies. They can't hurt you unless you invite them in. David is not here for my blood or my ranch. But he does want something.*

Me.

Oh God.

This is a bad idea.

A really bad idea.

I swore I would get back control of my life and my ranch.

Is this a test? To see if I'll take the easy way out again? I won't. No matter what my sex-starved body thinks, I won't say yes this time.

I need to free myself from owing anyone anything. "I have work waiting for me or I would."

He made no move to end the conversation. "Your home business? Sarah told me you were starting one."

Thank God I didn't tell Sarah the details. I'll have to talk to her about how much she's sharing with David. "Yes. Hopefully it'll bring in enough revenue after the first few months to pay you the rest of what I owe."

"I'm not worried about the money, Lucy."

"You should be. We didn't even sign anything."

He held her gaze. "Contracts don't matter with honest people, and crooks will always find a way around them. I trust you, Lucy."

"Trusting people is the quickest way to lose everything."

"Is that what you believe?"

"It's a hard truth, but I'm learning to deal with it. What do they say? 'Fool me once, shame on you. Fool me twice . . .'"

"You're no fool, Lucy."

"Not anymore, I'm not. I'm done letting others decide how things should be done. I'm going to save this ranch, and I'm going to do it my way."

David leaned in, his mouth hovering above hers. "You don't have to do it alone."

Lucy licked her bottom lip and let out a shaky breath. It would have been so easy to forget everything else and give in to him. *Then what?* "Yes, I do. I won't make the same mistake again."

His breath was a soft caress on her lips. "Would it be a mistake?" His voice held strength and a confidence just as attractive as the rest of him. What would life be like with a man like him at her side?

Even as her eyes began to close in preparation for his kiss, she told herself she didn't want this. She couldn't risk losing herself again . . . no matter how strong the pull between them was.

"A package for you, Miss Lucy," an amused male voice said from the bottom of the steps. She and David jumped apart. "I would have left it without interrupting, but it's a heavy box, and I'm supposed to have you sign for it." The postman smiled as he handed the box to David and took out a tablet for Lucy. "Sign right there, if you don't mind."

Lucy scanned the box in David's arms. It had to be from Technically Anonymous Pleasure. After seeing the poor-quality photos for some of the items in the catalogue, Lucy ordered one of everything with the intention of taking pictures for her website. The company was normally discreet with its labels, but Lucy wanted to rip the box away from David just in case. She reluctantly turned her attention to the tablet, signed the electronic form, then handed it back to the postman, who thanked her and left.

Looking at David, she said, "I'll take that now."

He bounced the large square box against his chest. "It's too heavy for you."

"I don't want or need your help. Give me the box." She reached out for it and pulled before he had a chance to release it. Meeting resistance, she pulled harder. His release of the box, along with the way she'd braced herself to pull harder, sent her stumbling backward beneath the weight of it.

And this is how I die, crushed beneath a box of sex toys.

David was beside her in an instant, stopping her fall by putting an arm around her waist. Once she was steady on her feet, he reached for the box. She clutched it to her and started to retreat, but was blocked by the arm still supporting her. Opposing emotions rushed through her. She loved the feel of him against her, loved his strong touch. At the same time, she'd just learned the risk of leaning on anyone, and she was furious with herself for being tempted to do it again.

"Easy, Lucy. I told you it was too heavy." His amused tone only confused her more.

There is nothing funny about my whole life falling apart and nothing amusing about how desperately I want to make the right choices this time. "And I told you I could handle it."

David frowned. "Was I supposed to let you fall on your ass?"

"If that's what I wanted—yes."

"I can't do that, Lucy. I'm not the kind of man who can walk away when someone is in trouble."

Sweat began to bead on Lucy's forehead from the exertion of holding the ridiculously heavy box. *Do they wrap their toys in bricks?* She turned to the side and bent to put the box down, but dropped it, barely missing both of their feet. She hated that she hadn't been strong enough to make her point by holding the box. Tears welled in her eyes.

She knew enough about David's history with Tony to believe David was sincere. Sarah had told her how David had hunted Tony down when he thought the horse trainer had gone unpunished for a tragedy David had felt was Tony's fault. Tony had been drinking himself to death when David found him. Another man might have gloated over the irony, but David had not only stayed and sobered Tony up, he had also guided the man back to a career he was gifted in.

But I don't need to be saved.

I need to do this on my own.

She met his eyes, and for a moment her resolve wavered. He had the kindest eyes she'd ever looked into. *What would we be to each other if we'd known each other before all this? If I wasn't already a tangled mess on the inside?*

Why ask myself what might have been, when all I have is here and now?

"Keeping this ranch is my priority now. My only priority. I know how ungrateful that sounds, but I asked you not to come. I warned you. Good-bye, David."

He bent closer again, so close Lucy's resolve began to dissolve. "I'm not leaving until I'm sure you're safe, Lucy. Wyatt hired me to help look after the outbuildings, and I agreed to bring some of my horses over to give work to some of the men who were here today. Wyatt seems to think they'll need it."

The room spun. "Wyatt can't hire you. This is my ranch."

David caressed the side of Lucy's face, running the back of his fingers down one side of her neck. "Wyatt's worried about you. He thinks you need someone to watch over you. I agree."

The pleasure of his touch confused Lucy. She felt vibrantly alive, and her miserable morning was too easy to forget. *No. No. No.* She pushed his hand away. "I don't care what Wyatt thinks, and I don't care what you do, either. I'm telling you to leave. I don't want you here."

"Then why do you look like you want to kiss me so damn much?" he asked.

Lucy turned away from him. She wrapped her arms around herself. She could lie to him and say he was wrong, but they'd both know it wasn't true. "You say you want to help me, David, but you don't listen to me. I will save this ranch, and I will do it myself." She turned back to face him. "Haven't you ever needed to prove something to yourself so badly that an easier way of doing something was impossible to consider?"

David nodded. "And that was usually right before I fell on my face."

She sputtered angrily and was about to tell him off when he raised his hand to caress her cheek again. "We're at a standoff, you and I. My daddy always said the secret to solving a disagreement was finding a compromise both could live with. Wyatt needs help outside, the men who were here today need jobs, and I need to know you're okay."

He ran a mesmerizing thumb across her parted lips. "You need to save the ranch on your own. What if I promise I won't step in to help again unless you ask me to, and in return you let me pay for the use of your barns and fields to train my horses."

"You can't pay me. I owe you money."

"Then charge me and deduct as we go. I'll pay you a fair rate for the lease of your facility."

"Why would you do that?" *Besides to sleep with me, because that can't happen.*

As if he heard her, he dropped his hand and stepped back. The sadness she felt at the absence of his touch was as confusing as fighting the pleasure from it had been. "I've been thinking about getting my own place for a while. This would be a way to test how I like it. Working with Tony has been good for me, but like you, it's time for me to see what I can do on my own."

"You can't stay in the main house." Lucy blushed right after she blurted her thought out.

A slow smile spread across his face. "Wyatt suggested I stay in the old workers' quarters. None of the men who were here today will be looking to stay there. It'll be perfect."

Perfectly crazy.

Am I honestly considering this? "If I say yes, it doesn't mean I'm agreeing to anything else. I want to be clear about that."

A twinkle lit his eyes. "Why, Miss Lucy, what else might I think you were agreeing to?"

A reluctant smile pulled at the corners of Lucy's mouth, but she pressed her lips together and told herself to be strong. Knight-in-shining-armor David was difficult enough to resist, so any hint of naughty playfulness put Lucy at risk of stripping right then and there and begging him to take her. She hoped he couldn't see the need in her eyes when she said, "I really do have a lot of work to do."

He replaced his hat, tipped it politely, and sauntered out the door.

After he was gone, Lucy sat down heavily on the box in her hallway. *I said David could work here.*

It's proof that I've lost my mind.

She remembered how perfectly his Levis had hugged his tight ass and muscular thighs. David would likely be working with his horses in the paddocks across from her house.

Talk about an office with a view.

David smiled his way back to his truck to get the overnight bag he'd thrown in there impulsively that morning. He could have left his things at the hotel he'd checked in to, but a smart man was prepared for all possibilities. He'd shower, change, make a few calls, then collect the rest of his things from the hotel after Wyatt returned.

She said yes.

His expression sobered when he thought about why he didn't want Lucy to be alone. He studied the main house. The sheer size of it was testament to the success Lucy's family must have once had with cattle ranching. Years of neglect, though, had diminished its value. Alone, it didn't seem valuable enough to merit York's level of interest.

Wyatt had said York wanted the land. David scanned the rolling fields beyond the house. During his first visit, he'd heard the ranch was over ten thousand acres. Once again, a nice setup, but there had to be more for someone like York to be willing to blackmail Lucy to get it.

When in doubt, follow the money. David didn't know what York thought would be so profitable about owning Lucy's land, but with a few phone calls he was confident he could find out—and soon. Unlike Lucy, David had no problem turning to others for help. He was a better man because of the people who had come into his life when he'd been in need, and he gladly paid that kindness forward whenever he could.

Accepting help didn't take away from a person's achievements. Lucy would see that in time.

David never took his natural intuition for granted when it came to working with horses. Many of the same rules of interaction overlapped species. Trust needed to be earned. Any rider who thought a horse should trust them just because they held the reins was quickly disappointed. Riding was a partnership acquired through clear communication, consistency, and mutual respect. He was betting the same recipe could win Lucy's trust.

David smiled as he walked into the bunkhouse and chose a room. The building was old but had been well cared for until recently. The walls were bare, but the furniture was good quality and the bedding spoke of a family who cared about the people who had worked there. He liked the physical evidence of what he felt he knew about Lucy already. She was a good woman who'd come from a good family. She'd pull through this rough patch just fine.

And then she'll be mine.

David pushed back a curtain to see the main house. He wondered what Lucy was doing. Was she wishing as much as he that he'd taken that kiss she seemed to want to give him?

There'll be plenty of time for that later.

He thought about the business she was starting. She'd told Sarah she wasn't ready to talk about it yet. He knew she'd gone to school for marketing. Most likely she didn't want to say much about her business until she knew she could do it. He could respect that.

I'll have her telling me all about it by the end of the week.

He turned and began to strip for the shower. He'd removed his shirt and shoes when his phone rang. When he saw the caller, he considered ignoring it but knew she was genuinely concerned. "Hello, Sarah."

"So, did you get there okay? What was it like seeing her again? Did you ask her out? Are you still there with her? I know I should have waited for you to call, but I'm dying from curiosity here."

With her barrage of questions delivered in her fast Northern accent, David held up a hand to calm Sarah even though she wasn't in the room with him. "Easy. I didn't call because there's nothing to say yet."

Sarah exclaimed, "Nothing? You drove out to see a woman you've been heartbroken about practically the whole time I've known you. I want to hear everything."

"I wasn't heartbroken. I liked her, that's all."

"Really? So you're on your way back?"

"I'm staying here."

"What was that? Could you speak up? You're staying with Lucy?"

"In the bunkhouse. Sarah, don't go making a big deal over this. She has an empty barn here, and I've been considering finding a place of my own. I've decided to lease the barn and work some horses here—see how it goes. That's all there is."

Sarah let out a gleeful sound. "I can't wait to tell Melanie. She and Charles had better get married soon, because we'll probably have another wedding on the horizon by the end of the year. I am so happy for you. You and Lucy are perfect for each other. I'll call her and say so as soon as I hang up with you."

"No!" David barked. He then softened his voice. "It would be bet-ter if you don't say anything to anyone right now." A thought came to him, and he went with it. "We're working things out. If you push Lucy, she may ask me to leave. *Again.* You wouldn't want to be the reason we don't work out this time, would you?"

Sarah gasped in horror. "No. I hadn't thought of that. I talk to her all the time, though. I can't not call her. Should I pretend I don't know you're there?"

David rolled his eyes skyward. Stopping Sarah was like trying to hold back the weather. "Don't lie, just don't make her feel weird about having me here. Also, have Tony call me. Normally, I would come back and settle things on that side before shipping some horses out here, but I can't leave right now."

"Can't? Is something wrong there?"

"Yes, Sarah, but I don't have the full picture yet."

"I'll have Tony call you. Hey, Mason is flying in next week with Chelle. They'd love to see you, and I'd love to see Lucy."

"I'll see what I can do," David promised.

Chapter Five

Later that evening, Lucy stood by the stove in her kitchen, waiting for the water to boil. She'd spent the late afternoon tweaking her website and telling herself she didn't care that David was one building away. *I doubt the bunkhouse is stocked with anything perishable. I should ask him to join me for dinner.*

Bad, bad idea.

I could make him a plate and take it to him.

Or I could do what I know I should, and stay the hell away from him until I get myself under control.

She'd moved the box that had been delivered to her father's office, but she hadn't opened it. She didn't want Wyatt to walk in and see what she'd ordered because she was afraid he'd think she was turning the ranch into a brothel. And if David saw it? *He'd think I'm the type of woman who uses those things.*

And I'm not.

Am I? She'd been raised to think such things were shameful, but she'd purchased a small vibrator for herself when she moved to the city. She'd looked at it as a private declaration that she was a modern woman—independent and self-sufficient, even in the bedroom.

She'd used it, but that's where her experience with toys ended. Lucy glanced at the still-cool water. *How the heck am I going to market something I know nothing about? I should have chosen to sell candles or bath products. At least I know about those. What was I thinking?*

That I need money, that's what.

Sex is a natural part of life—like breathing. That's how I should look at this. I'm a modern woman. Forget what my mother would have thought or what my neighbors might think. These are just devices to help a person breathe easier.

They aren't a replacement for men. Lucy closed her eyes and pictured David. There wasn't an inch of him that didn't feel as good as it looked. He had the muscular stature of a man who worked outdoors. His hands were strong but gentle. She shivered with pleasure at the idea of how they would feel on her bare skin.

A knock on the door made Lucy jump and quickly turn. She hit the pan with the side of her hand and expected a burn but felt nothing. She glanced down at the burner and realized she hadn't turned it on. *See, this is a problem. David is a distraction I can't afford.*

Lucy ran a hand through her hair and went to open the door. "Oh, hi, Wyatt."

Wyatt removed his hat and stepped through the door. "Thought you'd be happier to see me, considering the sale went through. The money was deposited to your account. Here is your receipt."

Lucy gave herself an inner smack and forced a smile. The sale was done. Relief flooded her. "Sorry, you know I'm glad to see you. It's been a long day, that's all." Wyatt handed the receipt to Lucy. She glanced down at it, then back at him. "Thank you, Wyatt. Do you need a check tonight?"

Wyatt shrugged. "I ain't worried. Me and the family are moving into the back house tomorrow. My wife is looking forward to being back here. My grandbabies are a bit on the wild side, but if you have a problem with them, bring it to me and not my son and his wife. They don't believe in disciplining children. Everyone has to feel good about everything all the time, or they think the world is ending. Life ain't like that. I find that taking them on hunting trips and talking about what they're doing wrong while I'm skinning something turns them right around."

Lucy's eyes rounded, then she burst out laughing. "You're pulling my leg."

Wyatt flashed a quick smile. "Yes, ma'am. It's good to see you laughing, Miss Lucy. The kids are better behaved than I ever was, better than even you and your brother were, but they're missing their old life. My son and his wife were in Dallas until he lost his job. They moved in with us in our rental in town, but no one was happy there. The kids play video games and hide in their rooms all day. I'm hoping it'll be different for them here."

"How old are they?"

"Brianna is eleven. Cooper is nine. I'd love to see them get into riding. I tried to take them out once, but they don't know teeth from tail on a horse. I get that my son doesn't want this lifestyle. He's working with some big headhunter, and as soon as they land him a job, he says they're gone again. They like to live large, and that's why they had no savings when he lost his job. But you can't tell him that, can't tell his wife that, neither. There is a whole lot of living that could be done while waiting for that perfect job, but I didn't have a place where I could really show them what that means. I appreciate you letting us come back."

Tears of gratitude filled Lucy's eyes. "Don't you dare make me cry, Wyatt. I'm already a mess."

"You'll be fine soon enough. Things are already turning around. Was that David's truck I saw in the drive?"

Lucy wagged a finger at him, although it was impossible to be irritated with him. "You know good and well it is. He said you hired him."

Wyatt took his time answering. "I'm not as young as I used to be, Lucy. There's trouble brewing, and I want to do right by you, but I have my family to think of, too. My son's a good businessman, but he couldn't fight his way out of a brawl with kittens. This town needs a David. York doesn't scare him, and seeing that reminds the men around him that we all had a life before York took over his daddy's place and did his best to make sure he was the only game in town. He's slowly buying out all the ranches in the area."

Lucy glanced at the door, then back at Wyatt. "You think having David here will change that?"

Wyatt replaced his hat. "Hope is a powerful thing. When you ain't got it, you got no fight in you. Everything changes as soon as you believe it can. Do you believe you can keep this ranch?"

Lucy clasped her hands in front of her. "I'm going to try my damnedest to."

"That wasn't answering my question, and if you can't say yes, I don't know what we're all doing here. Good night, Miss Lucy."

Ouch. It was impossible to be upset with Wyatt for speaking so bluntly because Lucy knew his concern was genuine. "Good night, Wyatt."

No longer hungry, Lucy left the kitchen and went to her father's office. She unlocked it, flipped on the light, and then stood over the large box she hadn't yet had the nerve to open. *If I don't believe I can do this, then I don't know what I'm doing here, either.*

She knelt, opened the box, and took out the largest package inside. It wasn't labeled. Opening it, she unwrapped a rose-colored velvet base a woman was apparently supposed to straddle. Included in the box were several screw-on dildos in an assortment of colors, shapes, and sizes. The front of the base had enough buttons on it to make Lucy laugh out loud. A woman could kill herself on that thing trying to program it. *Stop laughing. This is a career, not a joke.* No wonder the site didn't have a clear photo of the product; there's not much that's sexy about it. Lucy frowned, but with determination, reached for the directions. *I can do this.* She read the highlights listed in the description. "Remote control included. Bluetooth ready." *Bluetooth?* "Downloadable apps to increase your pleasure and your fantasy. Write your own interactive story or use one of ours."

Lucy sat back on her heels and threw the directions along with the base back into the box. *I need to start simpler.* She leaned back into the box and pulled out a smaller parcel. She opened it and took out what at first looked like a tangle of wires and Velcro. There was a remote control attached to a larger band of Velcro. Lucy figured the large band would fit on a wrist, so that was where she put it. She untangled the wires and saw attachments for three fingers. *Which three?* She glimpsed another control device in the box. It was the size and shape of a phone with a label that read "Waterproof." *Because it's not intimidating enough as is, why not add the chance of getting electrocuted in the bath?* She reached for the directions, then tried and failed to figure them out. Either the first device recorded what the phone-sized device told it to or it was the other way around. Once again, there were apps to download and directions that weren't written for regular people to understand. Lucy threw the toy back into its container in frustration.

Whatever happened to a good, old-fashioned vibrator?

She shoved the box away from her.

I wanted to sell something with a high profit margin. These are supposed to be the wave of the future.

Lucy sighed and stood.

I'm screwed.

Hopefully all of this will make sense to me tomorrow. She closed and locked the door behind her. *I know you're right, Wyatt. If I don't believe I can do this, we're all wasting our time here.*

Lucy slipped off her boots and placed them in the hall before heading up to her bedroom. She stripped to her underwear, slid a light nightgown over her head, then tucked herself into bed.

Mom. Dad. I know I've spent enough nights asking you to watch over me, but I need you to look away for a little bit while I sort this out.

And, Dad, do yourself a favor and stay out of your office. There's nothing there you need to see.

Lucy turned onto her side and fluffed her pillow with a punch. Had Wyatt gone over to talk to David after leaving her place? Probably. He'd make sure David had everything he needed.

Lucy's eyes began to close, and just before she fell asleep, she admitted to herself that she felt safer knowing David was in the bunkhouse. She didn't agree with much he'd done that day, and she wasn't proud of the ungracious way she'd responded to his help, but still, it was nice knowing someone was watching over her. She hugged her pillow closer and fell into the first peaceful sleep she'd had in a long time.

David was outside and ready for a day's work at the crack of dawn. His stomach was rumbling, though. He considered going to town for supplies, but he wasn't leaving until Wyatt came back with his family later that day. He'd worry less about Lucy once there were people around to keep an eye on her.

Until then, I'll settle for a cup of coffee.

He knocked on the kitchen door of the main house, but there was no answer. He was about to turn away but impulsively tried the door. It was unlocked.

Not safe. I'll have to talk to her about that.

He opened her kitchen door. Lucy would hide from him if he let her, and this time he wasn't giving her a chance to find someone else. She wanted to deny the attraction between them. If his intention was to bed her and leave, he would have respected that, but seeing her again had confirmed his initial gut reaction upon meeting her: *She belongs with me.*

She felt the same. He'd seen as much in her eyes the night before. *She'll come round.*

David called out to Lucy. She didn't answer, and he was turning to leave when an idea came to him. Could have been the way his stomach was protesting the length of time since his last meal, but making Lucy breakfast suddenly seemed like a good idea.

He started coffee and hunted through her fridge for eggs, bacon, and toast. He was no stranger to cooking for himself and prided himself on being better than most. His parents had made cooking a family event when he was young, and even though he didn't talk to them nearly enough now, cooking was a way of remembering happier times.

He was sliding a second omelet onto a plate when he heard the familiar sound of a shotgun being cocked. He shut the stove off, set the plate down on the counter beside him, and turned. Lucy was pointing a shotgun in his general direction and shaking.

"You scared me," she accused. "I thought someone had broken in."

"Do criminals in these parts feed you before they rob you?"

Lucy uncocked the shotgun and lowered it. "I thought you might be—"

It was then that David felt like an ass for not realizing she might be afraid of her ex-fiancé. "Ted."

Lucy shrugged a shoulder. "I wasn't sure if he'd give being nice one more try."

A thought occurred to David that he didn't like one bit, but he couldn't stop himself from asking. "Did he make you breakfast often?"

Lucy held his eyes for a long moment. She knew exactly what he was asking. He should say it was none of his business, but he didn't. He didn't want to picture her with Ted that way. Which wasn't fair since she'd been engaged to him. Of course they'd—

"Never," she said, then wrapped her arms protectively around herself.

His relief was short-lived. Her stance opened the front of her night-gown enough to give him a glorious glimpse of cleavage so that he almost forgot he'd asked a question. He shook his head as her answer sunk in. "Never?"

Lucy dropped her arms. "Not even close. That, by itself, should have been a warning sign that he had other reasons for wanting to marry me. I saw only what I wanted to see, I guess."

David stepped toward her. "Lucy . . ."

"Please. I don't want to talk about it." She waved a hand through the air, then looked at the table he'd set and the fresh pot of coffee. "What happened to you staying outside?"

David flashed a smile at her. He was having the damnedest time trying not to focus on how the sunlight was making her nightgown near transparent. "A man could starve out there, but I made enough for two." He placed the plates on the table and held out a chair for her.

Lucy sat in the chair and frowned up at him. "You can't just come in and out of my house."

He poured them both a cup of coffee and took his place across from her. "Door was open. Try the eggs, Lucy."

She blinked a few times quickly, then slowly did as he instructed. The moan she made was just about the sexiest thing he'd ever heard. "These are good. What did you put in them?"

"Family secret. If I tell you, I either have to marry you or kill you." Lucy went white, and David cursed his idiot mouth. "It's a joke, Lucy. Well, partly. My grandma used to say that to her dates after my grandpa died."

That seemed to calm Lucy. She took a sip of coffee. "How old was she?"

"A young eighty-two, and believe me, she never had a shortage of suitors. She had a smile that lit up a room. When you have that, it doesn't matter how old you are, you're beautiful." He sighed.

"It sounds like you were close."

"We were. I miss her every day."

Lucy rested her chin on her hand. "My grandparents died while I was too young to remember them, but I used to imagine what they'd be like. I shouldn't miss what I never had, but I do sometimes. I miss the idea of having someone in my life like that. Does that make sense?"

There she was, the woman David could imagine spending the rest of his life loving. Although she didn't see it yet, she was restlessly yearning for more—just as he was. They could be that more for each other. "It does. Do you have any family besides your brother?"

"Both of my parents were only children. If I have family somewhere, I don't know them. How about you?"

David wasn't used to talking about his family, but he wanted Lucy to know him. "My parents retired in north Texas by Amarillo. My father was a doctor. My mother was a teacher. They both wanted me to go to college and take over my father's practice. When they pushed hard, I left and joined the Marines. Funny how important leaving feels when you're young."

Lucy nodded in understanding. "I went to college in Rhode Island and never pictured myself coming back, but here I am." She took a bite of bacon, chewed, and then asked, "Are you close to your parents?"

"Not as much now as I was before I left. I'd like to say they got over the initial disappointment, but no matter what else I achieve, it wasn't what they wanted for me."

Lucy nodded again. "Wouldn't it be nice if life came with a road map? Then we wouldn't have to waste so much time being confused."

David reached out and took one of her hands in his. "I'm not confused." Their eyes met and held for a long sexually charged moment. He hadn't imagined the yearning in her face the night before, because it was back, but she was fighting it.

She snatched her hand away and moved both hands to her lap. "I don't want either of us to get confused by what you're doing on this ranch. So we should set some ground rules."

David sat back in his chair and kept his expression blank. She looked so serious; it was adorable. "Shoot."

She laid one hand flat on the table beside her plate. "First, you need to stop looking at me like I'm an item on a menu, and you're hungry."

It took all the control David had not to smile at that. "I will if you promise to do the same."

"I do not—" She stopped, took a deep breath, and narrowed her eyes. "I was emotional yesterday. If my expression of gratitude seemed like more than that, I'm sorry." She played with the fork beside her plate. "I realize this is an awkward conversation, but it needs to be said."

David nodded. She wasn't asking him to leave, so it was progress.

"There is nothing personal going on between us. You're leasing my barn and outside grounds. This is a business deal. I'll have papers drawn up today with an agreement on how I will pay off the balance. I'm heading to the bank today. I should be able to give you more than half of what I owe you."

"Lucy, I told you, there's no rush."

"It's important to me, so yes, there is. Second, don't come in the house unannounced. I can understand today, but it can't happen again. And at no time, no matter what you may need, do you ever go into my father's office. If you can't agree to that, then this won't work."

David arched one of his eyebrows but nodded again. *What is she hiding?* Instead of asking her a question he knew she wouldn't answer, he asked, "Isn't it your office now?"

She frowned as if that idea hadn't occurred to her. "I guess it is. It's hard to think of them as being gone forever, but they are." She pressed her lips together and looked down at her plate as if gathering her resolve. "Once you settle in, there won't be much reason for us to interact. The new business I'm starting will keep me busy, as I'm sure your horses will keep you busy once they arrive. I appreciate that you made me breakfast, but we shouldn't do this again." She looked up at him and then her eyes narrowed again. "What are you smiling at?"

David considered not sharing what he was thinking, but he was curious to see her reaction. "I'm imagining how we'll laugh about this conversation when you're waking up in my arms every morning."

Lucy stood, nearly knocking her chair over as she did. "That's not funny."

David stood and leaned forward over the table, giving her what he hoped was his sexiest smile. "I'm not joking."

Lucy stepped back. "It's time for you to leave."

David straightened. He remembered something an old-time trainer had told him when he'd first started working with horses. He'd said, *"Son, there are two ways to get a fearful horse across a bridge. One way is to use a whip. It gets you across the bridge faster, but you end up with a horse who hates whips and bridges. Or you can take that horse to the bridge every day and invite it forward a little bit more each time, letting it decide when it's ready to cross. When it finally does, you'll have yourself a horse who'll cross anything for you because you worked through it together."*

David smiled at the whip reference. Some women liked them. The old horse trainer's logic didn't translate literally to how a man should deal with a modern woman, but the idea of taking things slow and easy seemed to be what Lucy needed. Unless she *was* into whips. He was reasonably sure he wouldn't say no to much if she asked him to do it while standing there in something as sheer as what she was wearing, with her nipples puckered in excitement as they were.

Lucy folded her arms over her chest, which deliciously opened the bodice of her nightgown again. The outline of her petite form was *Penthouse* worthy. "I would ask what you're thinking, but I'm sure I don't want to know. Shut the door behind you as you leave, David."

David closed the distance between them and briefly kissed her open mouth. Her lips moved against his hungrily. When he lifted his head, her face was flushed and her eyes burned with a need that mirrored his own. He whispered in her ear, "You didn't say I couldn't kiss you.

That should have been your first rule. But then I would have suggested you not wear that nightgown again, because kissing you is all I've been thinking about since you walked in, and it practically disappeared beneath the bright morning sun."

Lucy gasped, stepped back, and grabbed a napkin to cover herself. "Get out."

David laughed and did as she said. She was losing the battle with herself. He paused on the steps outside her kitchen and smiled. Women had always found him attractive, and winning them over had never taken much effort. Lucy was different, and figuring her out was exciting.

A little while later, David was driving one of Lucy's tractors to clean up a large paddock he would use for his horses when his phone rang. It was Mason Thorne, a man he'd initially thought he would never get along with, but who was fast becoming a friend.

"David, so you're out at Lucy's place. How is that going?"

Instead of answering the question, he turned the tables. "I hear you'll be back in Fort Mavis. I expect to hear you're moving there soon."

Mason laughed. "It's a bit too small for me, but it has a certain charm. Will we see you?"

David wiped his forehead with the sleeve of his plaid shirt. "I can't see why not."

"Both of you?"

"My own mother isn't as interested in my social life," David said with humor.

Mason sounded shamelessly unrepentant. "We're all rooting for it to work out with Lucy. I'm here if you need advice on how to not screw it up this time. I understand women."

David chuckled. "That's a kind offer, but I'm doing just fine."

"So, you're dating her now?"

"No."

"Friends?"

"Sort of."

"But you're staying at her place?"

"In the bunkhouse. I'm leasing the barns and the land."

"What was the last thing she said to you? Be honest. I need to assess the situation."

"She told me to get out of her house."

"What did you do right before that?"

"I kissed her." *This is ridiculous. Why am I telling him anything? Because I don't want to fuck it up this time, either.*

Do I honestly believe Mason could have a helpful insight?

"And you're not at all concerned that you may have crossed a line?"

"She likes me; she won't admit it yet."

Mason groaned. "I used that line once when I played a stalker in a movie."

"I'm not stalking her, but I'm also not sitting back this time and letting another man swoop in while I do nothing. She's mine, and she's close to seeing that."

"I have excellent lawyers if it turns out you're wrong."

"Shut the fuck up."

Mason laughed again. "I'm not actually worried. I've seen Lucy around you. She likes you, but seriously, keep me on speed dial. Charles wouldn't be with Melanie if it weren't for me. If things go south, don't be too proud to come to the master of romance for advice."

Master of bullshit. "Hey, before I hang up on you, which I will gladly do in a minute, I need to ask a favor of you. Do you have any political contacts in the Mavis area? I want to know if there is anything being proposed for this area behind closed doors. Lucy's neighbor is buying up land and wants hers. I'm real interested in why."

"I'll ask around."

"Do it quietly. I don't want anyone to know who is asking."

"Is that the same neighbor who she was engaged to?"

"He's bad news, Mason. The more I hear about him, the nastier the stories get. I want to know what he's up to and anything I can use to stop him."

"I played a detective once. I'm all over this."

David sighed and shook his head. "I'll swing by when you're in Fort Mavis."

"Great, and bring Lucy—unless she's still throwing you out of her house."

David laughed and hung up. Mason was a sarcastic son of a bitch who played dumb because he liked to be underestimated. His time in the California State Senate had come to an end and, even though he hadn't made an announcement, there was talk about a potential presidential run. The country could elect a hell of a lot worse.

Chapter Six

Lucy refused to reflect on how good David's kiss had felt, or how eager her body was to feel more of his. She stomped up to her bedroom and looked at herself in the mirror. Her nightgown looked perfectly respectable, as far as nightgowns went. Normally, she didn't parade around half dressed in front of anyone, but he was the one who had decided to scare her half to death by making her breakfast. *The last thing I was thinking about was what I was wearing.*

Well, at least he was only joking about it being see-through.

She stepped back into the light from the window, and her mouth rounded. "Oh no." The material became completely translucent. She covered her suddenly hot cheeks with both hands. She might as well have been standing there in nothing but her panties. "No wonder he smiled his way through breakfast."

Recognizing a light of passion in her own eyes, she frowned at her reflection. *Don't be stupid. No matter how wonderful sleeping with him might feel, it would only make this situation more complicated.*

She told herself that even though she owed David money, she still had her pride. *If I sleep with him, what's the difference between me and any woman who accepts financial compensation for sex?*

Sex. Sex. Sex. Since when is that all I think about?

I'm spending my time reading about and thinking about sex toys. That could be enough to muddle any woman's common sense.

She ran one finger across her bottom lip and closed her eyes in pleasure as she remembered the feel of his mouth on hers. *Did he have to be such a good kisser?*

She turned away from the mirror, shed her nightgown, and stepped into the shower. By the end of her shower, she'd convinced herself the only reason it felt like he kissed better than any other man she'd ever been with was because it had been such a long time. By the time she was dressed and hopping into her truck, she'd put their morning flirtation behind her and was determined to focus on the day's errands. David stopped when he saw her across the driveway, turned the tractor off, and got down. Lucy started her truck quickly and peeled out of her driveway like a criminal running from the law.

I'm not afraid I'll melt at his feet if I talk to him again or stand there staring at him, wishing he'd kiss me again. No, I'm smarter than that. I just don't see what we have to say to each other right now.

She glanced back in her mirror and saw him standing in the middle of her driveway, shaking his head. *No matter how good he looks, he must smell like cow manure after working out there.*

I wouldn't mind washing him off.

A nasty crunching sound snapped Lucy's attention back to driving, and she realized she'd driven right over her mailbox, which had thankfully been on a thin post.

This has to stop. I'm lucky it was only a mailbox; there will be kids here this afternoon.

Snap out of it, Lucy.

David is just a man, no different than any other. When has deciding to be with one ever made things better? Doesn't it always end badly? I refuse to add another layer of shit to a situation that is already out of control.

Lucy kept telling herself this, and by the time she arrived in town, she believed it. She checked in with the bank. Even though she believed Wyatt would never cheat her, she needed to confirm that the money was there. Afterward, she met with the same lawyer her father had always used. He wrote up a simple loan paper for her and David without blinking an eye. In a town as small as Mavis, he'd probably heard all about David staying at her place, but he didn't ask. His discretion was what her father had always liked about him, and Lucy was grateful for it then and now.

She was walking out of his office when she literally bumped into a friend from high school. "Michelle."

A concerned look spread across the petite brunette's face. "Lucy. I heard about you and Ted; are you okay?"

Lucy scanned her friend's face and found no sign of anything but genuine worry. "I'm fine. Sometimes things just don't work out. You know how it goes."

Michelle Hughes nodded and gave her nearly flat stomach a pat. "I haven't heard from you lately, so you don't know that we're expecting another baby." Her expression twisted with embarrassment. "I'm sorry. This was the wrong moment to bring that up."

Lucy took her friend's hand in hers. "I'm okay and really, really happy for you. Ron must be thrilled. I know you both wanted to try for a boy."

"He is, and we're hopeful this time. The doctor thought he saw a . . . well, you know. It's hard to say when they're so little, but Ron already bought a football."

"That's great," Lucy said, then hugged her friend. She'd known Michelle since kindergarten. Seeing her happy brightened Lucy's mood. "I have work to do today, but I have time for lunch. What about you?"

"I'd love that."

They linked arms and walked to the town's diner together. *I was wrong. I do have friends here.* The people at the bank and her father's old lawyer had both not only seemed to care but also sounded as if they believed she could succeed. She was glad she'd come into town.

Over sandwiches, the two women caught up with what Michelle had been doing. When they finished, Michelle sat back and took a sip of her water. "Did I mention how good it is to see you? I've missed you." She put her glass down. "I was so sorry to hear it didn't work out with you and Ted. There is someone special out there for you. My mother always says, 'There's a lid for every pot.' You'll find yours."

Lucy twirled her straw in her drink. "I'm not focusing on that right now. I'm working on saving the ranch."

"I'm surprised you want it. You always said you couldn't wait to get out of here."

"People change," Lucy said quietly. "They grow up and realize what they thought was important isn't, and what they tried to leave behind is really all that matters."

"Leave something behind? Sometimes I wish I could."

Lucy's eyes flew to Michelle's, and her friend instantly began to backpedal. "I'm happy with my life, but we all have our challenges. You'll work yours out. You always were able to do anything you set your mind to."

Lucy smiled ruefully. That wasn't at all how she felt lately. She wanted to ask what troubles had momentarily put a sad look in Michelle's eyes, but she didn't. Michelle would tell her when she was ready. Instead, she asked a question that had been burning inside her. "Michelle, what do you think of toys?"

"Like for kids?"

"No, for adults."

Michelle leaned forward and whispered, "What kind of toys are you talking about?"

"You know—like vibrators and stuff like that."

Michelle's face turned bright red. "Well, I don't know anything about them. But there are shops for them in Dallas. Are you feeling that lonely?"

"It's not about being lonely." Lucy had been curious about what her friend would think of what she was selling, but she was regretting bringing the topic up. Michelle looked mortified. "I'm sorry. I don't know what I was thinking, asking you such a personal question."

Michelle was quiet a moment, then said, "Buying one would be a waste of time for me. I've never been able to . . . Ron says some women can't . . . and after all the sex we've had, I tend to agree with him. Even when it feels good, it never feels as good as they write about in those steamy books. I'm okay with that, though. I'm okay with how things are, and so is Ron." She laid her hand on her stomach again. "Plus, we must be doing something right."

Lucy leaned forward and exclaimed in a loud whisper, "Wait, you've never had an orgasm?"

Michelle smacked Lucy's arm. "Don't put it in the paper for God's sake. A lot of women can't. Everyone is built differently."

Lucy lowered her voice, but she was firm in her reply. "No, we all have pretty much the same parts. You've been married for five years. I can't believe you've never."

Michelle's eyes teared up. "Are you trying to make me feel bad?"

No, I'm wishing I knew which toy would cure that. "No, I'm just surprised, that's all. And I don't believe some women can't. I mean, maybe someone has a condition, but to me it sounds more like an excuse than a diagnosis."

"Are you suggesting Ron is not good in bed?" her friend asked, sounding suddenly angry with Lucy.

"No. No. But there might be some things he doesn't know. Things about you that if you knew, you could show him."

Michelle gasped and whispered, "I would never mas—do what you're suggesting. I'm a married woman."

"Exactly. You should be just as happy as your husband is. Aren't you at least curious if you can be?"

Michelle's anger dissolved somewhat. "I'm not like you, Lucy. I never dreamed of living in the city or having wild orgies. I wanted a simple life, and I have one. Of course things could always be better, but sometimes you have to accept what you've got."

"First, just because I moved to a big city doesn't mean I dove into orgies. Second, I'm tired of accepting that life has to suck. I don't think it does. I've made up my mind to make my life one I'm happy with— really happy with. You could do the same."

Michelle waved a hand nervously in the air. "I don't know how we even got on this topic."

Lucy made a face, grateful her friend didn't sound angry anymore. "I brought it up, sorry."

The waitress came over, and Lucy paid the bill. After they were alone again, Michelle said, "And besides, even if I wanted to try something like that—where would I get one?"

Not from me. I have a feeling if you saw what's in my office, you'd pass out. "Everything is online, Michelle, and they send the items discreetly packaged, so no one knows. Buying them has become commonplace."

"I wouldn't even know what to buy."

There's an irony to this. A good salesperson would convince her to spend four hundred dollars on the stuff I have in stock, but that's not what she needs. "I'd start with something small like a silver bullet. Something simple."

Michelle blushed and hugged Lucy. "You are never allowed to tell anyone we had this conversation."

"I won't. It's really not a big deal, Michelle. You'll see."

They walked out of the restaurant together. "I'm pregnant. I can't believe I'm even considering this."

Lucy stopped walking and sought to put into words what she was feeling. "Being a mother shouldn't mean you aren't still a woman. And being a woman shouldn't mean that enjoying sex is wrong. I can't picture a man who'd have sex if he thought he'd never orgasm from it. Don't ever be embarrassed about wanting the same."

Michelle smiled shyly. "This feels like old times. We used to talk about everything, remember? I've missed that."

"Me too." And she realized in that moment just how true that was. Michelle had loved Lucy's parents and had been a frequent extra daughter in their house throughout the years. Friendships like that should be sustained. Their season wasn't over.

They came to a stop beside Lucy's truck. "I know it was rough for you after your brother left, Lucy. I hope things are going better for you now."

"They're turning around," Lucy said with a smile, then stepped inside her truck.

As Lucy drove back to her place, she thought about what she'd said to Michelle about toys. Was there really a difference between the large mechanical device she'd giggled like a schoolgirl at the night before and the regular vibrator she'd owned since college?

I can do this.

Lucy was still smiling when she drove back up her driveway. She waved to David, who was standing near the barn with Wyatt, parked her truck, and walked into her house without stopping to talk to either of them. She didn't want to risk ruining the positive energy. She went inside her office and pulled down all the blinds.

I've been letting a little thing like a crazy number of controls intimidate me when I should . . . embrace the challenge, so to speak.

David pushed his hat back and fought the urge to follow Lucy into her house. She'd bolted that morning, and he'd had trouble concentrating since. All day he told himself she'd be fine in town by herself, but he was relieved when she pulled into the driveway, missing the mailbox he'd fixed.

He didn't know what to think about how happy she looked as she waved to him before heading inside her house without a word. Could be visiting the bank had put her mind at ease, and that was the reason for her smile. He wanted her to be happy, but he felt a pang of jealousy at the thought that someone else might have put her in such a good mood.

He didn't realize he'd grunted until Wyatt said, "If you let yourself get worked up this early, you'll be a wreck by the time you're actually dating. Let her come to you."

David could have denied his level of interest in Lucy, but he didn't see the point. Wyatt cared about Lucy and had known her a long time. His opinion wasn't one to be carelessly dismissed. David leaned a hip on the porch railing as he continued to look at Lucy's house. "I gave her space the first time, and she went off and got engaged."

Wyatt laughed. "You're not afraid to tell it like it is, are you? I like that about you. I know Lucy well enough to say she's not looking to get engaged anytime soon. And she likes you, but that won't be enough. Women and men aren't as different as they like to claim they are. They both find it hard to appreciate anything that comes too easily to them. Give the girl some time to pine for you."

David glanced at Wyatt out of the corner of his eye. "What is it about me that makes everyone think I can't do this on my own?"

Wyatt took a moment to seriously consider the reason before he said, "You're a good man, David. Those are few and far between. Lucy's always been a sweet girl. We were all holding our breath when she got engaged to that snake, York. No one wants to see you mess this up, son."

"I won't. Not this time." David rubbed a hand over his chin and sighed. "I consider myself a patient man, but I don't want to be out here when I could be in there."

Wyatt cackled another laugh. "I remember those days. Don't you worry, David, I've got plenty of boxes for you to unload from the last truck run. Come on, we'll feed you dinner for your trouble."

Pushing himself off the railing, David nodded toward the house in the back that Wyatt's family was moving into. "Does your wife make her own biscuits?"

"They're so good I would have married her for them alone."

David's stomach rumbled, reminding him that he hadn't eaten since breakfast. "Then you'd better treat her well, or my sights might turn in that direction."

"Try it and you'd live only as long as it took me to find the right corner of the field to bury you in."

David's eyebrows shot up. The man was in his sixties and so was his wife. He had to know he was joking. "I'll keep that in mind."

He laughed again and gave David a pat on the back. "You do that. Something tells me you'll be the same way with Lucy when she's yours. My daughter-in-law has my son getting manicures and waxing off hair from where God intended for it grow. She might as well geld him. It's good to have a man's man around. Hopefully some of you will rub off on him."

David let the waxing comment pass. He didn't want to know. "What you're saying is that you want your son smelling like he spent the day cleaning out paddocks?"

Wyatt's nose wrinkled. "Now that you mention it, I'll ask my wife to hold supper until after you shower. Let's get my truck unloaded first."

David agreed. What Wyatt had said about giving Lucy some time made sense, and he could use a distraction. He had a feeling that if Wyatt's family was anything like him, it would be highly entertaining.

Chapter Seven

A week later, feeling calmer than she had in a long time, Lucy walked between her piles of inventory and tried to pick the next one she'd try. Her initial embarrassment with them gone, she was taking a much more practical approach.

There was nothing wrong with a woman enjoying herself as much as a man did, and if these items helped women do that, she was actually doing them a service by making them available. Sure there were some toys in the room Lucy was convinced she'd never use, but she was okay with that.

She started asking herself what a woman would need to know about each selection and what they would like about it. Once she did that, a classification system easily followed. She was glad the company was new enough that she'd be able to have an impact on how they represented themselves, because she was beginning to get excited.

The more she thought about it, the more she recognized the flaws in the company's website. The descriptions read like they were selling computers, and the directions were written in geek jargon the average person would struggle with.

Lucy now understood why Technically Anonymous Pleasure had looked for a female to partner with. They needed to find a way to convince women like her that their products were not only worth the money but also not cold and mechanical.

Hiding in her house, Lucy sorted the items from the least intimidating to the most. *I was rushing myself when I didn't have to.* She'd valued Michelle's level of knowledge with toys and guided her to what she thought she'd be comfortable with. *I will value my own journey the same way. I don't have to try everything in this room, but if I decide to, that's okay, too.*

The founders of the company had taken items people might be familiar with and added a level of technology that needed to be demystified. Most of the toys were for women, but a few were for men. Each night, she would take a toy into her bedroom and document her progress.

On the first night, she chose a simple-looking vibrator with a chip that synced with an app she'd downloaded to her phone. The app contained short video clips of men, some clothed and some not, talking into the camera. It was designed to allow a woman to simulate having phone sex with a man. Lucy downloaded two videos that walked her through a sexy session of self-exploration. The geeks might not know how to market their toys, but they had obviously thrown money at every detail of production. The men were attractive and sexy, without being creepy. Lucy had watched two videos—one to learn the process, and one to see if it was as good as the first. She came twice, but decided it was easier to orgasm while imagining David than watching a video.

On the second night, she tried the vibrating panties that synced with erotic reading material. During the sex scenes in the story, the vibrating panties would automatically turn on. It was nice, but perhaps because she was reading, her mind kept wandering to David. As the story heated up, Lucy would find herself closing her eyes and imagining

David's hands on her, David's tongue replacing the vibrator. Lucy wrote her findings next to the item number.

By Friday, she'd gone through all the tame options. She wrote to the company and shared her thoughts regarding website descriptions and presentation of the items. By giving a few examples of how she thought they could market the products differently, she felt her confidence grow when they responded positively. *Perhaps my degree has not been for nothing after all.*

They needed to take a much more personal approach. Lucy added each product she'd tried to her website and wrote a blog to accompany it. She shared her thoughts about each one, but also started writing short erotic stories about a woman who used the toy. Her stories mirrored her reality. The character she used in each story was a single woman who wanted to be with a man but presently wasn't.

The more she wrote, the more her confidence soared. Since her website and her blog were completely anonymous, she didn't worry about offending anyone. She came up with a pen name and became bolder about sharing what she discovered about herself as she tried each toy. The feedback was instant and positive. Women started thanking her for her candor. Merely by chance, another blogger came across her site and mentioned it to her many followers. Her in-box quickly flooded with e-mails from women who were not only buying the products but also connecting with her stories.

Lucy was feeling good about herself and her growing business bank account. After only one week, she had made a few hundred dollars. The orders shipped directly from the company; all she had to do was find and engage clients.

There was only one area she wasn't feeling good about—she'd avoided David for an entire week. No matter how she spun it, she didn't like what it said about her. He'd stepped in to help save her ranch, and she'd delivered his money to him via Wyatt. She'd gone to say hello to Wyatt's family only when she heard David had run to town on an errand. David's horses had arrived a few days ago, and she hadn't gone out to help.

I'm a coward, sitting in here, hoping if I keep my head down long enough, I won't have to deal with my feelings. Doing anything I can to keep my mind off a man who probably wouldn't even be here if he knew what I'm selling. It's one thing to use a toy or two, but another thing entirely to make selling them a profession.

I used to face life head-on.

I've been avoiding Sarah because I don't know how to answer the questions she'll have about David.

I can't tell her how I spent this week or what I've been doing to distract myself.

Or how ineffective it was.

She found herself watching him from the window while he worked. She'd tried to tell herself being around sex toys had made her ripe for any man, but there were several men working the horses with David, and she felt nothing when she looked at them. Two orgasms a night should be enough to make a woman forget about any man, but that had only made Lucy yearn for David.

Lucy kicked one of the boxes in her office. This is where toys, even the best of them, fell short. They didn't have eyes that were full of laughter one minute, then burned with passion the next. The scent of them didn't make her want to tear off her clothes and taste every inch of them. Nothing in her office would ever pick her up, carry her toward her bedroom, only to stop and take her passionately on the stairs because it had to have her and couldn't wait. They couldn't wake her with a kiss or make her breakfast.

A sex toy, even the best one, would never be David.

She tried to tell herself David could never live up to the fantasy she'd built around him. For all she knew, he'd be awful in bed. Some men were. *Look at Michelle. Her husband is perfectly happy accepting that he can't fully satisfy her.*

Lucy left her office and locked the door behind her. *David is a distraction, and one of the few ways I could mess up something that is finally looking like it might work. If I let him close, let him in, I'll want to be honest with him. But what if he tells someone what I'm doing? It won't matter how much money I make; I couldn't look anyone in the eye. This ranch would no longer be worth saving.*

He doesn't seem like someone who would say anything, but my track record with reading people hasn't been that good lately.

I should be happy that the gamble I took looks like it will work. I should be celebrating the realization that I may actually be good at online marketing.

But I have no one to tell.

No one to celebrate with.

Lucy walked onto her front porch and sat in the swinging chair. David was talking to a ranch hand while they both watched another man work one of the horses in a round pen. As if he could sense her, David looked over his shoulder, and Lucy's breath caught in her throat.

He still wants me, and God help me, I want him just as badly.

He waved to her.

Lucy hesitated. Their attraction was too strong for things to stay innocent for long. Highly combustible. The only way to not burst into flames was to stay far, far away from the heat source until it gave up and went home.

Is that what I want? For him to leave? To know that the next time I see him will be at Melanie's wedding and, likely, with a date on his arm.

No. God, no.

Is it just that I'm lonely? I wake up and talk to no one. I go to bed alone. Would I crave him like I do if I were back in the city booked with social engagements?

I would.

He was watching her intently with those blue eyes she found impossible to look away from. *He's waiting for a cue from me, a sign that I'm ready.*

I'm not. Not for what we both want.

All or nothing. That's how this feels, but does it have to be that way? I could say yes to time with him. I don't have to give in completely.

Where would the harm be in a walk together? In dinner?

Is anything I'm doing worth it if I become some kind of weird recluse whose only companionship comes from devices with batteries?

Lucy lifted her hand and waved back. David said something to the man beside him and started walking toward her. This time, Lucy didn't run. She stood and met him on the top step of her porch.

He stopped at the bottom step, rested a foot on it, removed his hat, wiped his forehead with his sleeve, and then held his hand out to her. "Come see what I do for a living."

Lucy bit her bottom lip and let her eyes wander over him. He was covered with dust, but she doubted there was a woman in Texas who would have minded. The simple act of raising his hand in her direction flexed the powerful muscles in his arm and shoulder. He was ridiculously handsome, but without the air of conceit that usually came with such good looks. She looked him over hungrily. No man should fill out a pair of jeans as well as he did. As soon as she realized where her gaze had settled, she raised her eyes to his and blushed. Her hesitation lasted long enough that most men would have dropped their hand, but David didn't. His eyes danced with humor that made it impossible for her not to smile back at him. She finally placed her hand in his and said, "I'd like that."

Another man might have asked her why she'd hidden from him all week or rushed to apologize in case he'd offended her. David did neither. He acted as if their last awkward conversation had never happened, and Lucy was grateful.

As they walked together, he kept her hand in his. A week earlier, Lucy would have pulled away. Today, she let herself enjoy the pleasure in that simple touch.

That is what I have missed. When was the last time someone held me? Touched me? Cherished me?

He led her to a round pen where a young man with red hair was standing in the middle with a lead line, encouraging a horse to circle him. "That's Lucas. He's helping me not only with the horses but with the new men I hired. Ask ten cowboys how to train a horse and you'll get ten very different answers. I don't break horses; I gentle them. What men do on their own time with their horses is none of my business, but any man who works with me will follow my philosophy."

Lucy looked the large horse over. If she had to guess, it was around five years old and still wild. "Is that a mustang?" To a cattle rancher, mustangs were direct competition for resources. Government land was leased to ranchers, and the time they were allowed to graze their herds on that land was often dictated by how much the wild mustangs grazed an area. In the past, the mustangs were culled through hunting, but animal protection organizations had made that illegal. Now many of them were rounded up and kept in holding facilities where they spent the rest of their lives in large overpopulated paddocks. Lucy's father had often said what people do out of kindness is often a cruelty of its own.

"It is. This one is a quarter horse mix. As you likely know, so many breeds have been released into the wild that mustangs now can be any pedigree. Their only commonality is their wildness." David watched the horse as it trotted around the young cowboy.

"My father never had much love for them."

David looked down at her with that accepting, patient look of his. "I can understand why he'd feel that way, but these horses were brought to Texas by people. Some lines have run free for hundreds of years. Some came to it more recently, but still by no fault of their own. They aren't vermin to be exterminated. They are spirited, beautiful creatures who are healthier and more intelligent because they are bred and survive by natural selection. They deserve a chance to be valued, and I give them that every time I send one home with a family."

I sell high-priced sex toys and am working my courage up to try some of the multi-motored advanced ones. That's practically the same thing, right?

Lucy closed her eyes briefly and groaned. *I always considered myself a good person. No one's perfect, but I've always tried to be kind to others and not shy away from my responsibilities. David is a whole different level of good.*

She opened her eyes and pulled her hand free from his. "I should get back to my office."

David blocked her retreat. "Mason will be in Fort Mavis this weekend. He and Chelle will be there. Sarah asked if you were going. I said I had no idea. Mason must really want us both there, because he said he'd have a private plane waiting for us at the airfield tomorrow morning."

"Oh, that's really generous of him, but I can't . . ."

"Don't let me be the reason you don't go. I don't mind driving back."

Lucy met his eyes and was instantly sorry she did. He was being sincere, and she felt lower than low. He would actually drive all the way to Fort Mavis and let her take the plane. He was that fucking nice.

I should tell him the truth about how I'm saving the ranch. Let him see that although he's vying for sainthood, I'm quickly slipping in the opposite direction.

"Take the plane, David. If I decide to go, I'll make the drive. I've done it before."

He kept her corralled against the round pen and leaned down so his lips hovered just above hers. "Are you afraid to fly?"

She swallowed hard. "No."

He ran a hand lightly down her arm, sending shivers of pleasure through her. "Then what is it? Are you afraid if we're alone, you won't be able to keep your hands off me?"

Yes. "That's ridiculous."

"Then say yes. There's no reason you and I can't share a private plane ride to see our closest friends, is there?"

His voice. His touch. The promise of his lips on hers. Lucy was helplessly mesmerized. "I guess you're right."

"I am," he said with a slow, sexy smile.

Striving to hold on to some semblance of sanity, she said, "We have to be back by Sunday night. I have a conference call scheduled."

His breath tickled her cheek. "How is your business going?"

"It's coming—" She blushed at the double meaning that was accurate. "It's coming along. I've already generated some revenue. Not enough to break even, of course, but I'll get there."

"That's great. New businesses are tough. I bet you're working all hours of the night right now."

Lucy tried to look away but couldn't. Memories of how she'd spent the nights last week would have been much more exciting if David had been there with her, watching her, taking the toy from her and bringing her to climax himself. Her body clenched, and she grew wet.

It didn't matter that it was the middle of the day, that they were not alone, or that she'd just told herself she wouldn't sleep with him. If he pulled her against him, claimed her mouth beneath his, she would have given herself over to him completely.

"Lucy?" David asked gently.

"Yes?"

"I want you. I don't give a damn that everyone is watching us right now, but I do care what they think of you. Be ready by nine tomorrow morning. You're getting on that plane even if I have to carry you onto it."

Imagining that did nothing to calm the hot desire pulsing through Lucy. She told herself she should say no. If she couldn't control herself now, in public, what would happen when they were finally alone? She licked her bottom lip. "You wouldn't do that."

"Then you don't know me well enough yet." He bent and kissed the spot just below her ear. His excitement pressed against her stomach, proof that their conversation was also turning him on. "I want you, Lucy, and I will have you. Maybe not today. Maybe not this weekend, but soon. We both know it's inevitable."

Lucy arched back from him, which only succeeded in pressing her more closely against his bulging cock. Her lack of ability to think when he was that close sent panic through her. "Let me go."

"Say yes."

"About the plane?"

"If that's where you want to start."

"Fine. Yes. Now let me go."

David released her, and she bolted back into her house. Once inside, she leaned against the closed door and let out a long shaky breath.

So much for being able to keep things casual.

I'm going away with David.

Oh my God, I'm going away with David.

David rested an arm on the railing of the pen and stared at Lucy's front door long after she'd disappeared through it. Of all the things he'd meant to say to her, announcing that he would soon fuck her wasn't one of them. Something happened to his brain when he was around her.

He didn't notice Lucas until the younger man was beside him. "It's not hard to see why you decided to stay."

David glared at Lucas. "Get back to work before I decide you are not, in fact, the best choice for this job."

Lucas smiled. "You won't fire me. You need someone to take over here while you pursue other interests."

David grunted. He had no intention of letting Lucas go, but that didn't mean he wasn't tempted to slug him. "I do need you this weekend. I'm heading back to Fort Mavis. Can you handle everything while I'm gone?"

"Does the job come with a pretty girl I can moon over, too?"

David snarled, "Lucy's coming with me."

Lucas laughed and raised his hands in mock surrender. "I was only hoping there was more than one woman in town."

David relaxed and was reminded of how he'd felt with Wyatt when he'd made a similar joke. Some things never became funny. "Just watch over the ranch and the horses."

Lucas was quiet for a moment, then said, "I might not look like it, but I've had my share of girlfriends. If you need any advice, don't be shy about asking."

David's temper rose again. "I am perfectly capable of working things out with Lucy on my own."

Lucas raised his hands again, but this time his expression was serious. "I know, but you've been good to me, and I want to see you happy. Everyone wants it to work out this time."

"*Everyone* needs to step back and mind their own fucking business."

Undeterred, Lucas retorted, "We would, but no one wants you to—"

"Fuck it up again?" David snapped. He advanced on Lucas. "I did nothing wrong the first time, and she is coming around just fine. I don't need or want anyone's help with this. Why do all y'all find that difficult to understand?"

"Because no one wants to see the mopey, lovesick David again?" Lucas said, then ducked and retreated back into the round pen. "You didn't have to deal with you."

David swore and strode off. Lucas was wrong. He did have to deal with that side of himself. He'd lain awake night after night, asking himself why one woman could matter so much. He'd spent month after month doing whatever he could to convince himself she didn't, only to find himself wanting her more instead of less as time went on.

If he had known when he first met Lucy that she was sadder and more desperate than she'd let on, he never would have returned to Fort Mavis. He would have stayed and made sure Ted York didn't take advantage of her. He'd thought he had more time.

He'd been wrong.

His friends were well-meaning, but they didn't see the difference between then and now. The first time, he'd played nice.

This time, he was playing for keeps.

Chapter Eight

That night, Lucy avoided her office and its contents. It would still be there on Monday when she returned. What she needed now was a dose of sanity, of calm. She tossed and turned until dawn and started the next day with a cold shower. She had no idea if it would be effective, but she was a wreck on the inside. With just enough makeup to conceal the circles beneath her eyes, she wavered back and forth while choosing outfits.

The practical choice was boots, jeans, and a blouse. She was going from one ranch to another. This wasn't a date; it was a trip to see a good friend of hers. Although she didn't know Mason well, she'd gotten to know his fiancée, Chelle, through Sarah. That couple lived a very different lifestyle than Lucy. They were often photographed at big events. They might want to go somewhere expensive. *I should have asked. I need to call Sarah.*

Thankfully, her friend picked up. "Lucy. Is everything okay? I've been calling you all week."

In her underwear and bra, Lucy paced her bedroom. "I know. I'm sorry. I've been so busy with the new job. I saw your messages, and I meant to call, but time flew by and I didn't."

Sarah made a small sound, like she didn't believe Lucy. When she spoke, she sounded hurt. "I've been dying to hear what it's like to have David there, but I don't want to bring up something you clearly don't want to talk about."

You just did. "Sarah, I didn't call you because I didn't know what to say."

"Aha, I was right: not calling me was a decision. I thought we were getting close again, but sometimes I wonder. You didn't tell me when your parents died. You didn't turn to me for help when you needed it. Whenever something big happens in your life, you shut me out. How can we be friends if you won't let me know you?"

Lucy sat on the edge of her bed, and her shoulders slumped. "Are you saying you don't want me to come this weekend?"

Sarah made another sound of displeasure. "I'm saying I might slap you before I hug you. Or I might hug you, then slap you, then hug you. I'm not sure which. You have this idea in your head that people won't love you if you're not perfect. Have you looked at the rest of us? Whatever stupid thing you think you might be doing, chances are I've done just as bad. Talk to me, Lucy. Don't shut me out."

Lucy took a deep breath and a leap of faith. "If I tell you something, you can't tell anyone. Not even your husband. Do you understand?"

"I tell Tony everything."

"So that's a no?"

"It's a yes under duress. What is it? If you're in trouble, I can't promise I won't enlist Tony's help. We're a team. But I won't say a word to him unless I absolutely have to. How's that?"

With a whoosh, everything Lucy had held in poured out. "David paid off my debt to Ted. I'm selling high-tech sex toys now to pay him back. I'm actually making money at it, but I can't tell David. He is the nicest man I've ever met. I thought Ted was nice, too, and I was wrong. Am I wrong about David?"

"No," Sarah said slowly. "David's a good guy."

"Too good, right? Too good to want to be with someone who would sell sex toys."

"Whoa, wait. First, I can't believe you didn't tell me that was what your new business was. I write romances. Why do you think that would shock me?"

"You haven't seen some of these toys."

"Exactly. Research. And, second, how do you know David wouldn't be into them?"

Sarah's really okay with it. Is it possible that I'm the only who is shocked by what I'm trying to sell? The only one who is embarrassed? No wonder I left Mavis. When I'm here, I feel like I have to be the daughter my parents thought I was. I have to find my way back to not seeing myself through their eyes.

"Is Tony into toys?"

"Not really, but he would be if I wore the right outfit and asked him to be. You have to give David a chance. He wouldn't leave over something like that."

And there it was, the reason Lucy was so afraid to move forward with David. "I don't know if I could handle another person leaving me, Sarah." Tears filled her eyes and spilled down her cheeks. "It's why I have trouble leaning on people. If I don't need you, I won't be devastated if you leave, too."

"Oh, Lucy. I'm not going anywhere."

"I know. At least my head knows, but I never pictured myself alone like this. I had a family, and it was a good one. I thought it was, anyway. I loved Rhode Island. Life was fun, full, good. Then my dad died. I felt like I'd lost a quarter of my heart. Then I moved back here to help my mom, but what good did that do? And then Steven left. Every time something went wrong, I told myself to stay positive. All I had to do was be strong and keep going, but something happened inside me when Steven left, too. I can't explain it. I want to hide from the world, but I feel so alone when I do. Horribly, utterly alone. I used to know what to do. Now, I don't know who to trust, what to believe."

"You. Are. Not. Alone. And David really cares about you. You have to know that."

"I want to believe he does."

"He stuck by Tony at his worst. If that didn't run him off, nothing will."

"I'm scared, Sarah. I don't like feeling this way. I never used to be afraid of anything. How do I get back to being that person?"

Sarah was quiet for a bit. "I don't think anyone ever gets 'back' after they've experienced loss. It's terrifying when you realize how little of your life you're in control of, that, at any moment, you could lose anyone or anything you love, and there is nothing you can do to stop it."

"You think that way, too? You're always so happy."

Sarah sighed. "Of course I do, but I use that knowledge to make me stronger. What's the alternative? Giving up? Wallowing in the past? I could have been that person, but I refused to be. When I accepted how temporary everything is, something beautiful happened. I started to see time as a gift. Every day I have with Tony is a day I am thankful for. I can't think about what will happen if it ends. I can't spend every day worrying that he might die or leave me for someone else. We want to have children. I won't be able to enjoy them if I'm constantly afraid of losing them like I lost my little brother. I don't want to live like that. Happiness is a decision to believe that we're more than this—that despite what we know, being here is worth it. It's a little like believing in Santa Claus. Once you know the truth, you never go back to waiting up to catch him come down the chimney, but you believe in the spirit of him, so the magic continues."

She makes it sound so easy, just as she's always made life look. But she's experienced loss, too. She had issues with her family and survived them. All I have to do is believe? I wish I could snap my fingers and do that. "Should I tell David about my business?"

"Have you been on a date yet?"

"No."

"Then I'd hold off on that. Let the man woo you a little before you bring out the dildos. Hey, that's a great line. I may use that in a book."

It was difficult to do anything but smile when talking to Sarah. "Thanks, Sarah. I can't wait to see you."

"Me too. Now, when are you coming?"

"Mason is flying us in this morning."

"Is he? He is so cool."

"What should I take to wear? Is any part of the weekend going to be formal?"

"I don't think so. Pack a dress if you want, but you're so tiny, you can fit into any of our clothes if you need something."

A knock on the downstairs door made Lucy jump to her feet. "That must be David. I have to run."

"Tell him I said hello."

"I will."

Lucy sprinted down the stairs and opened the door. This time she wasn't afraid of the passion she saw blazing in David's gaze as it raked over her. "Sorry, I was talking to Sarah about what I should wear."

A slow, I-like-your-choice smile spread across his face. "And you decided to keep it simple?"

Lucy looked down and realized she was still only in her bra and panties. While turning three shades of pink, she turned and bolted up the stairs. "Oh my God, I'll be right back."

"No rush," he called back with humor.

A few minutes later, dressed in jeans and a blouse, Lucy returned with a small piece of luggage. David grinned at her. She waved a finger in his direction. "We will pretend that never happened. I'm ready now."

"I'm not," he said, pulling her into his arms. He kissed her like a man who was returning home and couldn't get enough of the woman he'd missed. She dropped her luggage at her feet, and her arms went up to circle his neck. His tongue plundered her mouth mercilessly, and she opened wider for the claiming. He pulled her against him, molded her to him, crushing her against his erection.

When he lifted his head and rested his chin on her forehead, his heart beat under her ear as wildly as hers. "You taste too damn good," he growled.

You too. Lucy stood stiffly in his arms, wishing she could turn off her head and let herself simply enjoy him. *I want to believe—in myself, in him, in happily ever afters.* In a husky voice, she said, "We should go."

David nuzzled her neck. "You're right. Everyone is excited to see us. They've been calling all morning. That mattered to me—before you answered the door."

Lucy pulled back from him. Even though she wanted to give in to how she was feeling, she thought about what Sarah had asked her earlier. They didn't have a relationship. Not a normal one. He'd never asked her out on a date. She knew very little about him. All they had so far was an attraction neither one of them had proven successful at denying. "I need you to know that just because I said yes to the trip doesn't mean that—that I am saying yes to anything else."

He studied her face for a moment, then said quietly, "We can take this as slowly as you need to. Come on, we have a plane to catch." He held out his hand to her.

Lucy put hers in his and felt a jolt of pleasure at how natural it felt. They walked together to David's truck. Lucy watched his expression for a sign that he was displeased with her, but he was smiling. So many other men would have been frustrated with her. David was confident but patient. He wasn't shy about what he wanted, but he cared about how she felt. Lucy had doubted men like him existed, but here he was. Not only was he good-looking, smart, and kind; he was also openly interested in her.

Good things can happen—if I believe they can.

Right?

It's supposed to be that simple.

He caught her looking at him and paused before starting the ignition. "What is it?"

Focus on the positive—the part of the experience that feels like a gift. She didn't have the words to articulate everything she was feeling, so she said, "You're a pretty amazing man, David."

He shot her a smile that set her heart beating double time again. "You ain't seen nothing yet, darlin'."

As they drove to the airport, David kept the conversation light. They talked about Wyatt, his family, and how happy her manager looked now that he was working on her ranch again. They discussed the clear weather and how it was nice to be flying out on such a beautiful day. He could see Lucy relaxing the more they spoke.

Taking Lucy back to Fort Mavis would be good for her. She had a tendency to withdraw and hide. She did it with him, but also with her friends. She hadn't left her house once in the past week. That wasn't healthy. He knew all about hiding and how a person's life could get smaller and smaller until it was suffocated. *And, if I am being honest with myself, I've done my share of hiding. I keep adding layers of good deed on top of good deed, but does a lifetime of good wash away a person's mistakes—even if those mistakes cost someone's life?* David pushed those thoughts back.

Lucy needed to get out of her house and away from that ranch. She needed to surround herself with people who cared about her. He'd known plenty of men who pulled their women away from the people they loved. Isolating women made them easier to manipulate. David had no respect for such men. No person or creature should ever stay somewhere because they were too broken to leave.

Lucy said she wanted to save her ranch, but David was no longer sure she should. She wasn't happy there. Anyone could see that. If she had female friends there, he hadn't heard about them, and they weren't rushing forward to help her.

Away from that ranch, Lucy might flourish—find the easy smile Sarah said she used to have. David considered himself a good judge of people and horses. He looked for a spark in their eyes. If it was there, he knew there was more to them than whatever they were presenting. He'd rescued many haggard horses and sold them a year later in stunning condition.

Lucy was far from haggard, but when she thought no one was watching, her expression was one of a woman with the weight of the world on her shoulders. *Like a mustang kept in a tiny corral for too long, she's forgotten how to run free.*

He smiled and wondered what Lucy would think of being compared to a horse. She might not take it as the compliment it was intended to be.

Lucy shifted in the truck seat to watch him as he drove. "What are you smiling about?"

He flashed a guilty grin. "I'd tell you, but it's not wise to tempt you to hit me while I'm driving."

"I would never—" Lucy stopped as she seemed to remember the time she had hit him. "I've never hit anyone besides you."

He winked at her. "So I was your first."

She rolled her eyes but looked as if she were fighting back a smile. "You like to push your luck, don't you?" He loved how comfortable she was becoming with him.

He wiggled his eyebrows and shot her a lusty grin. "Only with you."

"You're impossible," she said with a laugh.

"And you are gorgeous when you laugh." Lucy's smile fell away, and if David hadn't been driving, he would have hugged her. It was as he'd suspected: somewhere along the way, she'd stopped seeing herself as beautiful. He reached for her hand and brought it to rest beneath his on his thigh. "Do you remember the first time we met?" he asked.

Lucy's hand shook beneath his. "Tony had sent you to see if you could help out."

"That was why I was here, but that's not what I remember about that day. You answered the door, and everything I'd planned to say flew clear out of my head. I'm not a young boy. I've met a fair share of women, but you were stunning. You worried if I was tired and hungry from the drive, but all I could think about was how beautiful you were."

Lucy's hand felt cold beneath his, but she didn't withdraw it. "I don't have good memories from that day. I had just accepted the loan from Ted. I was feeling pretty low about that and then felt worse when I realized you also wanted to help me. I didn't want to ruin what I thought was a solution. I wish I could go back and not have been such a gullible—"

"Don't beat yourself up over something that's done, Lucy. Everyone regrets something. I don't trust anyone who says they've never done anything they're ashamed of."

In a heartbreakingly raw tone, she asked, "Could we please not talk about it anymore?"

He tightened his hand on hers. "What are you so afraid of?"

Lucy turned her face to look out the window, and he cursed himself for pushing her too far too fast. They rode in silence to the small airport. Soon after they parked, they met the pilot and were led to a six-seater plane. Though Lucy was polite, her answers were short. They settled into seats that faced the same direction with a narrow aisle between them. As they taxied down the runway, David was tempted to take her hand in his again, but he told himself to be patient.

They were above the clouds by the time she met his eyes again and spoke. "I used to be brave. In fact, my parents called me fearless. I would decide to do something, and nothing would stand in my way. I flew cross-country by myself without thinking twice. Moving away was an adventure, and I used to love the excitement of not knowing what would come next. Back then, I thought if I worked hard and was a good person, nothing bad would ever happen to me."

"That's not the way life works."

"No, it's not. When my father died, my mother was so sad. I thought having us around would make her happy. I promised her whatever I thought it would take to make her see how much we loved her. It wasn't enough. I'm guessing you heard about how she died."

"I did." He kept his answer short, hoping it would encourage her to keep talking.

"I don't know why my brother waited until it was too late to tell me about our financial problems. Maybe I could have done something. Maybe he knew I couldn't have. I don't know. By the time he told me, he'd already given up on the ranch and me."

He hated that there was nothing he could do to change what had happened to her. She didn't trust people to stay with her, because they hadn't. "Lucy, none of that was your fault."

With a pained expression, she closed her eyes for a moment. "That's what I tell myself, but believing it is the hard part. I can only imagine what you must think of me for taking money from Ted—and then you."

This time, David did reach for her hand. "You were a person in need, and he took advantage of that."

Lucy looked down at their linked hands. "I don't like to see myself as weak, but I let myself get engaged to a man I didn't love, so I don't know who I am anymore." She weaved her fingers with his. "You asked me what I'm afraid of. I'm afraid I may not be the person I thought I was. I might be so much less." She blinked back tears, and David's heart clenched in his chest at the sight, but he kept silent. "I know you like me, David, but I don't know if I have anything to offer anyone. I'm afraid of being alone. I'm afraid of being with someone. You scare the hell out of me. I like you, but I don't know if I could handle losing someone else. Sometimes I think it would be a whole lot easier on both of us if we never saw each other again. I'm not myself right now, David, and you need to know that, because I don't want to hurt you."

David was glad, right then, that they hadn't slept with each other yet. She had some healing to do before she'd trust what they felt for each other. "I'm not going anywhere, Lucy, but you don't have to believe that today. And before you worry about hurting me, I'm a grown man. I know the risks. Worry less about me and more about what you need from this trip. If you could wave a wand and have these few days be any way you wanted, what would that be?"

Her eyes met his and were full of such yearning, he would have promised her anything. "I'd want to forget about everything back in Mavis and enjoy the weekend."

He brought her hand up to his lips and kissed her fingers gently. "So do it."

She looked deeply into his eyes and bit her bottom lip. "Just like that?"

"Just like that. Lucy Albright, let's go see people we love and have a few laughs."

With a shaky sigh, she said, "That sounds perfect." She smiled, and it lit up her face. "Sarah has been asking me to come visit, and I've been putting it off. It'll be wonderful to see her."

David nodded. "I'll enjoy watching Tony sweat a little about the fact that all his help wants to join me in Mavis."

"They do?" She looked so concerned that he rushed to reassure her.

"Not really. A year ago they would have, but things are better there now. He's a damn fine horse trainer, and they'd stay just to learn from the best, but even a good man needs his ego trimmed back a bit now and then."

She looked across at him through her lashes. "Even you?"

As serious as he could force himself to sound, he said, "No. I'm the perfect combination of humble and amazing."

Her eyebrows shot up, then she laughed and it was music to his ears. "It's hard to see the humble."

David kept smiling, simply happy to see her smiling.

She shook her head. "I know the story about how you met Tony, but I can't imagine the two of you working together for as long as you have. You're so different. He's closed off, but you're easy to get along with."

It was a question David had been asked many times. "On the surface, Tony and I seem different, but in ways that matter we have similar philosophies. You can tell a lot about a man by how he is around creatures that depend on him. On his worst day, in his darkest of hours, Tony made sure his horses were respected."

Lucy nodded. "I can see that. What about Mason Thorne? He's an interesting bird."

David thought that was a good assessment of the ex-actor turned California State senator. "Once I looked past the bull he spouts, I began to appreciate that he's often the first one to show up when someone is in a bind. He and Chelle are the perfect pair. She grounds him, and he puts a sparkle in her eyes that wasn't there before."

Lucy's expression closed, and she turned away from him. He didn't know exactly what he'd said that upset her, but he let her withdraw. He'd bring her back to that bridge again and again until she was able to cross it fearlessly.

Chapter Nine

Lucy stared down at the blanket of clouds below the plane and gripped the armrest. When David had mentioned how good Mason and Chelle were for each other, she'd thought, *I want that.*

That's all it had taken to send her into an emotional tailspin. *Could David and I be that for each other? What if he hates the idea of me selling sex toys?*

Stop.

I'm overthinking this.

David's a nice man.

He's fun to be with.

None of that means we'll spend the rest of our lives together or even date. I don't need his approval.

Enjoy the weekend. Flirt a little.

Nothing has to happen.

She glanced across the small aisle at David. He was reading a magazine, but he looked up and met her eyes. She opened her mouth to apologize. She wanted to say she knew how ungrateful she seemed and how much she appreciated his kindness, but she closed her mouth without uttering a word and turned away from him again.

The pilot announced they were preparing to land, and Lucy let out a sigh of relief. After landing, she unbuckled her seat belt, gathered up her purse, and forced a smile to her face. "I can't wait to see Sarah."

When David didn't say anything, she raised her eyes to his. In one strong, incredibly sexy move, he dug his hand into the hair on the back of her neck and kissed her until she was arching against him wantonly. He released her and said, "Me too," as if they hadn't just exchanged a soul-rocking kiss.

Lucy swayed on her feet and brought a shaking hand to her lips. David stepped back and motioned toward the door. "Ready?"

She searched his face for what he was thinking but couldn't read his expression. "What are we doing, David?"

A gentle smile stretched his lips. "Forgetting about everything else and enjoying the weekend."

The pilot opened the door of the plane, and before Lucy had time to think much about what David had said, Sarah was bolting up the plane's steps to hug her. "It is so good to see you," Sarah exclaimed.

Lucy hugged her back tightly. "You too."

Once released, Sarah threw her arms around David and gave him what looked like a bone-crunching embrace as well. "It feels like you've been gone forever."

David laughed. "Hardly more than a week."

Sarah's smile was infectious. "Tony missed you, too, although he probably won't say it." The three of them walked down the steps of the plane together.

Tony pushed himself off from the front of an SUV and came to greet them. He wasn't the huggable type, but Lucy gave him one anyway. He hugged her back, proof of Sarah's influence on him.

David and Tony shook hands with warmth. "How is the Double C surviving without me?" David asked.

"It's barely holding together," Tony said. That description might have fit the ranch before Sarah came into Tony's life, but not since. Still, it was probably nice to think he'd been missed.

"So nothing has changed," David joked.

Tony made a face. "I've lost count of how many people came to see you but settled for talking my ear off. How did you ever get anything done?"

Sarah wrapped an arm around Tony's waist and smiled up at him. "Poor Tony. It's a burden being so popular."

He attempted to look irritated, but failed. Instead, he swatted her behind playfully and said, "Don't mock me, woman, or you'll ruin my ability to intimidate people."

Sarah laughed up at him. "That's already shot to hell. Even Jace isn't afraid of you anymore."

David nodded in the vague direction of Tony's ranch. "How is he?"

The pilot interrupted the conversation briefly to place the luggage in the back of the SUV and to give David and Lucy a card with his number on it. Tony suggested they continue the conversation while driving, and all agreed.

Sarah sat in the front seat with Tony. Lucy was with David behind them. As they drove, Sarah half turned in her seat so she could see them as she spoke. "Jace is still in New York with Charlie and Melanie. He's anxious for the renovations to be done so they can move back into their house, but he says he's having fun. We haven't told him that you left. No one wants to be the one to break that to him."

David's expression tightened, and Lucy watched in wonder at his affection for someone else's child. "He'll always be welcome wherever I am. He knows that. I'll make sure I have a man-to-man talk with him when he returns."

"Can you do that with a six-year-old?" Sarah asked. David grunted as his reply, and Sarah reached back to give his knee a sympathetic pat. She directed her next words to Lucy. "He probably can. David has helped take care of Jace since he was a baby. He's going to be an incredible father."

David and Lucy looked at each other and then away. An awkward silence dragged on for several minutes. Eventually, David cleared his throat and asked, "Did Mason and Chelle fly in yet?"

Sarah shook her head. "They were supposed to be here already, but Mason had something come up at the last minute. They should arrive early tonight. They're staying at a place in town, but I made up the bedroom with the queen-size bed in case—you know. David has his own room in the bunkhouse, but you two can do whatever. We're all adults."

Lucy's face burned with a blush.

David's eyes danced with amusement when they met hers.

Tony reached for his wife's hand. "You might want to let them figure all that out for themselves."

Happily oblivious, Sarah answered, "They shouldn't feel awkward. We're fine with whatever. As long as they don't use that tree in the far field. The one with the low branches that has our names etched in it. That would be weird."

David covered his mouth with a fist and choked back a pained laugh. "I won't ask."

"That'd be for the best," Tony answered gruffly, but the look he gave Sarah was hot with old memories.

Lucy felt completely off-kilter. Part of her wanted to sink into the seat and disappear, but another part was tempted to laugh along with David. She settled for swatting the side of his leg.

David took her hand and settled it beneath his on his thigh. With a playful grin, he nodded at her as if to ask if she wanted to test out a tree of their own. A collage of erotic possibilities flew through Lucy's head, and she suddenly found it difficult to think of anything else.

She pictured herself naked with her legs spread at just the right height for David to feast upon. When they kissed, his tongue was strong and bold. Would it be the same as it adored her eager sex? Would he circle her clit or tug at it with his teeth? She closed her eyes briefly and imagined how that powerful tongue would feel plunging in and out of her.

David's thigh tensed beneath her hand, and when she looked back at him, she saw a mirroring need in his eyes. The front of his jeans bulged, and Lucy fought the impulse to move her hand over to caress him. Although Sarah had turned to face forward and was chatting with Tony, she could turn back at any moment.

David leaned over and spoke softly into her ear. "When you look at me like that, all I can think about is fucking you. I was enjoying the heaven between your legs, and you were begging me not to stop. Tell me you were imagining the same."

Lucy's mouth went dry as she fought the desire to turn and kiss the lips that were caressing her ear as he spoke. Saying yes would open a door she wasn't ready to walk through yet. *Even if my body feels ready. So ready.*

Sarah saved her from having to answer by turning in her seat again. "We thought we'd have dinner at our place tonight, then do something together in town tomorrow. How does that sound?"

In a somewhat strangled voice, Lucy said, "I'm game for anything."

"I like the way you think," David said softly to her, then straightened. Heat spread through Lucy until nothing else mattered but David and every place where they were touching. "I'm surprised Melanie and Charles didn't come back for the weekend."

"Mason and Chelle are heading to New York next, so I'm sure they'll meet up then," Sarah answered.

Tony added, "Mason said he has news."

Sarah's smile shone. "Maybe they picked a wedding date."

"As long as they don't have it here."

David smiled across at Lucy. "Tony always did like his privacy. If you think he's bad now, you should have seen him before he met Sarah. At least now he knows the names of his employees."

Sarah smiled at that. "Lucy, he really was that bad. He'd fire some of the hands, and David would rehire them without Tony even realizing they were the same men. He refused to talk to anyone but David and Melanie. Then I came along."

Tony bemoaned, "And ruined my plan to die a lonely, miserable bastard."

David laughed.

Tony shot a quick glare over his shoulder. "Push me, and we'll see if we can line up some charity riding lessons while you're here."

"God, no," David said with such disgust that it piqued Lucy's curiosity.

"I thought you liked giving riding lessons," Lucy said.

The car fell quiet again.

When no one else looked as if they would explain, Sarah made an awkward face and said, "I may have taken advantage of David's good nature a teeny-tiny bit, but it was for a good cause."

Lucy looked back and forth between David and Sarah. "Now I'm curious."

Sarah waved a hand expressively beside her. "Remember that you were engaged to someone at the time."

Lucy watched David's expression closely. "What did you do, Sarah?"

"I encouraged women to pay to fly in from all over to meet David. They said they wanted to learn how to ride from him, but really they came to flirt with him. You wouldn't believe what they were willing to pay simply to meet him. It was steady money for the children's hospital. I'm glad you two are a couple, but it'll be tough to find another fund-raising gig like that."

"No need to; we're not a couple," Lucy said curtly and was just as shocked at her own announcement as Sarah looked. *What did I think David was doing while I was engaged? Pining for me?* She pictured him laughing and meeting different women every week, and just as quickly as desire had rocked through her, jealousy darkened her mood. *How gullible can I be? He talks like he fell for me the moment he met me, but it's obviously an exaggeration. What is it going to take to learn that people lie?*

I shouldn't have come.

I'm slowly patching myself back together, and I'm doing it on my own. Why would I want to hand my fate over to someone else again?

Do I really want to do that to myself? Unlike Ted, I could fall for David. I could believe in him. And then what? If I discover my judgment still sucks and he leaves me, will I be strong enough to pick myself up again?

Or will I shatter into a million pieces?

Is anyone worth that risk?

Lucy glared at David. *Why did you have to come into my life now?*

Out of the corner of her eye, Lucy saw Sarah open her mouth to say something, then shut it and turn to face forward in her seat. Tony kept his thoughts to himself, and although David's eyebrows rose at Lucy's declaration, he didn't argue the point. He looked down at where their hands were still entwined, then up into her eyes again. Lucy was a tangle of emotions—angry, scared, sad. She slid her hand away from his and turned to look out the window of the car.

If they had been alone, she might have apologized. She knew she was sending him mixed signals, and she didn't want to hurt him, but she also had to protect herself.

Life had taught her some harsh lessons recently, and one of them was that at the end of the day, she was the only one she could depend on.

Leaning on anyone else was a recipe for disappointment.

Lucy glanced back at David. He gave her a sad smile, and she turned away from him again.

I warned him that I'm a mess. If he gives up, it's probably for the best.

One step forward, two steps back. David gave Lucy the room she seemed to need during the ride to the Double C. He carried her luggage to the bedroom Sarah had made up in the main house. He left his things in the SUV. Things would be different between them soon enough.

David pushed those thoughts out of his head and made his way downstairs. Lucy was in the kitchen talking to Sarah, so he headed outside. There was no reason not to make himself useful while he was there.

Tony was on the porch as if he'd been waiting for him. He nodded for David to walk with him to the barn. "We need to talk."

David fell into step beside Tony. "Shoot."

Tony came to a halt just inside the shaded main aisle of the large horse barn. "Once you and Lucy sort yourselves out, are you relocating to Mavis permanently?"

David scanned the area without actually registering much of what he saw. "I don't honestly know. It'll depend on how happy Lucy is out there."

Without looking at David, Tony said gruffly, "Thought you might want to know that Ribblan Ranch will be hitting the market soon. That's two thousand acres of nice hayfields. When the time comes, you might want to mention that option to Lucy. She might find she likes this area more than where she is."

"You afraid you'll miss me?" David joked.

Tony met his eyes and said frankly, "I understand the desire to get a place of your own, but we're all kind of attached to you round here. Sarah, Melanie, Jace—me. You've been a good friend, David. Better than I deserved for a long time. Yeah, I'd miss your sorry ass if you moved away."

A declaration like that meant even more when it came from a man who had once been a recluse. When David thought about it, bringing Lucy to Fort Mavis might be what they all needed. "The Ribblan Ranch, huh? It's a mite fancy for my taste, but I'll look into what they're asking for it."

Tony nodded, and they started walking toward the paddocks.

David stopped and raised a hand. "You're not going to tell me what you think I should do to win Lucy over?"

Tony gave him an odd look. "You need me to?"

David lowered his hand. "No, there's enough who seem to think I need guidance."

Tony arched an eyebrow, then picked up a lead line and opened a gate to one of the paddocks. "Sounds like you're talking to people who don't know you well. I've never met a man with more sticking power than you. You don't give up on people or horses. I wouldn't be surprised if you announced the two of you are getting married this summer."

David lifted and dropped one shoulder. "She's skittish after her engagement to Ted."

Tony attached the lead line to the halter on one of the young horses in the paddock, then handed the rope to David. "Work will help you clear your head."

David looked at the horse. "Is she new?"

"Came in while you were gone. The owners thought they could train her themselves and gave her enough bad habits that she's dangerous now. More than one person has been caught unawares from a sly kick. She could use some of your magic as well. The family has a young girl who wants to ride her. I'm ready to tell them to find another horse; I won't risk—"

Tony didn't finish the sentence, and he didn't have to. Kimberly Staten's death had forever changed both of them. "I'll work with her, and if I agree with you, we'll find that family a horse that will fit them." David looked into the horse's eyes and didn't like what he saw. She wasn't scared; she was angry. Most horses could be brought around to seeing the benefits of partnering with humans. A few couldn't. Tony had said David didn't give up on people or horses, but he was wrong. He'd come across a handful he couldn't gentle. Each had been a humbling experience that still haunted him. He'd spent countless sleepless nights asking himself what else he could have done. The hardest part had been finally letting the horse go and admitting he couldn't reach it.

After all that Lucy had been through, David understood her reluctance to trust anyone. She'd told him she had nothing to offer him, but he refused to believe that. Last night and during the flight to Fort Mavis, David had felt they were making progress.

The look she'd given him on the ride over, though, had mirrored the expression in the mare's eyes. She'd been angry with him, resentful. For the first time, he asked himself if it was right to pursue her.

He led the mare into a round pen and frowned at her. He didn't like the potential failure the horse represented. Forcing his negative thoughts aside, he stepped into the horse's space and laid a hand on the side of her neck while unclipping the lead line with his other. "I'll do my best, my friend, but in the end, your fate is something only you can decide."

With a defiant shake of her head, the horse stomped the ground in front of him. He recognized a warning in her eyes and spun the rope between them to move the horse back from him before she kicked out. He worked the horse in circles, then demanded her attention each time she stopped. Each time she turned her haunches to him, David moved the horse off again. Most horses would begin to stop and face him, but this mare didn't. At the end of their session, she pinned her ears and lowered her head at his approach.

Tony leaned on the railing of the round pen and said, "My gut tells me that horse needs a field, not a family. And that's assuming she can get along in a herd."

David relaxed his shoulders deliberately and walked up to the mare to reattach the lead line. Her ears rose along with her head. He looked into her eyes again, seeking some sign that she was salvageable, but saw nothing conclusive. "Mine says she needs more time. It took more than a day to make her this angry. The road back can take time."

Tony shook his head and walked away. Although David understood why Tony was cautious with abused horses, it saddened him at how quickly Tony had written off this mare.

As David walked the horse back to its paddock, he recalled with painful clarity a friend he'd lost during his one tour of Iraq. Sergeant Andrew Clarendon and David had bonded during basic training but were sent to different units. He had been cocky and self-assured, but a damn good soldier.

They'd met again when David and a four-man fire team had gone into an Iraqi town on a public relations trip. Along with three other fire teams, they were delivering toys and supplies to local families when he met up with Andrew and his platoon who were in town, following a tip about hiding insurgents.

Andrew and his men had headed down an alley, and David had suggested to his team leader that they join them as backup. His gut had told him Andrew needed him, but the officer in charge of the supply delivery told him to follow orders and focus on the purpose of their trip to town. Moments later, all hell had broken loose. Shots were fired, and a wounded marine came out of the alley yelling that it was an ambush.

RPGs and small weapons fire rained down from the rooftops. As they were returning fire and running for cover, David had made his way toward the alley. With their backs to the wall, his buddy Andrew and his men were cut off.

David remembered thinking, *Shit, we are all going to die bringing supplies for these ungrateful bastards. The whole town should be bombed out of existence.*

It was then that David had seen a man waving to him to come inside. David had shaken his head. He needed to find a way to get Andrew out.

The man continued to wave frantically to David. He was someone David had given supplies to in the past, but there was no reason to trust him, nothing beyond a look in his eye that said he wanted to help. He led David through his house and the home that adjoined his until they were behind where Andrew was. It was too late to save Andrew, but David and his men carried his body out of the line of fire.

David was one of several men heralded as heroes that day, but he regretted not following his instincts. Andrew might still be with them if he had. Eventually, the town was secured, and the next supply trip went without incident. David never again saw the man who had helped him, but in his mind, he was the hero.

After one tour, David left the Marines, but the lessons he learned there remained very much a part of him. *No one gets left behind. Ever.*

He'd let himself be persuaded to ignore his gut instinct a second time, years later. Kimberly Staten's death hung as heavily on David's conscience as Andrew's death had. He'd known the horse she'd chosen was dangerous, but when he told her rich father as much, he'd been fired. No one blamed David for the horse trampling her to death, yet he couldn't help but think he should have fought harder to protect her.

But Kimberly's father had told him to leave, and he had.

Not a day went by that he didn't regret that decision, and it had given him a stubborn streak when it came to doing what he felt was right.

Lucy needed him, and he wasn't going anywhere.

Chapter Ten

Lucy was peeling potatoes while Sarah chopped vegetables for dinner. There was a comfort in the mundane act that helped calm Lucy. "So what was it like to hit the *New York Times*?" Lucy asked.

Sarah smiled brightly. "Unbelievable. Crazy. Wonderful. I never dared to dream that big. When I think about how close I came to giving up on writing, it's scary. I have so many stories in my head that are dying to be shared. I can't imagine doing anything else. When my first book started selling well, my parents thought Tony and I would want to move to New York to be closer to publishers. They don't get it. My writing freed me. I'm exactly where I want to be."

"I'm happy for you, Sarah. You deserve to be happy."

Sarah put down her knife and gathered the vegetable bits into a bowl. "So do you. You can tell me it's none of my business, but what happened in the car? One minute you and David looked like lovebirds. Then a moment later you were angry. Was it because of the riding lessons? They weren't his idea. He only went along with them because I begged him to."

Lucy put her own knife down, turned her back to the counter, and covered her face with her hands briefly. Sarah had asked her to share instead of hide from her. It wasn't easy, but Lucy lowered her hands and met her friend's eyes across the kitchen island. "I was jealous, I guess. Then scared when I pictured him with all those other women. How could he want me when he could have his pick of women? I don't want to blame Ted for anything, because everything I did with him was my choice, but I trusted a man who ended up being nothing like I thought he was. I want to believe David is different. I want to believe this time my instincts are right, but all it takes is the smallest hint that I could be wrong to send me into a full panic."

Sarah walked around the kitchen island and then rested against it beside her friend. "David is one of the nicest men I know."

"Then he deserves someone who knows what they want."

Sarah shook her head and made an impatient sound. "Do you want to be with someone or do you want to go back to living on your ranch alone? Because I can't figure you out. This isn't about who David could get or what David deserves. This is you letting your fear rule you. I grew up in a house where everyone was too afraid to say how they felt. They were afraid to talk about my brother's death, afraid to face their guilt. Fear like that is a disease. It festers and grows. If you're holding out for David to prove to you that you can trust him, you might as well end it now. He'll never be able to, because the problem is in you, not in him."

Lucy tried to blink back her tears, but one escaped anyway and rolled down her cheek. She wiped it away impatiently. "I don't know how to be like you, Sarah. I don't know how to simply put my fear aside."

Sarah laid a sympathetic hand on Lucy's forearm. "You take it one day at a time. You tell yourself—I will not be afraid *today*. Not here. Not in this moment. You don't worry about all the tomorrows and everything that might come with them. You make your stand right here and now. I know you have it in you, Lucy. I've seen it."

"And if we're wrong about David?"

Sarah put her arm around Lucy. "You will still not be alone. You'll always have me. Hos before bros." She made a face. "I've never really liked that saying. I don't usually call myself a whore, but it's hard to find something that rhymes like that. Girlfriends before dead ends? You'd think that because I'm a writer, I could come up with something better—but it's not easy."

Lucy hugged Sarah back. Nothing had really changed, but she felt a hundred times lighter than she had a moment before. *That's what good friends do—they leave you feeling better than they found you.* "Chicks before dicks?"

Sarah laughed. "That's worse."

Lucy turned and picked up a potato. "Fries before guys?"

"I've created a monster."

"Would you mind if I steal this idea for my blog? I'll ask if anyone can come up with something better. It might make a fun contest."

Lightening the mood, Sarah returned to dicing vegetables. "I didn't realize you have a blog now. What do you write about?"

Lucy's cheeks flushed. "I just started the blog, but it's doing better than I thought it would. I asked myself what would get me to try a new product. People tend to buy things they feel a personal connection to. My stories give them that connection."

"I need to read this blog."

"Oh no. It's anonymous so I can be very honest about my experiences with the products," Lucy said.

Sarah waved the knife in the air. "I won't tell anyone it's you. Come on, I write sex scenes. Nothing you put in your blog will shock me."

Lucy brought her latest post up on her phone and handed it to Sarah. Sarah leaned over, holding the phone in one hand, and immediately started reading.

"Oh, wow." She scrolled up, and spent the next few minutes skimming Lucy's other posts. "Oh my God." Finally, she put the phone down. Her eyes were round with surprise. "You really are selling sex toys."

"I told you."

Sarah glanced back down at the phone with a blush. "I pictured—well, nothing like this. So, let me get this straight, you strap something to your hand that you use on yourself while you're reading and getting video phone calls, too? Do you have to answer the call? Seems like there is a lot going on there."

Leave it to Sarah to look beyond the potential embarrassing aspects of the exchange and give the content serious consideration. Now that Sarah brought it up, the complexity of multitasking while trying to orgasm had been a little frustrating, but Lucy had thought it was just her. "What would you suggest?"

Sarah reread the post calmly as if it weren't an intimate retelling of Lucy's encounter with the toy. "You definitely want an option of text to speech, and it has to be with a sexy voice. Also, I hope the app allows you to not receive phone calls. I'm imagining what a mood killer it would be for Tony if we're using this and hot guys start calling me."

"This is perfect, Sarah. Why didn't I think of any of this?"

"Because you're looking at these toys like a single woman. You test-drove everything alone. To increase your customer base, you should write about how couples interact with them." She smiled. "I'm sure David would love to help you. You should ask him."

Lucy had been typing furiously, but stopped as Sarah's suggestion sunk in. "I could never do that."

"Why not? What a great way to find out if you're compatible."

Lucy swallowed hard. "What would I say? 'Uh, David, yes, I do want to sleep with you, and would you mind if we also try out a few sex toys while we're at it?'"

Just then David entered the doorway of the kitchen, cleared his throat, and asked, "Sarah, could Lucy and I have a moment alone?"

"Absolutely," Sarah said with a huge grin as she fled the kitchen.

Lucy swayed and gripped the counter behind her, imagining how unsexy fainting would be. She braced herself for a conversation she didn't feel ready to have and raised her eyes to David's.

He walked toward her slowly, with that easy confidence of his. He stopped just in front of her, so close, Lucy's body warmed for his. It was impossible to look away, and Lucy's heart beat wildly as she waited for him to say something.

The longer he was quiet, the more nervous she became. Finally, in a rush, she said, "Taken out of context—"

He placed a hand on either side of her hips and leaned down so his mouth hovered above hers. "Don't backpedal, Lucy. You didn't say anything we both don't already know." His eyes twinkled with humor. "Except the last part. That was a surprise, one I liked."

Lucy searched his eyes, but saw only patience *and* desire. "Why aren't you upset with me for earlier? You've been so good to me, but I've done nothing to deserve it. You have women paying to meet you. I don't understand why you want *me*."

He raised a hand to gently run through her hair. "If I were an artist, I would paint how you make me feel so you could see it. If I were a poet, I'd have the words to explain it. All I have is this." He lowered his mouth to hers and kissed her.

His lips teased hers at first, warm and comfortable. She brought her hands up to his shoulders and relaxed into the kiss. David's hands grasped her hips and brought them against his, grinding her erotically against his erection. His tongue slid into her mouth, inviting hers to dance. She went where he led and lost herself in the wonder of how good he made her feel. By some standards, it was an innocent enough kiss, but every inch of her was alive and begging for more. He kissed his way to her ear, then down one side of her neck.

With one hand, he swept the food off the counter behind her and easily lifted her so she was seated on it with him between her legs. He ran his hands up the sides of her thighs, then up to the front of her shirt. With one strong move, he pulled the front of her shirt out of her jeans and then deftly undid the buttons.

He cupped one of her lace-covered breasts and brought his mouth to her nipple, blowing on the material it was eagerly pushing against. Lucy quivered with pleasure and arched herself closer to his mouth. His teeth grazed her nub while his other hand began its own mind-blowing assault on her other nipple.

Lucy moaned with pleasure. Emotionally, she might be a train wreck of indecision, but her body didn't waver on what it wanted. It hated every layer of clothing that stopped her from feeling his bare skin against hers. Every layer that prevented his cock from driving into her. She reached feverishly for the buckle of his belt, but he stopped her by taking her hands in his.

"Not here," he said huskily.

"Here?" she asked, then opened her eyes and looked around. Vegetables were strewn on the floor around them. *I would have fucked him right here in Sarah's kitchen.* "What is wrong with me?"

Lucy made a move to grab the edges of her shirt, but David held her hands in his and brought them to her sides. His breathing was as heavy as hers. "Not a single thing. We belong together, you and I." He kissed the valley between her breasts. "Your heart knows it." He brought one of his hands to the crotch of her jeans and caressed her through it. "Your body does, too." He kissed her temple gently. "When you decide to trust me, we're going to be fucking fantastic together."

Lucy was shaking with a mix of emotion and sexual frustration. David casually buttoned up the front of her shirt as if she were his to dress. She felt like a woman being asked to jump off a cliff into the arms of a man below. "I'm trying, David. It might not look that way, but I am."

He eased her off the counter and pulled her into a hug. "I know you are, and you're worth waiting for."

His words were so unexpected, tears of gratitude filled Lucy's eyes and spilled down her cheeks. She wrapped her arms around David and hugged him tightly. They stood in an embrace that was very different from the one a moment before, but it was just as intimate in its own way. This closeness wasn't about sex. In his arms, she felt safe—loved.

Memories of times she'd felt that way swirled through her. She remembered huddling in her mother's arms the first time a boy had broken her heart. Her mother's love had been unconditional. Lucy thought back to the day when she'd told her father she wanted to go to school in Rhode Island. Her father had hugged her this tightly, telling her he'd always support her no matter what she decided to do. A memory of the comforting hug her brother had given her the day of their mother's funeral came back with painful clarity. Even if David loved her, and he hadn't gone as far as to say he did, but even if he did—it didn't mean he wouldn't leave her.

Love hadn't been enough to keep anyone with her.

Lucy hugged David so tightly her arms hurt, and she wept against his strong chest. She cried for the parents who had left her, for the brother she didn't know how to reach, and for the woman inside her who desperately wanted to find a way to believe in forever again.

David rocked Lucy gently against him, murmuring to her that everything would be okay. He hoped he sounded like a better person than he felt. A few moments earlier he'd almost taken her in the kitchen. His cock throbbed painfully from the denial of that pleasure. His body was having a rough time understanding that she was clinging to him for an entirely different reason now.

Lucy needed to face her fears, and he hoped her tears meant she was doing that.

He wanted to tell her he would fix everything that was broken in her life, but he knew he couldn't. He couldn't bring back her parents, go back and give her brother the brains and courage to stay with her, or turn back time and stop Ted from ever entering the equation.

He pushed back the passion that was raging inside him and told himself the most important thing was that she was beginning to trust him.

After a few minutes, she sniffed loudly and started to roughly wipe her tears away with her hands. Still in the circle of his arms, she said, "I need a tissue."

He stepped away only long enough to grab a few paper napkins. He handed them to her, then pulled her back into his arms.

She blew her nose twice, then leaned over to drop them into a trash can. "I sure know how to kill a mood, don't I?"

He lifted her chin gently until her eyes met his. "I'd still fuck you on the table in a heartbeat."

She gasped.

He chuckled and brushed away the last of her tears with his thumb. "Is that wrong?"

A myriad of emotions passed over her face, then her lips curled ever so slightly in a smile. "A little."

Sensing humor was making her feel better, he joked, "They say honesty is good for couples."

She shook in his arms and searched his face. "Is that what we are?"

He let out a slow breath and chose his words with care. "You tell me. You're brave enough to tell Sarah what you want, but I'm the one who needs to know what's going on in that beautiful head of yours."

They had visited this place before, and he wouldn't have put money on one outcome over another. She looked into his eyes for a long moment, then said, "Being with you reminds me of how much I've lost, how good things used to be. I don't know what to do with how you make me feel. It's wonderful and painful at the same time. Does that make sense?"

He breathed in her scent and thought how easy it would be for her to walk away from him, for this to be the last time he held her. "It does. More than you know."

They took a moment to simply hold each other, then Lucy arched an eyebrow at him. "When I was talking to Sarah—"

"Yes?"

"What did you hear?"

"Just the part about you liking sex toys and wanting to try them with me."

"That's it?"

"Was there more?"

"So you have no problem with them?"

David's cheeks flushed, and his blood rushed south to his cock again. Lucy sure knew how to guarantee he was barely capable of speech. "Why would I? Aren't they all about pleasure?"

Lucy smiled up at him and shook her head in wonder. "How do you always know the perfect thing to say?"

He pulled her hips forward until she was once again positioned perfectly against his swollen member. "Because we fit, Lucy."

Desire flashed in her eyes.

From the other room, Sarah called out, "Tony and I are heading into town for pizza. We'll see you later."

At the sound of the front door closing, David swept Lucy into his arms and carried her out of the kitchen. She clung to his shoulders, but didn't protest.

He strode into the bedroom Sarah had made up for them and kicked the door closed. He lowered her to her feet and, holding on to the last of his control, demanded, "I know what I want, but I need to hear you say you want it just as much." He gave her lips a light kiss and ran his tongue over her bottom lip. "Say yes, Lucy, and I'll make love to every inch of you."

Her eyes were blazing with need. "Yes."

He grazed her cheek with his lips and whispered into her ear, "Then strip for me."

Chapter Eleven

Lucy froze for a second. It would have been easier if David was the type of man who took what he wanted. He wasn't willing to settle for her simply giving in; he wanted it all. She stood there at the edge of the imaginary cliff and remembered Sarah's advice.

This is not about everything that could go wrong.

This is about making a stand.

I refuse to be afraid today.

With trembling hands, Lucy began to unbutton her shirt. She dropped it to the floor and raised her chin bravely. He surprised her by keeping his eyes on hers. Suddenly, Lucy understood why. Yes, he wanted her body, but he wanted *her* more.

Her fear fell away. No matter what happened next, she was where she belonged. She stepped out of her boots and socks and was working on her pants when an idea came to her. "This will be disappointing if I'm the only one who gets naked."

A lusty grin spread across his face. He shed his clothing with impressive speed, then stood there, his huge cock displayed proudly before she'd finished taking off her jeans. She would have laughed at his enthusiasm, but there was nothing funny about the perfection of his muscular thighs and work-hardened body. She faltered while stepping out of her underwear and almost fell, but he caught her. With an experienced flick, he unfastened her bra and helped her out of her last remaining piece of clothing.

He dropped it to the floor, then held her face in his hands. "The last thing I want to do is disappoint you." He kissed her slowly, tenderly. The tip of his shaft grazed her stomach, but he took his time.

He ran his hands up and down her arms, across her back, and down to cup her bare ass. His touch was adoring rather than demanding. Lucy wrapped her arms around his neck and opened her mouth for him, rubbing her nipples across his bare chest. The move excited him as much as it did her.

One of his hands slid between her legs and between her wet lips. He circled her clit with his middle finger while he dug his other hand into the hair on the back of her neck. His mouth was hungry and demanding while he arched her backward over his arm.

His mouth closed over one of her breasts at the same instant he thrust a finger inside her. Lucy's senses were overloading. His thumb continued to brush back and forth against her clit as he pumped his finger in and out of her. His mouth loved both of her breasts with a combination of light nips and licks that had her head spinning.

She wanted to run her hands over him, to bring him the same pleasure he was bringing her, but the way he held her kept her just off balance enough that she was at his mercy. But, oh, what mercy he took on her.

He brought his mouth back up to hers, and this time his tongue was bold and demanding. He thrust a second finger inside her sex and increased his speed. Heat spread through her, lashing at her sanity, and she cried out in ecstasy into his mouth. *None of the toys make me feel like this. Alive. So turned on. Ready to explode.*

And still he didn't stop. He kept his magic fingers moving inside her and kissed his way up and down her neck. When his mouth began to suckle on one of her breasts, it sent her over the edge. She needed to touch him. She adjusted her position so she could reach down and close her hands around his rock-hard dick. He was huge, and she could have come again just from the thought of how good he would feel inside her. "I can't wait, David. Now. Now."

With a sexy growl, David withdrew for a moment, leaving Lucy standing there in a sexual daze. She heard him rip open a foil package, and then he was back. With a condom on his glorious cock, he advanced on her like a conquering pirate. She backed away playfully until she felt the bed on the backs of her legs. She sat on the edge and began to inch backward across the bed.

He crawled toward her, enjoying the short chase, and pounced. They rolled together until he was on top. He kissed her passionately again, running his strong hands over her. Lucy wrapped her legs around his waist and met him kiss for kiss. She couldn't get enough of him. Every touch, his and hers, sent flames of pleasure through her.

He settled himself between her legs, the tip of him nudging for entry, and raised his head to watch her face. His first thrust was deep and sure. Slow. His next was faster and more powerful. He kissed her lips lightly, and she adjusted her legs so she would thrust upward to welcome him deeper. Their rhythm was natural and primal.

Like two pieces of the same puzzle, they fit, and everything else fell away. There was nothing other than the taste and feel of each other. Lucy had enjoyed sex in the past, but even when she'd climaxed, she'd always felt in control. With David, thinking was impossible. She was a slave to how David made her feel, and thankfully, he seemed just as out of control with her.

Her orgasm hit with a cry she normally would have held in. He joined her with a curse and then collapsed beside her. He turned, disposed of the condom, and tucked her into his side. He kissed her forehead, and she laid a hand on his chest.

They came back to earth slowly. David pulled a sheet over them and smiled. "Next time we'll go slower—"

Lucy silenced him by placing her fingers lightly over his lips. "It was perfect."

He kissed her fingers. "I won't argue that, but I have techniques that will blow your mind."

Lucy chuckled against him. "Mind-blowing techniques, huh?"

He rubbed her back lazily. "Give me a minute, and I'll show you."

Feeling playful, Lucy joked, "How good could they be if they only take a minute?"

He rolled so he was above her again. "Oh, now you're in trouble."

"Hello? Is anyone here?" Chelle called from downstairs.

"We're—" David started to answer her, but Lucy put her hand over his mouth again.

"Don't you dare," Lucy whispered.

With the thin walls of the old house, it was easy enough to hear Chelle. "Didn't they tell us to meet them here? I'll text Sarah and see where they went. Strange, though. I could have sworn they'd asked if we wanted to eat dinner here."

"Maybe they're in the kitchen," Mason said.

Lucy's mouth rounded as she remembered the condition they'd left it in. "No." She pushed at David. "Do something."

Laughing, David climbed out of bed and quickly put on his jeans and shirt. "I'm good, but I doubt I can beat him there."

"Hey, Chelle," Mason called out. "Come here."

"Is something wrong?" A second later Chelle said, "Sarah says they're on their way to town for pizza. Do we want to join them?"

"Sure. We're not eating here anyway." Mason called across the house.

"Why?" Chelle asked.

A moment later, Mason said in a loud voice, "David? Lucy? You have fifteen minutes to wrap it up."

"Mason," Chelle said in reprimand.

"We'll wait in the car, but hurry it up. I'm hungry."

"They may not want to go to dinner anymore."

"Do you?" Mason called out.

Part of Lucy felt mortified that they knew what she and David had been up to, and part of her really wanted to see her friends. She asked David with a look if he wanted to go.

He nodded.

She waited for him to say it, but he gave her an angled brow that said, "You do it."

She sat up in the bed, loving how his eyes raked over her hungrily. He didn't let her stay in her comfort zone, and she was beginning to appreciate that about him. She raised her voice and said, "We do want to see you. We'll meet you at your car in a few minutes."

Whatever Chelle and Mason said next was spoken softly enough that Lucy didn't hear anything but the door close as they left. Lucy got off the bed and strode over to David, wagging a finger at him. "I can't believe you made me do it."

He looped his hands behind her waist, pulled her to him, and shrugged. "I like hearing you say what you want."

"Really?" The confidence she was beginning to feel with David was heady. "And if I said I'm a little sad I have to wait to sample one of your techniques?"

David again stripped off his shirt and jeans and was beside her in a heartbeat. "I'd say I hope Mason is a patient man, because this may take a while."

A while later, David and Lucy finally made their way out of the house. If either Chelle or Mason minded, they didn't say. David's appreciation of the couple deepened when they acted as if nothing had happened.

Lucy had been tense when she'd climbed into the backseat of their car with him, but within minutes, she relaxed against him.

As they pulled out onto the road, Lucy glanced back at the car that followed them. "Do you have to have security wherever you go?"

Mason said to Chelle, "If it were just me, I might not feel it was necessary, but my whole world is sitting in the seat next to me."

Chelle took Mason's hand in hers. "We had a scare a few weeks ago. Nothing serious, just enough to make us realize that there are crazy people out there."

Mason added, "Speaking of crazy—David, remind me to tell you what I found out on that matter you asked me about."

"Sure," David answered, hoping Lucy didn't make a connection. Her expression hadn't changed, so she likely hadn't. "How was the flight in? Ours was very nice, thanks to you."

Chelle smiled back at them. "I thought Mason was crazy to have two planes, but he said the price of two small ones was just about the same as one large one. I think it's a case of men loving their toys."

Remembering their earlier conversation, David shot for a serious tone and said, "We do love them."

Lucy started laughing and slapped his leg. "Stop."

With easy humor, David said, "In Texas, we say bigger is always better, but tell yourself whatever you need to, Mason."

Mason rolled his eyes and shook his head in tolerant amusement. "Chelle, this is the thanks we get for waiting for them."

Chelle laughed. "I had no idea David was so funny."

"Fucking hilarious," Mason said, but he was smiling. "Lucy, why don't my friends respect me?"

David leaned forward and gave Mason a pat on the shoulder. "We would respect you, but we *know* you."

Deciding to have a little fun with David, Lucy said, "Mason, David actually says very nice things about you when you're not around."

Chelle turned in her seat and smiled at David. "Mason speaks highly of David, too. It's a bromance. How sweet."

Both David and Mason grunted at the same time, which made the women laugh. David laced his fingers with Lucy's and pulled her in for a quick kiss. He could pretend to be irritated, but he felt too damn good about life for anything to change his mood. Lucy was at his side, the taste of her lips was still on his, and she was happy.

Nothing was more important.

Chapter Twelve

Seated beside David at a long table that had been hastily engineered by pushing two rickety square ones together, Lucy took a sip of beer and smiled. These were her friends, and she knew how lucky she was to have them. Regardless of their financial status or level of fame, they had remained genuine and down-to-earth. Even Mason, whom Lucy often saw on television in a suit, was dressed in casual jeans and a T-shirt.

Their meal had been a series of interruptions from townspeople, but the group had handled them gracefully. Some came to ask Tony a question about a horse, some to ask Mason if he would run for president, and one woman even brought a book over for Sarah to sign. For Lucy, though, the most fascinating interactions were between David and everyone who came to the table. He might not have been the one who drew them over, but while they were there, they spoke to him with open affection. Time and time again, they thanked David for his help with something and asked why they hadn't seen him and when he next planned to come around.

David always looked over at Lucy before explaining that he had been spending time in Mavis lately, and then he would introduce Lucy to the person. Their reactions were anything but subtle. The most common responses were "About time" and "I'm so happy for the both of you." But a couple of the comments were more personal. One woman told Lucy she was nuts if she let David get away. Another asked when the wedding would be. After the first few, David began to look uncomfortable, but he didn't stop introducing Lucy.

Chelle asked everyone at the table to raise their glasses in honor of the fact that she and Mason had finally chosen a wedding date. They toasted and clapped as she and Mason exchanged a dramatic kiss that left the table laughing.

A few minutes later, Lucy excused herself to go to the ladies' room and got a taste of a darker aspect of town. The waitress who had served their pizza and drinks with a smile all evening cornered her when she came out of the bathroom and said, "If you break David's heart again, I wouldn't bother coming back to Fort Mavis. You won't find it a very friendly place."

Lucy's first impulse was to tell her to mind her own business, but she held her tongue. *What does she mean "break his heart again"?* Lucy met the woman's eyes. "I have no intention of hurting him. I care about him."

The woman's fake smile returned. "There's plenty of women willing to help him get over you. I'd keep that in mind."

Lucy returned to the table. Apparently, David hadn't been kidding about having feelings for her since they'd first met. She joked nervously, "The people in this town are pretty intense, aren't they?"

David frowned, looking protective and ready to take on anyone who might have offended her. "Did something happen?"

Lucy decided it was best to keep some conversations to herself. She was still trying to figure out how to take in the whole town seeming to know how he felt about her. On one hand, it was reassurance he wasn't lying about his feelings. On the other hand, it was pressure she didn't feel ready for. "No, just a notion I have."

Tony looked at the waitress who had spoken to Lucy and said, "If that notion is that this town has its share of assholes, it does."

Mason shook his head. "Tony, have you ever heard of the law of attraction? What you put out in the world comes back to you."

Tony didn't look bothered at all. He took a sip of his soda before answering. "Then I must be a saint, because I married one."

Sarah laughed and hugged her husband. "I love you."

Chelle touched her fiancé's cheek lightly and teased, "Are you going to let Tony get away with being the most romantic man at this table?"

Mason narrowed his eyes at Tony, then laughed. "I hate that I can't think of something awesome to say." He kissed Chelle briefly on the lips and joked, "Is smelling better romantic? Because I have him beat in that area."

This time everyone laughed.

Lucy's phone rang. She let it go to voice mail, but then it rang again. She checked the caller ID. It was Michelle from Mavis. With an apologetic wave of her phone, she said, "I should probably take this."

"Hello," Lucy said, turning slightly away from her friends so her conversation wouldn't interrupt theirs.

"Lucy, I went by your house, but Wyatt said you were gone for the weekend."

"Yes, I'm in Fort Mavis visiting friends."

"With David?"

Lucy glanced at David. He smiled at her, and she looked at him apologetically. He shook his head as if to say it was no big deal. That was David, always understanding. "Yes."

"You'll have to tell me all about it when you get back. Promise?"

"Sure. Is that why you called?"

"No. I have something I want to tell you, but I don't know how to."

"Just say it."

"I don't know if I can."

"Now you're scaring me. Is it bad?"

"Oh no, nothing like that. This is good, but embarrassing. Lucy, I had my first orgasm all because of you. I did it. I used that toy you told me about, and I waited until I was home alone. At first, I was so nervous and afraid Ron would walk in on me, but then it started to feel good and then it started to feel great. I didn't know anything could feel that good. Is it always this good? Does it get even better? I have so many questions."

Lucy lowered her voice. She was happy that her friend had made a self-knowledge breakthrough and wished she were able to say more. *I don't know what the appropriate thing to say is when your friend has her first orgasm, but I'm pretty sure whatever it is shouldn't be said now, right in the open.* "Can we talk about this later?"

David didn't plan to eavesdrop, but when Lucy's voice had risen with concern, all conversation at the table ceased. Whoever she was talking to, it was obvious the conversation was an uncomfortable one for Lucy. She looked . . . guilty.

He didn't like the possessive feelings surging within him at the possibility that she might be talking to a man. When her eyes met his again, he mouthed, "Is everything okay?"

She nodded, but waved one hand in the air in mild panic. He told himself he trusted her. Just because her body language looked like it was proclaiming she was hiding something, it didn't mean she was. Or that it was a man. She'd never lied to him.

I've never asked her if there is anyone else.

Fuck.

No. This has to be about something else.

The more the caller spoke, the more Lucy averted her face. "I really can't talk right now; I'm out at dinner with friends." Lucy pushed her chair back so there was an even greater distance between her and everyone at the table. "I don't know. That's a decision only you can make." She suddenly sounded sad. "I've asked myself that very question. We'll talk when I get home."

Don't let it be another man.

I'm willing to wait, but I won't share her.

Lucy pocketed her phone and pulled her chair back beside David. "Sorry about that."

David placed his arm around the back of her chair. "Is there a problem back home?"

Lucy didn't meet his eyes. "No."

Sarah leaned across the table. "Who was that?"

Lucy shrugged. "Just someone with a question."

Sarah smacked the table as an idea came to her. "Oh, a client."

"Sort of," Lucy hedged.

Chelle leaned forward with interest. "A client? That's awesome. Sarah said you were starting a home business. She wouldn't tell me what it was. Mason thinks you're selling makeup. I said there wasn't enough money in that, but I thought maybe health products. Really, neither of us knows much about either, but it was fun to guess. Were either of us close?"

Lucy glared at Sarah, then smiled, but it looked forced. "You both were close, but I feel weird talking about it. I'm just starting out."

Chelle reached out and laid a hand on her arm. "I know how you feel. I sold candles one year. I hated asking everyone if they were interested in hosting a party or buying something. They'd say yes, but I was never sure if they felt pressured. You don't have to feel like that. Whatever you're selling, we'll buy ten. Right, Mason? Just to get her started."

"You don't have to do that," Lucy said, shooting what looked like a save-me look at Sarah.

Sarah clearly knew what Lucy's new business was, and Lucy apparently didn't want anyone else to know. He watched her squirm and told himself a better man would step in. *I'm only human, though, and dammit, I want to know.*

Tony added, "No reason why we shouldn't all do what we can. Sarah, buy as much as you want. We'll find a purpose for it."

Sarah gurgled and bit her knuckle. "Anything you say, sweetie."

Chelle clapped her hands. "That reminds me. I donated baskets to the church raffle, and that brought in some business. I can help you with ideas like that if you want."

Sarah burst out laughing. "Sorry, I'm picturing everyone's face if you donated a basket at church."

Lucy threw a piece of crust at Sarah and stood. "Thanks for the support, Sarah."

Sarah instantly stopped laughing. She stood and made a grab for her friend's arm. "I'm sorry. I wasn't thinking."

Lucy pulled her arm away from Sarah. "No, you weren't."

Frantically, Sarah waved at their friends. "They don't know anything. I didn't tell anyone, I swear. Not even Tony."

Tony frowned.

David knew exactly how he felt. He didn't like being on the outside either.

Lucy was shaking her head angrily. "No, but now they *want* to know. It didn't have to be an issue."

Mason raised both hands. "I don't need to know."

Tony nodded in agreement. "I heard nothing."

Chelle went to stand with the other two women. "We love you, Lucy. As long as it's legal, does it matter what you're selling?"

Lucy threw her hands up in the air. "It's sex toys. Okay? Satisfied? That's how I plan to save my ranch—by selling high-tech vibrators."

A man at a nearby table said, "No wonder he likes her so much."

David rose to his feet, and the man meekly went back to eating. "Lucy—" David didn't know what to say, but moved to stand beside her in support.

Mason said, "We'll still take ten."

Chelle swatted at him and shook her head. "This is no time to joke."

Mason shrugged, with big innocent eyes. "Who's kidding?"

Lucy moved to walk away, and David stepped in front of her. "There's no need to leave. No one will judge you here."

She waved her hand at everyone in the restaurant and tears filled her eyes. "You don't think so?"

David looked pointedly at the nearest man to him. "Will *you*?"

The man shook his head.

He scanned the nearby tables of people who were watching them. "Does anyone here have a problem with what Lucy is doing?"

Tony stood, as did Mason. David didn't need their help. He was more than ready to take on the first person who said anything.

From across the room, one man called out, "My wife wants to know if you have a catalogue."

Laughter erupted, and the tension in the room eased.

Lucy looked fragile, but hopeful. He felt like an ass for letting her friends push her into sharing something before she was ready to, but she had a choice to make. She could hide or be proud of who she was.

She raised her chin and answered, "Not yet, but I'll have some for my next visit."

Two young men at a corner table said something, but David didn't hear exactly what it was. He turned toward them. "If you've got something to say, be man enough to say it to my face or smart enough to keep your mouth shut."

An older man from another table walked over and slapped one of the young men in the back of the head. "Sorry, David. That one is mine. I'll talk to him."

David nodded at the old man. "Thanks, Pete."

Mason whooped and clapped a hand on Tony's back. "I always thought this town was afraid of you, but I think it's David they're afraid of."

Clara, the waitress, chirped in, "That's not fear, Mr. Thorne, that's respect. There ain't a person in here David hasn't helped one way or 'nother. When my daddy lost his retirement, David helped him find a fancy lawyer in Dallas who got it back for him." She looked at Lucy. "A smart woman doesn't walk away from a man like that."

David's cheeks warmed. "Your family has been just as kind to me."

Tony grumbled, "Life was a whole lot less complicated before we all started sharing so much. Are we staying or going?"

Not caring who was watching, Sarah said, "Lucy, I really am sorry."

Lucy gave her a quick nod, but her attention remained on David. She searched his face. "I didn't mean for it to come out like this. The last thing I wanted to do was embarrass you."

"You didn't. Now, what do you want to do—stay or go?"

Lucy looked at Clara, then back and said, "I want to stay."

"Then let's have another round of beers. In fact, how about a round for everyone—on Mason. Vote Thorne for president!" David smiled.

Mason called out, "I'm not announcing anything, but I will buy all of you a drink."

General applause filled the room while David, Lucy, and their party sat back down. Once everyone was settled, David took Lucy's hand in his. He spoke softly into her ear. "You could have told me."

"I was working my way toward it."

"Is there anything else I should know?" *Now is the time to tell me if there is someone else.*

"No, that's the only secret I had."

Thank God.

Chapter Thirteen

A few hours later, Lucy was tucked against David's side on the porch swing of Sarah and Tony's house. The evening air had cooled off just enough to make the thought of going inside something neither were ready to consider.

There was also the hanging question of how and if they would part for the night. Lucy wasn't comfortable enough with David to share a room with him in the main house. She couldn't imagine going back to the equally not-private bunkhouse with him. Eventually, they'd have to come to a decision, but at the moment, Lucy was right where she wanted to be.

As if he could hear her thoughts, David kissed the top of her head. "I had fun tonight."

With her head resting on his strong shoulder, Lucy looked up at him from beneath her lashes. "Me too, if you can believe it. I'm glad I didn't leave. I like Fort Mavis."

David caressed her arm as he talked. "No town is perfect, but there are enough good people here to make up for the trouble that sometimes bubbles."

"And they love you. If you ran for an office here, you'd win hands down."

He shrugged. "Like I said, it's a good town. We watch out for each other."

"I was born in the town I live in, and I could count on one hand the number of people who like me." It wasn't something Lucy was proud of.

"So why stay? Why not sell the ranch and move on?"

"I promised my mother—"

"I don't know a mother who would want her daughter to stay where she's not happy."

Lucy raised her head and sat up straight. "You don't understand."

He kept his arm around her. "Then explain it to me."

Lucy pressed her lips together for a moment before speaking. She wasn't sure she could explain something she was still working out for herself. "For a while, I told myself I was saving it for my brother. I also told myself I had to hold on to it because of the family history. I'm not sure either was the real reason. When I came home, David, I lost so much. I was ready to give up—" David's eyes snapped to hers and she quickly added, "Not kill myself. Well, not physically, but I was dying on the inside, and I had started to think maybe it was for the best. Maybe feeling nothing was better than hurting so much. Thank God, I spoke to Sarah. She gave me the kick in the ass I needed. I knew I had to make a decision, and saving the ranch was what I decided to do."

"That's why you were angry when I stepped in." David rubbed his cheek in memory.

"Yes. I need my business to work out. I need to pay you back. Not because it will save the ranch, but because it will save me." Lucy laid a hand on his thigh, praying what she was saying made sense to him. "I want to be with you, but I'm so afraid of losing myself again."

David turned to look out over the darkened driveway. "I want you to have that win, Lucy. Being with me doesn't mean you can't save your ranch on your own. There are no rules. We define what we have."

Lucy wanted to believe that. She wanted to so badly. "Why are you so good to me?"

When David looked down at her again, the fire in his eyes made Lucy question why she worried about anything when it came to him. All the answers were right there for her to see. "We belong together. I knew that from the first moment I met you."

Lucy leaned her head on his shoulder again. Her emotions were still too scattered to be able to say anything that would match the intensity of how he felt for her. She didn't want to hurt him by saying less and didn't want to lie, so she remained quiet. After a short time, she said, "You were right about how good being with my friends would feel. I needed this."

David rested his chin lightly on her head. "It's obvious Chelle and Sarah felt the same. Poor Sarah, she says whatever is on her mind, and we love that about her, but I bet she has trouble sleeping tonight."

"I'll talk to her tomorrow. I was angry, but, in the end, I'm glad it's out there, I guess."

David sighed. "I am." He nuzzled the side of her face. "So, tell me, what exactly is a high-tech vibrator?"

She described some of them to him, and finished by saying, "I know it may be an unconventional way to make money, but I'm actually pretty good at selling them."

"I don't doubt it for a minute," he murmured into her ear.

Even though her body was heating up, she gave him a slight push. "I'm serious. I went to school for marketing, but I've never really applied what I had learned. When I came across this business and heard they wanted someone to design the marketing plan, I wasn't sure I could do it. But I know I can now. I get it. It's not just putting products up on a website. It's connecting with potential clients."

David raised his head and arched an eyebrow. "And how do you do that?"

"Through a blog, and it's working. It's anonymous so I can be honest."

"What do you write about exactly?"

Lucy blushed. "I try out one of the items, then share my experience with it online. That way, women know what to expect when they use it."

David shifted and adjusted his jeans. Lucy glanced down at the bulging evidence of how the topic was arousing him. Knowing how easily she excited him was a turn-on for her, too. Lucy licked her bottom lip. "Sarah suggested I try them out with you so potential buyers would know how they work with couples. I know you said you were into toys, but now that you know what they're like, are you still game?"

David closed his eyes for a second, a lusty grin on his face. "Fuck, yes." He looked over at her, his eyes blazing with desire. "Getting a room in town at this time of night would be obvious."

Lucy almost said she didn't care, but it was also exciting to see what else he suggested. "Yes, it would be."

"The walls in the main house are thin."

"Definitely."

"The bunkhouse is the same and full of men."

Lucy bit back a smile. "Looks like we have to wait."

"Or get creative."

I love the way he thinks. Lucy could barely breathe. "How?"

He kissed her deeply until they were both shaking with need. "Your blog sounds like a perfect bedtime story. If I can't have you by my side tonight, I'll settle for coming to the sound of your lovely voice." He kissed his way to her ear. "On one condition."

Lucy was on fire and ready to promise him anything. "What?"

He whispered, "You have to come, too. I want to hear you bring yourself that pleasure."

They kissed again, losing themselves to a passion so intense it threatened to toss all sanity to the wind—making love right there on the porch became a real possibility. Lucy tore her mouth away from his before she suggested that herself. She rushed to the door. "Good night, David."

"Talk to you in a few," David said, then hopped over the railing of the porch and walked off into the dark toward the bunkhouse.

Lucy stepped inside. Sarah and Tony were in the living room talking. Sarah waved her in. Lucy walked toward the doorway. Her body was trembling with anticipation.

Sarah stood. "Lucy, I just wanted to say again how sorry I am about spilling the beans. I promise it'll never happen again."

Lucy hoped she didn't look as excited as she felt. Still breathless, she said, "It's all good, Sarah. I'm over it. No worries."

"Did you want to hang out and play a game of Scrabble?" Sarah asked.

Lucy shook her head vehemently, then forced a yawn. "I would, but I'm so tired. I'm heading right to bed. Good night, y'all."

Her friend gave her a funny look, then sat back down beside her husband on the couch. "Okay, see you tomorrow for breakfast."

"Perfect. Okay. See you then." Lucy sprinted up the stairs. She turned on the radio in her room just loud enough to block out the sound of her voice and called David.

He sounded as out of breath when he answered. "I'm torn. We could still go to a hotel."

Lucy pushed aside her usual shyness. "I've never done this before. I'd like to try it."

"Oh yes." David let out a sexy hiss. "Take off your clothes and describe yourself doing it."

Feeling a little ridiculous, Lucy swept her shirt up over her head and said, "I took off my shirt." She unhooked her bra and let it fall to the floor. "Okay, I took off my bra, too." She paused, feeling uncertain. "I don't know how to make this sexy. I'm sorry."

David's tone was excited and encouraging. "Anything you say is hot to me, Lucy. There is no way to do this wrong. I want you so badly, I could come from the sound of you reciting the alphabet. Just talk."

Confidence brought the sexiness back to what had momentarily felt ridiculous. She stepped out of her shoes, jeans, and panties. "I'm sliding my legs out of my jeans, and it feels so good. It reminds me of your hands on me. I'm kicking my silk panties off. They went flying onto the bed, the bed where I'll be in a minute, spread out, touching myself, wishing you were with me."

"Fuck, Lucy, you're good at this."

I am, Lucy thought. She remembered a boyfriend who had once asked her to talk dirty to him. She'd tried, and after a few minutes, he told her to forget it. They'd had sex, but it was as mediocre as her sexy monologue had been. The two experiences couldn't be compared. Lucy saw why now. It wasn't about doing it right or wrong. It was about how much pleasure she found in pleasing David. This wasn't for him—it was for *them*.

Just like couples who use toys on each other.

Lucy walked over to the bed and lay down on top of the blankets. "The air in the room is cool, but I like it. You'd like how my nipples are already jutting out, begging to be in your mouth. I'm on the bed now, and I'm already wet for you. Can you feel how wet? I'm touching myself the way you touched me. It's not the same, but it's good. My hand should be your hand. I know exactly how you'd rub me. You'd start slowly, then move faster. Oh yes. You'd do it just like that."

David was breathing heavily. "Those gorgeous tits would be in my mouth. Tell me what you'd want me to do. Lick your fingers, and use them like I'd use my tongue."

Lucy did just that, and it was so much more exciting than anything she'd ever done to herself. Memories of his mouth on her breasts just a few hours ago were so vivid, they mixed and intensified the pleasure her own hand was capable of bringing.

"Now read to me."

Lucy didn't want to stop. Everything she was doing felt too good. "Really?"

His voice was a demanding growl. "Read your blog, Lucy. I want to hear what you do with your toys. Now."

"Yes." Lucy was used to the softer side of David, but he was also a man who knew what he wanted, and he didn't settle for less than everything. Submitting to his will brought a whole new level of excitement to the exchange. Lucy scrolled through her phone for a blog entry from when she'd tried a toy she imagined working better with two.

With his cock in one hand and his phone in the other, David lay across his bed, stroking himself while Lucy chose an entry to read to him. She was the ideal woman in his mind. She was kind, intelligent, funny, and sexually adventurous, without taking it to a level he didn't want to go to. He had been well acquainted with Internet porn since he'd gotten his first computer at sixteen. Some men might deny it, but he doubted many were different.

Some people saw it as societal corruption; David viewed it as nothing more than a visual menu of what people had always been doing behind closed doors. Seeing something didn't mean you had to do it, just like going to a restaurant that served octopus didn't mean you had to order it. A good sex life came from knowing your own personal taste and finding a partner who shared it. David's taste was already narrowing to one particular part of the menu—Lucy and whatever side dishes came with her.

"Are you ready?" she asked huskily.

David groaned. "Yes."

"When I opened the package, I wasn't impressed. It was smaller than I'd imagined and purple. I've never liked purple toys. They remind me of childhood television characters I'd rather forget. I put that thought aside, though, and read the instructions. It arrived precharged, thankfully. The directions were vague and without diagrams, so I took my best guess as to where the toy stimulates. I suggest using lube with this toy since the amount of thought that went into the how and where to use it didn't rev me up for the trial run. So how was it? I give it a four out of five, but only because I can see this one working much better with a partner. The C shape allows it to vibrate on the G-spot and the clitoris at the same time, which is amazing. The remote control option allows for a hands-free experience. It's small enough to be worn under clothing, but it's loud, so I wouldn't try it during your office break. The remote includes a timer option, which would allow you to take the boredom out of long commutes to work. This toy was designed small so it can also be used during intercourse as a way of enhancing pleasure for both. I haven't tried it that way yet, but I'd love to hear from anyone who has."

Still hard and excited, David chuckled. "It's not exactly what I expected."

Sounding more excited than insulted, Lucy said, "Hey, I wrote what women want to know. And they love it."

David pictured Lucy naked on her bed, one hand on her wet sex, caressing herself while she read to him. "It was good. Now, ditch the blog and tell me how you feel."

"Besides being insulted that you don't love my writing?" she teased.

David growled. "It was awesome, but you know what's better? Imagining you here with me, kissing your way to my cock."

Lucy's laugh was a provocative tease in his ear. "Are you sure? I could read you another entry."

"Do that only if you want me in your bed tonight. I'll have you screaming out my name, and I won't care who hears."

"And how would you do that?" She purred her request. "Tell me how you'd take me there. Every detail."

"Lucy?" Her name was almost a growl on his lips. *Not what I want on my lips right now. I want my mouth on her pussy. Licking. Sucking until she screams.*

"Yes, David," she answered, and there was a tremor to her voice that hadn't been there a moment ago.

"Open your legs. Wide. Now."

He was certain he heard her whimper.

"I'm so hard for you right now, and if I were with you on that bed, you would have your sweet, luscious lips wrapped around my cock. You would be licking and sucking, licking and sucking. You would be wanting my cum, as you used that sweet tongue of yours to work my head."

Fuck if her moan at that moment didn't almost make him come. *I wish I could see her face. See desire in her beautiful eyes.*

"Can you taste me, sweetheart? Can you feel how much you've turned me on?"

"Yes," she whispered. She was panting.

Fuck, I can barely breathe.

"You want my cock in your mouth?"

All David heard was a moan. *God, I should be in her bed right now. Fuck.*

"Put two fingers inside your pussy. Now. Push them hard into you so they hit you where you need it."

"Uh-huh. *David . . .*"

"And Lucy, while you're making love to my hard cock, do you know what I'll be doing?"

"No." He barely heard her, but he imagined the flush on her skin. Her sheen of sweat as she wrapped her mouth around him. *Sexy girl.* He could hear how wet she was. He could hear the slap of her fingers. So he went for it.

"I would have my tongue so deep within your pussy that you'd barely be able to breathe. I'd be licking, sucking, licking, and sucking. You'd be thrusting your sexy pussy up against my mouth so I could devour every last drop of your sweet-as-fuck juices as you come all over me."

Imagining his chin wet with her juices, and hearing Lucy give herself over to her orgasm, had David coming. Hard. Imagining her sucking every part of his cum down her pretty throat. He could hear her heavy breaths. Imagine her glazed expression.

And that's how it is done, darlin'.

David rolled over, cleaned himself off, and then, spent, flopped back down onto the bed.

"Lucy?"

"Yes?" she asked in a whisper.

"When we get back to your house, let's try that toy."

She chuckled. "See, I told you my blog was effective."

He could have told her that her writing skills had nothing to do with the fact that he was dying to try all the toys with her, but he kept that thought to himself. "It sure was. Lucy, I won't want to sleep in the bunkhouse in Mavis."

She breathed in audibly. "You want to move in?"

"We'll make love every night. You'll fall asleep in my arms. I'll wake you with a kiss each morning. It doesn't have to be more complicated than that. You want this as much as I do. Say yes, Lucy."

He waited for what felt like an eternity for her to answer. The longer she didn't say anything, the more he began to worry he'd pushed her for too much too soon.

"Yes," she said, then hung up.

David tossed his phone on the bed beside him and stared up at the ceiling. The last thing he wanted to do was go to sleep. He wanted to throw open his window and yell that she was his.

He wanted to join her in the main house and hold her until the sun came up.

He held himself back because he knew she needed more time before she could fully give herself to him. For now, he would bask in the relief that she wasn't unreachable.

She'd said yes.

Chapter Fourteen

The next morning, Lucy showered early and, although she dressed simply, took extra care with her hair and makeup. While applying the finishing touches, she paused and studied the woman looking back at her. There was a life in her eyes that hadn't been there for so long, Lucy had doubted it would ever return. She glimpsed the woman she'd been before her father died, and the thought brought a smile to her lips.

No, she couldn't go back, but she could go on.

And not just survive.

She could live and laugh again.

She thought about David.

Maybe even love one day.

The glow on her cheeks had nothing to do with the makeup she'd applied and everything to do with memories from the day before. When she thought about how hard she came last night—just from hearing David's incredibly sexy voice *demanding* she touch herself and imagining blowing him—she couldn't stop smiling.

David was a gentle soul, but he was also a confident, dominant man, and . . . and the more she was with him, the less she wanted to imagine her life without him.

So much had changed in one day. When she thought about how new everything was, fear nipped at her heels, but she refused to let it affect her mood.

The optimistic woman in the mirror deserved a chance to prove that happy endings were possible. She'd paid her dues. She'd survived more than she ever thought she could. Was it impossible to believe she might deserve someone as good as David in her life?

Lucy made her way downstairs and was surprised to see Chelle already there. She was talking to a still apologetic-looking Sarah. As soon as they heard her, they both turned.

Sarah said, "Lucy, I still feel awful about—"

Lucy closed the distance between them in a few long strides and threw her arms around her, swallowing the rest of what Sarah would have said in a tight hug. "You will never know how grateful I am to have you in my life." She turned and hugged Chelle. "You too. Let's not worry about something that actually turned out for the best. I'm glad it's out there."

The happiness Lucy had seen on her own face was reflected in the smiles of her friends. Sarah said, "Tony is showing David and Mason one of the horses. I told them to take their time. Let's make a big breakfast. We were supposed to head to town today, but what do you think about hanging out here?"

Chelle said she thought Mason would probably love being able to truly relax without worrying about who was watching.

Lucy agreed. She really liked Fort Mavis, but her friends were the reason she'd come, and having a stress-free day with them sounded perfect.

They headed into the kitchen together as Sarah joked, "Funniest thing about the vegetables we were preparing for dinner last night. They ended up all over the floor. I cleaned it up, but what do you think could have done that? Squirrels?"

Lucy slapped her forehead. "I meant to clean that up. Sorry, Sarah."

Chelle rounded her eyes in feigned innocence. "I don't know what else could have been on your mind."

Sarah winked at Lucy. "Details are not necessary, but I sanitized the whole kitchen."

Lucy sat on one of the stools that lined the kitchen island and wagged a finger at Chelle. "We contained ourselves until we got upstairs, but Sarah, you should have heard Chelle and Mason. I was mortified to be caught with David, and those two were calling upstairs to us. I was dying."

Chelle shrugged and smiled. "We wanted to see you. Besides, aren't you glad we waited for you? Last night was fun."

"It really was," Lucy agreed with a huge smile.

Sarah started taking supplies out of the refrigerator and cabinets, placing them on the island. "You and David are adorable together. I knew he liked you, but when I see him with you . . ." Sarah sighed dreamily. "Love is a beautiful thing."

"We're not in love," Lucy corrected quickly. "We haven't even been on a real date yet."

Eyes round, Sarah said, "Really? The way you were all over each other, I thought—"

Chelle shot a look at Sarah, then said, "Lucy, whatever is going on between you and David, you both look happy, and that's what's important."

Sarah handed Lucy a bowl and eggs to crack. "How *do* you feel about him?"

Lucy slammed the first egg against the glass so hard some of the shell joined the yolk in the bowl. She tried to dig it out and knocked the bowl over. Chelle righted it and handed her a napkin. Lucy wiped her hands nervously. "It's happening so fast my head is spinning."

Sarah took the bowl and started cracking the eggs absently. "David's not usually one to rush into things. I bet he's afraid if he looks away, you'll be engaged to someone else again."

Chelle shook her head and covered her eyes, but she was laughing. "Oh, Sarah. Is everyone from Rhode Island as blunt as you are?"

Wrinkling her nose at Chelle, Sarah replied, "I spent too many years worried about what I could and couldn't say. I don't care what you think; I'm not going back to that."

Lucy crossed over to hug Sarah. "We love you just the way you are, Sarah. And what you said actually makes sense. In a blink of an eye, David went from not being in my life to working on my ranch. After this weekend, he says he wants to stay in the house with me."

Chelle started making pancake mix. "What do *you* want?"

That wasn't an easy question to answer. "I feel like I'm coming back to life. I don't know how much of it is the business and how much is David, but he's part of why I'm smiling today. When I came home, I made too many decisions based on fear. I spent so much time worrying I'd lose everything, I didn't allow myself to enjoy what I had. I feel good when I'm with David. Good about myself and my life. If holding on to that feeling means saying yes to something that's happening faster than I would have planned, then that's what I want to do. I'm willing to risk the crash and burn if it means I can feel this good for even one more day."

Chelle sniffed and blinked back tears.

Sarah looked as if she were doing the same. She walked over to retrieve a box of tissues. "Breakfast will never get made if we keep this up. I should warn you that I'm also more emotional right now because . . ." She touched her still-flat stomach. "I'm pregnant. We weren't going to say anything yet, but I wanted to tell you in person, not on the phone."

Chelle dabbed away her tears with a tissue. "I guessed that last night when you were sipping soda right along with Tony." She hugged Sarah.

Life builds momentum, I guess. Just like things had gone from bad to worse, could they continue to get better and better? Lucy hadn't thought it was possible to be happier than how she'd woken up that morning, but she knew how much Sarah wanted a baby, and she couldn't have been more excited for her. Happiness came hand in hand with the knowledge that it didn't tend to last. Lucy pushed that thought back. "How did Tony take it?"

Sarah laughed and waved at the tears that were still brimming in her eyes. "At first, I thought he was going to faint, then his eyes got all misty. He's not good at expressing how he feels in words, but he's been glued to my side ever since. If I sit, he's there with a pillow for my feet. When we're alone, he hardly lets me lift a finger. He thinks we need to hire help for the house, because now he doesn't want me cleaning inside or out in the barn. I tried to tell him there is hardly anything going on yet, but pampering me is his way of showing me how excited he is."

Lucy hugged Sarah briefly. "I am so happy for both of you."

With a sad smile, Sarah cocked her head to one side. "I wish you lived closer. I'd love to share this with you." She put a hand on one hip and looked out the kitchen window. "Tony and I will both miss David if he stays in Mavis with you. I guess I always imagined that a child of ours would grow up being his shadow the way Jace was." Sarah turned back and made a face. "Not that I don't want it to work out with you two. That's the more important thing. It's just that David has a natural way of bringing out the best in people—even kids. You should see Jace with him. He's such a proud little man. Promise you'll both make the drive up here often enough for our little one to know you both."

Lucy nodded, but didn't promise anything. Instead, she started setting the table. A light panic whipped through her. Promising to visit the baby with David would mean Lucy knew they'd still be together. She was still getting used to the idea of being with him when they returned to her house.

I know I said I'm willing to risk the crash and burn, but is it wrong to hope that just this one time things don't end that way?

David stood with Tony and Mason near the paddock that held the troubled mare. Tony was updating David on things that had happened around the barn, but David wasn't listening. In his mind, he was already in Lucy's bed in Mavis, waking her with a cup of coffee and a kiss. He was pulling into her driveway and meeting her halfway, swinging her up into his arms, and kissing her senseless because they'd been apart for a few hours.

"How long is this going to last?" Tony asked Mason.

"What?" Mason asked.

"The stupid grin that tells me he's not listening to anything I'm saying."

Mason laughed and clapped a hand on David's back, bringing him back to the present. "You really should play it cooler, David. You're putting your heart right out there for her to trample."

"Speaking of trampling," Tony said in a can-we-get-back-to-business tone. "One of the hands was kicked pretty badly this morning while walking her from her stall to the paddock. Luckily, there were men around to stop her. She wanted to hurt him. I get most horses, but I don't get her. I've never said this before, but I'm ready to put that horse down. She's got a mean streak."

Mason looked from one man to the other. "Isn't that a little extreme for a kick?"

David looked the horse over again. "It is. You've had the vet out to look her over?"

Tony nodded. "He didn't find anything and said what I've been thinking. She's dangerous. I won't keep a horse like that here, and I'll be damned if I let her go somewhere else."

David stepped into the paddock and closed the gate behind him. He walked up to the horse and spoke to her softly. "What's going on, girl? What has you so angry?"

She pinned her ears back. Horses rarely kicked without giving plenty of warning that one was coming. She was giving him a not-so-subtle warning.

David stood where he was. He was in a better mood than normal, and that spilled over to how he felt toward the horse. He wanted to see her get past whatever was holding her back. He continued to talk softly to her.

She reared up, and if Tony hadn't pulled David back, she might have landed a direct front kick to his chest. Tony half dragged David out of the paddock and closed the gate.

"Holy shit, that was close," Mason said.

"Now you see why she has to go," Tony said.

David, his pride dented, said, "What's wrong with you? She's been here a week, and you're ready to give up on her? Put her down? Since when is that our policy?"

Tony's eyes narrowed. "First, it's no longer *our* policy. You moved on."

Mason interjected, "Do cowboys cry? Because this is really touching. David, he misses you."

Both David and Tony shot Mason a quick glare.

Tony continued, "Second, Sarah is pregnant. No child of mine will be around a horse like that. Ever."

David's irritation with Tony fell away. He smiled. "You're going to be a father?" As joy for his friend swept through him, he gave Tony a bear hug that surprised both of them. "I'm so happy for you."

Tony pushed him away, but smiled. "I'm going to be a father. No matter how many times I say it, I can't believe it."

Mason's smile was just as wide and genuine. "Looks like we have several things to celebrate this weekend. Tony, I'm happy for you, too. Really, this is the good stuff."

"Thanks," Tony said. "It is."

David looked over at the mare again. Tony's reaction to her made sense now, especially considering what had happened with Kimberly. Still, one week was nothing when it came to giving a horse a chance. "Ship her to Mavis. I'll see what I can do with her."

"Don't turn your back on her," Tony warned. "We were thinking about asking you to be the baby's godfather."

David's chest tightened with emotion. "I'd be honored."

They stood in comfortable silence for a few minutes before Mason said, "David, I looked into what you asked me to. No one had specifics, but it sounds like that area abuts one being assessed for a deep oil reserve. Nothing has been confirmed yet, but sometimes when a find like that is made, big offers come in for the land around it in case there are veins or other pockets of oil. I wish I had more to give you, but it sounds to me like Lucy's neighbor is a gambling man, and he is betting the land out there will soon be worth a lot of money."

Tony asked what they were talking about, and David brought him up to date with what had happened when he arrived on Lucy's ranch.

"What a piece of shit," Tony said.

"Couldn't have said it better myself," Mason concurred.

"Lucy's ranch manager, Wyatt, worked for York for a while. He thinks Ted's dangerous. I don't want to scare Lucy, but if that kind of money is involved, my gut tells me he's right."

"What do you need?" Tony asked.

"I don't need anything yet," David said. "But I appreciate knowing I have backup if I do."

"Always," Tony said.

Mason chuckled and lightened the mood with a joke. "For a miserable bastard, he has his nice moments, doesn't he?"

When both Tony and David gave Mason a look, Mason said, "I really wish I'd known both of you when I was making movies. I could have nailed that fuck-you-I'm-a-cowboy glare."

They continued to stare him down for a moment, then broke into huge smiles because really it was too good a day not to.

Chapter Fifteen

Later Sunday night, Lucy heard her phone ringing. She instinctively started to roll over to reach for it, without fully waking up, but was held in place by a strong arm across her waist. The call was instantly forgotten as David pulled her naked body back to spoon with his.

"Who calls at midnight?" he groaned into her ear.

"No one good," Lucy answered. Having David in her house, in her bed, was both wonderful and confusing. There was no denying how good being with him felt. They'd spent a comfortable day with their mutual friends, laughed and talked the whole flight back, and made love tenderly before falling asleep in each other's arms. It had been the perfect day followed by the perfect night—so good it was hard not to worry. Was she missing something, or was David truly as wonderful as he seemed?

The phone call went to voice mail. A moment later, her phone beeped, announcing a message. The persistence of whoever was trying to contact her birthed a hope that her brother might finally be reaching out to her. She eased out of David's embrace and turned on the light beside her bed. "I need to see if it's . . ." Her voice trailed away when she glanced back at David.

He was up on one elbow, and the beauty of him momentarily wiped all thought from Lucy's head. He wasn't one of those polished city men. He was ruggedly attractive. All man. And when he looked at her that way, she felt like she belonged to him in a timeless, primal way. His hair was still askew from her hands running through it, gripping his head while he'd worshipped her sex with his relentlessly talented tongue. *And it was even better than I'd imagined the other night when he'd described it to me.* Lucy shook her head to clear it and reached for the phone. "That's odd," she said.

"What?" He leaned forward to caress her bare shoulder with one hand.

"The caller ID says I called myself."

"Don't answer those calls. It's usually a telemarketing scam."

Lucy shrugged. Had she been home alone, she might have been nervous. That was the natural side effect of watching scary movies when she was younger. She couldn't imagine anything bothering her while David was there. Then she checked her texts, and a shiver went down her spine.

David was instantly beside her, looking over her shoulder at the phone.

Lucy read the message aloud. "It says, 'Burn in hell, whore.'"

David growled. "Who sent it?"

Lucy handed him the phone. "Me."

David took the phone and did a quick Internet search. A moment later, he typed in a symbol and numbers. A recording came on saying that the call had been traced and gave a department at the phone company to call if they had questions. David said, "The phone company website says it usually takes three calls for law enforcement to take it seriously, but I'll talk to them about this tomorrow."

Lucy took her phone back and, with a shaking hand, laid it on the bedside table. "Forget about it. It's probably a stupid prank." The last thing Lucy wanted was to make a big deal out of it and bring possible attention to the nature of her new business. Mavis wouldn't be as accepting as Fort Mavis had been.

David pulled her into his arms. "I can't forget it. We'll follow up on this tomorrow. People can't hide as well as they used to. They think they can, but there's always a way to figure out who they are."

Lucy arched back from him. "I'm not asking you, David. I'm telling you that this is my home, my town, my business. I don't want to involve the police in a prank phone call at this point. If you're going to stay here with me, you need to respect that." She thought about how Ted hadn't done anything in response to David showing up. He might be spiteful, but she doubted he was dangerous. Looking deeper into this would only bring more attention to her. That was the last thing Lucy wanted.

"If?" Emotion darkened his eyes.

There it was again, the panic that welled up inside her. *No matter how good being with him feels, I can't let my life spin out of control again just when I feel like I'm finally getting my footing back.* "I told you I need to prove something to myself, and you said you being here wouldn't stop me from doing that. Well, here's the first test of that. I don't want to tell anyone about the text or the phone call. I don't want you to do anything about it, either."

David ran a hand through his hair. "I won't sit back and pretend it didn't happen."

Lucy looked down at his chest and said, "Then maybe you should leave."

"That's it? You'd end what we have just like that?" He snapped his fingers.

Lucy imagined the worst-case scenario and asked herself if she could survive it. She didn't believe anyone in Mavis knew about her business, but if David riled up the law enforcement, they would. One prank message wasn't as scary as the idea of the whole town turning against her. There was a chance Wyatt would not want his family at her ranch if he knew. She'd lose him and the other men.

And where would that leave her? Alone. Scared. Vulnerable.

Not one step further than she'd been when she accepted help from Ted. She didn't want to be that person with David. She would not be that person ever again.

Lucy raised her eyes to David's. "I'm asking you to drop this. If you can't respect my wishes enough to do that, then what do we have? What exactly would I be ending?"

David's instincts told him Lucy was wrong. The text wasn't a prank; it was a warning. A sign that trouble was coming. He wanted to tell her that for her safety. And for that reason, he didn't care what she wanted him to do; he would protect her.

There was a chance he'd lose her. She wasn't making idle threats. He could see the desperation in her eyes and hated not being able to instantly fix all her problems. He couldn't understand why she wouldn't want anyone to know about the text, but he knew how people reacted when they felt their back was up against a wall.

If they'd met somewhere else, in different circumstances, he would have taken it slower. She was right to feel rushed. They should have dated first, taken more time to get to know each other before bringing their relationship to this level.

Circumstances were not different, though. If he were given a chance to do the last two weeks over again, he would make all of the same choices. Once Wyatt had told him he didn't think Lucy was safe, David's course had been set.

He'd spent too much time wanting her and thinking he'd lost her to have spent a week on her ranch and not end up right where he was.

He could have gone back to staying in the bunkhouse when they'd returned from Fort Mavis, but his need for her overshadowed his normally patient nature.

He didn't like the line she was drawing in the sand. It put him in a no-win situation. On one hand, he could respect her wishes and not get involved, but if the texts were from Ted, it meant he was becoming bolder and more dangerous. If David was going to protect her, he needed to know whom he was dealing with. Which meant he needed to find out more about the text. If he didn't want Lucy to throw him off her ranch, he'd have to do it without Lucy knowing he had.

Which meant deceiving her—something David hated introducing into their relationship.

He pulled her back into his arms and hugged her to him. The excitement of feeling her naked body flush against his faded momentarily against the emotions raging through him.

I'm sorry, Lucy. I know you need more time before you see us as a team, but time is something we may not have without this step.

He kissed her temple. "I won't say anything to anyone."

She searched his face. "You promise?"

His gut twisted. "Yes." Then he kissed her with all the feeling raging within him. She kissed him back just as passionately, as if the fire they lit could somehow burn away whatever wall was still between them.

They tore at each other: both angry and scared and just hungry enough for each other that it was an animalistic mating. They were two people trying to prove something to themselves while also giving in to a lust that could not be denied.

When they collapsed into each other's arms, sweaty and spent, David felt better.

And worse.

Chapter Sixteen

Two weeks later, in the office of her home, Lucy ended an invigorating phone call with Technically Anonymous Pleasure and closed her laptop. She was feeling good about the sales her website was generating as well as how responsive the founders of the company were to her suggestions. Word of mouth was spreading fast. All they had to do now was keep the momentum going.

A highly rated radio program had contacted TAP and asked to interview Lucy. They hadn't asked for her by name, but they'd wanted to speak to the woman who was writing the popular blog attached to the company. Lucy came up with an alternative. Her blog was growing in popularity, mostly because of the contributions from other users, so Lucy suggested the company hire a well-known sex therapist to take calls during the radio program. She said it would engage customers more. She sent the woman a generous basket of product and was pleased when she endorsed several on air. The show had been a huge success and titillating enough to be mentioned on every news station.

A few days after that, a national news show had sensationalized the story into a global threat against marriage, warning that if this type of technology were allowed to continue unchecked, everyone would soon have their own sexbot.

Completely ridiculous, but the most searched-for item on the company site the next day had been . . . sexbots. Lucy had joked that if they created one, she would not be the one to test-drive it.

I don't really want to try out any of these toys anymore.

She hadn't shared that last part with them. They'd been too busy watching the news about their company unfold to notice that she hadn't posted a new review of an item to her blog since she'd returned home.

David had said he liked sex toys. When they'd been in Fort Mavis, he'd even said he couldn't wait to come back and try some of them out. Somehow, and Lucy was at a loss for how, that had changed. Her business had become something neither of them talked about.

Lucy wanted to ask him why, but things were going so well between them that she didn't. She felt guilty about how she'd spoken to him the night she'd received the nasty text. He had been generous, kind, and open about his feelings for her. *And how do I repay that? By threatening to throw him out the first night he sleeps over.*

I'm a real piece of work.

She stood up and walked over to the box that contained all the toys she hadn't yet tried. *How am I going to review the rest of these if I don't try them out?*

She laughed sadly into her hand. *Talk about job stress I'll never discuss with my friends. How is work? Oh, too many projects piling up.*

Turning away from the box, Lucy walked to her window and scanned the area for David. He was in the round pen with the mare he was determined to reform. Tony had written the horse off. Wyatt had even warned his family to stay away from her, but David wasn't giving up that easily.

David couldn't turn his back on any creature in need, be it human or four-legged.

Is that why he's here with me? What happens when I do finally pay him back? When he thinks I don't need him anymore?

Don't leave me, David. Please don't leave me.

Two weeks with David in her bed, at her side, giving her reasons to smile each day, had changed some of Lucy's thinking. In the beginning, she'd been grateful to have one more day with him. She'd savored the meals they shared, the nights of passion, and the dates he took her on. All while fighting back small panic attacks because he'd end a phone call abruptly when she entered a room or went into town without telling her where he was going. But the more time they spent together, the less she gave in to those feelings. David wasn't hiding anything, except perhaps the name of the next restaurant he wanted to surprise her with. He was the good man he portrayed himself to be. *A better person than I am.*

David finished up with the horse, and Lucy turned away from the window.

I'm the only problem in our relationship.

Me and my fears.

I need to stop letting them control me.

Lucy walked back to the box and picked up the largest toy inside. It was the velvet base with the exchangeable mechanical dildo on top. She placed it on her desk, laid out the variety of attachable pieces in front of it, and sat down. She rested her chin on one hand and looked at it sternly.

You don't scare me, you know.

You're just a bunch of wires and silicone molds.

She glanced at the directions, then attached one of the dildos to the top. It had a tickler on its end that reminded Lucy of a mop of hair.

Not even sexy. More like something from outer space.

She absently ran her finger over the complicated arrangements of buttons on the front. *And seriously, how much does something like you need to do?*

As she brushed too hard against one of the buttons, the dildo started to spin. "Shit." She tried to turn it off, but the button she'd pressed had sent the base into a vibration mode so powerful, the thing was hopping on her desk. She made a grab for it, pressed another button, and the dildo flew forward, slapping her across the face. She swore and lost her grip, and it hopped itself off her desk and crashed to the floor.

She scrambled onto her knees, trying to grab the damn thing. It eluded her first attempt, but she finally caught it. Despite how it wiggled for its freedom, she righted it and located the "Off" button. Swearing, she sat back on her heels and wiped a hand across her now sweaty brow. It was only then that she noticed David standing at the door.

There are moments in life that test a man. The sight of Lucy chasing a hopping machine with a dick waving from the top of it like a flag was probably the funniest thing David had ever seen. The expression on her face warned him not to laugh. He told himself she was probably embarrassed, and he shouldn't have opened the door without knocking.

Then, because he was only human, he grinned and asked, "Tough day at work?"

She looked torn between laughing and crying. "Only a masochist would make something like this."

David closed the door behind him and came to squat in front of her. A thought occurred to him that wiped the smile off his face. "Don't ever try anything you don't want to. No matter what anyone says."

Lucy pushed the machine to one side. "They don't make me try them. I thought it would be a good idea to know as much as I can about what I'm selling, and some are still in development, so my feedback helps."

Feeling better, David bit back a smile. "What did you learn about this one?" She was still dressed, so he figured it couldn't have been that much.

She glared down at the velvet-covered base. "They should label the buttons better." She touched one of her cheeks. "And don't put your face too close to it." He coughed back a laugh, and her eyes narrowed. "It's not funny. I was trying to turn it off, and it slapped me."

There was no holding back the laughter then. David laughed until his eyes teared up.

Lucy took a moment but then joined in. She was soon laughing as hard as he was. Gasping to catch her breath, she said, "It literally slapped me across the face. Thank God I picked the small dildo."

David roared and then stood, offering Lucy a hand to help her up. "What a way to lose an eye. Try explaining that to our kids."

Lucy gave him a funny look for a second, then fell naturally against his chest and continued to laugh. "Why the hell would they give it spring action? And what do those other buttons do?"

The questions piqued David's interest. "Someone had to design that thing based on what people like. It's in the production phase, right?"

"It's already for sale on the company website."

"Is it selling?"

"Not well, but I haven't said anything about it yet, and that seems to drive sales." Lucy glared down at the machine again. "This might sound stupid, but I have a weird bond with this toy. It was the first one I saw when I opened the box, and it intimidated me. I've been avoiding it ever since. I'm half convinced it knows I'm afraid of it, and that's why it tried to kill me. It won today, and it knows it."

David held back another laugh only because she was speaking seriously again, not because what she was saying was any less funny. She really did hate that machine. He wanted to do something for her. He'd spent the last two weeks trying to find out who had called her and what trouble, if anything, Ted had brewing. So far his attempts to help her hadn't achieved much. This problem, however, was one that seemed easy enough to resolve. "Does it come with directions?"

She looked from him to the toy and back. "Yes, but they're impossible to make sense of."

David put his hands on her hips and shifted against her. "I'm sure we could figure it out together."

She frowned. "You'd want to try it?"

"Get on it? No," he clarified. "Figure out if it does anything you'd enjoy—sure. I told you I have no problem with toys."

She leaned back so she could see his face better, and at that, he moved her across his quickly hardening cock. "You don't have to pretend to like something you don't."

David hugged her tighter and tried to concentrate on the topic and not how good her breasts felt against his chest. "What makes you think I'm not being honest?"

He hated the question as soon as he heard himself voice it. He'd already lied to her about where he'd gone that day he looked up the properties Ted had purchased and compared them to the area being tested for deep oil pockets. He'd lied about whom he'd been talking to when she caught him asking Tony's brother, Dean, if he knew the sheriff in Mavis. He'd always considered himself an honest man. Lies were for those who weren't brave enough to stand up for what they believed in. Though he still thought it was necessary, the only way he could protect Lucy, it was beginning to get harder and harder to look her in the eye and not confess.

Lucy studied his face for a long moment. He looked away, hoping she couldn't see the guilt in his eyes. She touched his face gently. "You said you liked them, but I think you said that to make me feel better about what I'm doing. Otherwise, you would have asked to try one of them—"

David groaned. Although he'd had sex with Lucy almost every night since they'd come back from Fort Mavis, he hadn't pushed to use the toys. As crazy as it sounded, even to himself, he'd wanted her to get comfortable with where they already were before moving forward again. She'd felt rushed, and he'd tried to spend the last two weeks with her building a stronger foundation for their relationship.

This toy was different, though. It represented more than possible pleasure for her. She saw it as something that could beat her. He wanted to take the power away from the machine and give it back to her. He kissed her lips and rested his forehead on hers. "I didn't want you to feel any more pressured than you already did, so I figured I'd wait until you brought them into our bedroom. However, if you want to hog-tie and tame this one, I'm game."

Chapter Seventeen

Up in Lucy's bedroom, David and Lucy sat on the floor with the machine, all of its pieces, and the directions spread out on a towel. They were reading over the instructions like a couple about to build a cabinet together.

"It recommends using lube. Do you have any?"

Lucy blushed and went to open a drawer on the table beside her bed. She returned and put it on the towel beside the machine. "Check."

David picked up the remote control. "It seems safer to use this than try to control anything from the main panel once you're on it."

Lucy noted the look of concentration on David's face and laughed softly. "You're so serious."

He gave her a lopsided grin. "I don't want you to get hurt."

She leaned over the machine and planted a kiss on his lips. "That's sweet."

David kissed her back, then, like a kid figuring out a new toy at Christmas, he said, "It's not as complicated as it looks. Watch. These buttons are all for the top part. This one is for rotation. That one, vibration. This one moves it up and down. That's the face slapper. I'd avoid that while you're on it." He pointed to the second row of buttons. "This one gives the base that hop you discovered earlier. I bet the big button next to it turns it off in an emergency. They should make it red so people would know." He handed the remote to Lucy. "See if I'm right."

Lucy was reminded of the time she tried to learn how to fly a drone. There were a lot of possible combinations, but as she went through the various modes, she kept testing the big button, and David was right—it shut everything off. That part was reassuring.

What she couldn't yet see, though, was what anyone found sexy about it. She had no desire to sit on it and start it up, either alone or while David was watching. She put the remote down and sighed. *It'll be the shortest review ever: "Scary as hell if you're alone; a complete flop if you're not."*

Lucy looked across at David, ready to admit defeat. "Do you find anything sexy about this?"

His gaze warmed. "Yes. You."

She felt a familiar heat spread through her. Two weeks of David should have taken the edge off how much she wanted him, but it hadn't. All it took was one look, one glimpse at the hunger in his eyes, and her body began to hum for his. They didn't have to touch for her to get wet. Her body knew his so well now that she could lick her own lips and taste his.

Lucy pulled her shirt over her head, tossing it on the floor behind her. She unclasped her bra and did the same. While he watched, she suckled on one of her fingers until his lips parted, then brought it to his mouth. He took her hand in his and wrapped his lips around her finger. His tongue circled it.

He went up onto his knees and removed his own shirt, then kicked off his shoes and socks. Lucy slid off the rest of her clothing and then helped him out of his.

They rolled onto the floor together beside the towel. His mouth was hungry for hers, then for the rest of her. She couldn't get enough of him. Her hands ran over every inch of him, loving how he moaned from the pleasure of her touch.

Whatever else was wrong with her life, this was right. Being with David was something she'd never regret. He kissed his way down her neck, spent his time adoring and teasing each of her breasts, then moved lower.

He kissed her stomach while running his hands up and down her, wanting more and more of her. She knew exactly how he felt.

She parted her legs eagerly for him and cried out his name when he dove in and did what he'd learned she liked the most. This wasn't a man experimenting with what he hoped his woman liked, this was a man who knew exactly how to send his partner out of control. He used his tongue, his teeth, those incredible fingers of his, until she was just about to climax.

Then the bastard stopped.

He lifted his head and smiled. She wanted to kick him, but she didn't. She dug her hands into his hair and pleaded silently for him to finish.

He sat up and reached for the machine. While she considered all the ways she could kill him, he lubed it up, then growled, "Get on it, Lucy. We don't have to turn it on, but I want to see you on it."

Lucy shook her head to clear some of the sexual daze she was in. Part of her wanted to refuse, but she was also already so revved up that the thought of plunging something inside her was tempting. Knowing she would do it while he watched was suddenly such a turn-on that she almost came from the thought alone.

She moved to stand above the machine, and at first thought she would squat down and take it inside her, but it was low enough so that wasn't comfortable. She went down on her knees and hovered above it for a moment.

David dug his hand into her hair and kissed her deeply. His tongue plundered, and Lucy forgot all about everything but him. Easing herself down onto the mechanical shaft was like taking him inside her. It felt good.

David kissed his way to her neck again and whispered, "Should I turn it on?" He ran one hand down the front of her and caressed her clit while he waited for her answer.

"Oh yes," she breathed.

He started with the vibration of just the dildo. Combined with his intimate touch, it was so good, she threw her head back and cried out for him to keep going.

The shaft inside her began to turn and caress her in a way that sent her spiraling back toward an orgasm. David continued to kiss her body while moving his fingers back and forth over her clit.

Lucy was nearly out of her mind. David stood, then gruffly ordered, "Take me in your mouth. I want to come when you do."

She grasped his excited cock and brought him deeply into her mouth. The shaft inside her started to move up and down. Lucy did the same with her mouth on David. Having David in her mouth while feeling as if he were always plunging upward into her sex was excruciatingly exciting. Lucy came before David did, but she kept loving him with her tongue. The machine beneath her was relentless. It didn't care that she'd already come. It kept twirling and thrusting up into her, just as David's cock thrust deeper into her mouth.

"I'm going to come," he said, giving her time to withdraw if she wanted.

She took him deeper, took the shaft inside her deeper, and came for a second time while he exploded in her mouth. He stepped back and reached for the remote, hitting the big button. Then he offered his hand to Lucy and helped her to her feet.

She was shaken and could barely stand. He picked her up, carried her to the bed, and slid beneath the sheets with her.

"That was amazing," she said, then kissed his shoulder. *Understatement. Of. The. Year. If I review that one, sales will skyrocket. Holy. Shit.*

David nuzzled her neck. "You can say that again."

She smiled. "You didn't try the hopper."

He murmured, "Didn't want to push my luck, but we can next time."

Lucy glanced at the machine, then back at David. "I conquered that little fucker."

David threw back his head and laughed. "You sure did, honey. You sure did."

Chapter Eighteen

The next morning, Lucy was pushing a cart up and down the aisles of the grocery store, absently placing items in the basket. She couldn't stop smiling and had gotten a few strange looks from the locals, but she didn't care. Every time she thought about David and how good he was to her, she felt like she was floating on a cloud of happiness.

It wasn't that she didn't miss her brother, that she didn't still mourn her parents, but the weight of all that was no longer crushing her. She could breathe again. If she didn't think someone would call the police to cart her away, she would have thrown her arms up in the air and done a happy spin right there in the bakery department.

She picked up an individually wrapped special-occasion cupcake, one with a decadent mound of frosting on it. She imagined how she would hand it to David that night.

He'd ask her what the special occasion was, and she'd say, "Tonight is the night I want to smear frosting all over you and slowly lick it off." She shuddered as her body warmed and clenched in sexual anticipation.

"Lucy, are you all right?" a woman asked in a concerned voice that implied she might have tried and failed to get Lucy's attention already.

Lucy shook her head and brought herself back to the present. "Hi, Michelle."

Michelle kept her hands gripped to the handle of her grocery cart. "You never called me back."

Lucy was instantly contrite. "Oh my God, I'm sorry, Michelle. Things have been so busy with my new business and—"

"David." Michelle smiled, but it didn't reach her eyes. "I hear he's living with you now."

Small towns. "He is."

"That's good, Lucy. You deserve someone in your life." Michelle's face crumpled, and tears filled her eyes. "I threw Ron out."

Lucy didn't know what to say. She felt guilty about being too happy to have known her friend was going through something like that. Although she'd vowed to see her more often, so far most of Lucy's time had been spent with David or working. "I'm sorry to hear that."

Michelle sniffed. "He started drinking again. He used to when he first met me but stopped because I wouldn't marry him if he didn't give it up. He only has a temper when he drinks."

Lucy swallowed hard. "He didn't—"

"Hit me?" Michelle shook her head. "He's never touched me, but it was getting ugly at our house. I feel awful, though, because I think this time was my fault."

"Michelle, don't say that. Of course it wasn't."

She lowered her voice. "He's been a good husband to me, but I told him I wanted more. I asked him if we could figure out why I could orgasm with a toy but not with him. I thought talking about it would bring us closer. He walked out of the house that day and came back drunk. I tried to explain it to him the next day, but it escalated into a nasty fight, and he called me all sorts of ugly names. I gave him a chance to apologize. I mean, marriage is for better or for worse. His apology was to come home drunk and yell at me again. Sheriff Dodd helped remove him from the house that night. It was humiliating, but I didn't want him to do anything I couldn't forgive him for. I love him, Lucy. What if I drove him to this?"

"You didn't," Lucy said emphatically.

"We were happy before I bought that toy, Lucy. This is my fault."

"Were you? Happy, I mean. Or was *he* happy, and you were settling for the best you thought you could have?"

A tear rolled down Michelle's cheek. She wiped it away with a fisted hand. "I'm pregnant. This should be a happy time for me. I don't want to raise my children without a father." She whispered again, "Maybe this is God's way of punishing me for touching myself."

Lucy walked over and hugged Michelle. "If God punished people for that, Michelle, there would be no men on the planet. And hardly any women. God wouldn't push your husband to drink. Not the God I pray to. This will work out. You'll see."

Michelle shook in her arms. "What if it doesn't?"

Sarah's words came back to Lucy, so she said, "You are not alone, Michelle. No matter how this turns out. You have people who care about you, and that's what's important."

Michelle sniffed and wiped her cheeks again. "There's something I should have told you, but I didn't want to believe it. It's something Ron said to me while he was drunk."

The hairs on the back of Lucy's neck stood up. "What did he say?"

Michelle took a fortifying breath before saying, "Ted hates you. Ron warned me to stay away from you, or I could get hurt, too."

"Too?"

"I know. I tried to ask him about it, but that's all he would say. He's staying out at York's place now, and it scares me. Working for him is bad enough, but the men who stay with York—they change. It's like a cult out there. An angry mob of men who do whatever York tells them to do." She lowered her voice again. "Things happen when York wants someone's land, things that everyone calls accidents, but aren't. If he wants a family out of this town, they don't last long. Everyone is too afraid to talk about it. I couldn't say anything to you when you were marrying him because I didn't think you'd believe me. But I'm afraid for you now. You're smart to have David and Wyatt out there with you."

"It'll be okay, Michelle. Don't worry. Everything's going to be okay." She knew she couldn't really promise that, but surely Ted wasn't really as dangerous as Michelle suggested.

She talked to her friend for a few minutes longer before promising to call her the next day, but she was trying to wrap her head around what Michelle had said. Outside of the one prank call, nothing had happened at her ranch.

Was the warning nothing more than a drunk Ron trying to scare his wife into taking him back?

Ted no longer had a financial hold on her land. Even if he burned it all to the ground, he wouldn't get it. David held the note on the property.

And why would Ted want her property that badly? Why was he buying up all the land around him? It wasn't as if the price of beef was going anywhere.

On the way back to her ranch, Lucy stopped by town hall. She asked the clerk if she could see a map of the properties surrounding hers.

The woman said, "Sure, I still have that out. It's a popular request lately."

"Really?" Lucy asked, trying to sound as if she weren't interested in the topic at all.

The woman shuffled through some piles, then brought out a rolled plot map. "Sure, I even had your handsome boyfriend in here a few weeks ago. He said he was looking up something for you." She held out the roll to Lucy and let out a dreamy sigh. "What town did you find him in? Are there more like him? I'd move in a heartbeat."

Lucy took the roll. *Why would David want to see the land plots?* "Sorry, he's one of a kind." *And he's mine.*

"Oh well, I guess that's for the best, anyway."

Lucy laid out the paper on the large desk in the office. She didn't know what she was looking for, but she was hoping something would jump out at her. "Who else requested to see this map?"

The young woman seemed to question if she was sharing too much. "That's not confidential information, right? I'm alone today, or I'd ask."

Lucy shrugged. "It's not important. I was just curious." She dug through her memories for a name that would help her. "Hey, are you Nikki's little sister, Kelly?"

The woman nodded. "You probably don't remember, but I used to stalk the two of you. It drove Nikki crazy. We're close now, but she said I was awful when we were little."

"I remember. You'll have to tell her I said hello."

Kelly nodded and glanced around to make sure no one was listening, then said, "We had some men in suits come in last year—I can't imagine who would care that I told you—then a lawyer. Ted York was in here one day. Oh yes, and some of the families just before they sold to Mr. York and moved away. This job is usually boring, but I'm loving it this year." She stepped back from the counter so Lucy could see her dress. "I may have even met someone. Who knew coming to work would be where I'd start meeting men? He came in last week. Gorgeous *and* single. He wanted a list of all the properties that have sold in town in the last two years. I told him I'd have to research it. He promised to come back for it." She smiled. "I bought five new dresses." Kelly laughed.

Lucy smiled even though her mind was racing. "I'd be surprised if he can remember what he came in for when he sees you."

Kelly blushed. "Thanks." She nodded toward the table. "Did you find what you were looking for?"

Lucy rolled the paper back up and handed it to her. "I did. Is there any chance I could get a copy of that list of sales?"

With a shrug, Kelly said, "It's all public knowledge, so I see no reason why not. I'll make you a copy. Hang on, I'll be right back." Then she returned and handed Lucy the list.

"Thanks, Kelly. And good luck."

She left and tucked the list into the visor on the passenger side of her truck.

She didn't know how she felt about David going to town hall. She didn't want to believe that something was going on, and he wasn't being honest with her. She had more questions than she had answers, making her drive back to the ranch a very long one.

David started his day inside Lucy's house, making phone calls. He wasn't happy with the lack of progress with the mare, and it was weighing on him. He contacted the family who owned the horse and asked them where they'd gotten her.

They countered by asking when they'd get their horse back and how much all that training was going to cost them. David hated having to explain to them that the horse would never be suitable for a family. He offered to keep her.

They quoted a ridiculous price for a horse that would likely kill them if he sent it home to them now. He offered them a trade instead. He had an older mare who was as gentle as they came. It took a little convincing, but when he explained that this horse could be ridden bareback around their yard, they agreed.

David said he'd ship the horse to them at no cost, and the deal was set. All that was important to him, he stressed, was helping the mare they'd sent him. They had to know something.

It was only then that they opened up and admitted how little they'd paid for the mare. They said they'd gotten her at an auction. They'd thought they were saving her from slaughter, but she'd never been right, and the more they handled her, the worse she'd gotten.

"Do you know anything about where she came from before that?"

They didn't, but they gave him some information about where they'd bought her. David contacted the man who'd run the auction. And he gave David the name of who'd provided the horse.

Before David hung up, he said, "Did you know how dangerous she was when you sold her to a family with a child?"

The man didn't sound repentant. "I put the horse through as is. If you buy a horse dirt cheap, you know it has problems."

David could have said more, but wasting his breath on those who had no intention of changing had never been his style. Instead, he called the number the auctioneer had given him.

The woman who answered was curt at first until David explained that his intention was only to find out whatever he could to help the mare.

"She was a good horse," the woman said sadly. "I raised her from a foal. She wasn't mean at all."

"What happened?" David held his breath and waited.

"I told my husband we needed to replace that old barbed wire. He said it was good enough when his daddy had horses here, and it would work for us. Tia, that's what we called the mare you have, she got caught in it out in the far field. Got her neck tangled up in it real good." The woman paused, and her voice filled with emotion. "You probably think I didn't care about Tia, but I loved her. I used our savings on vet bills to heal her up. She was never right again, though. Her mane grew over the scars and made her pretty on the outside, but something changed in her. She'd turn on us when we were doing nothing but leading her to her field. She nearly killed my husband. He wanted to shoot her, but I convinced him to give her a chance. No one would take her but the auction." In a whisper, she said, "Tell me she didn't kill anyone."

"No, ma'am, she didn't, but she's still dangerous."

"Who'd you say you were? David Harmon?"

"Yes, ma'am."

"The one from the commercials who works with Tony Carlton?"

"That's me."

The woman let out a light sob. "You don't know how much I needed this call. I hated sending Tia to the auction, but things work out the way they're supposed to, don't they? She found you."

David's face flushed. "I haven't reached her yet."

"You will. I have to believe that."

David's throat was tight with emotion. "If I can't, I'll have to put her down."

"I understand," the woman said. "If you can't help her, I don't believe anyone can."

David paced the living room of Lucy's home long after hanging up with Tia's old owner. He hadn't noticed scarring on the horse, but there was a chance the mane had indeed hidden it. If that wound was where the horse's halter was, there was a chance that pressure on the halter hurt the horse. If Tia began to associate being handled with pain, that might explain why she lashed out.

Maybe.

He rubbed his hands over his face in frustration. He'd woken up in Lucy's arms, feeling like he could conquer the world, but when it was important, was he actually making a difference at all?

He'd found next to nothing that could help Lucy. When it came to York, the town was tight-lipped. Wyatt thought something bad was brewing, but he didn't have the details that would allow David to do anything. It was all rumors and gut feelings at this point. York hadn't done anything illegal or anything that would justify David going after him.

Threatening him was tempting, but that would help York. Right now, David had the advantage of York not knowing he was on to him. David was hoping that would leave York overconfident.

A knock on the front door was followed by Wyatt calling out, "David, you in there?"

David strode over and opened the door. "What do you need?"

"There's something in the barn you need to see."

David grabbed his hat and followed him. Seated on a wooden chair and holding a bloody towel to his head was a man David didn't recognize. "What the hell happened?" Two of the ranch hands were standing on either side of him like sentries.

"This here is Ron. First, before you attempt to talk to him, he's drunk. Second, he got it in his damn-fool head to try to take that mare of yours. She taught him a lesson he won't soon forget. I called the sheriff. He's on his way."

Even though his head was lolling to one side, he slurred, "I was trying to save the damn horse. It was too close to the barn, and I couldn't let it burn—I should have let it die."

David strode closer and stood over him. "What do you mean you should have let her die? What did you come here to do?"

The man's eyes couldn't focus on David's face, but he snarled, "People like you need to be run out of town. You and that whore of yours."

Despite the condition of the man, David lifted him up by the neck of his shirt. "Say one more word about Lucy, and I will kill you with my bare hands."

Wyatt, at David's side, said softly, "Put him down, son. The best thing you can do is let the fool speak. He won't remember much of this later, but his tongue is mighty loose right now."

David dropped the man back onto the chair. The man groaned and looked like he was about to pass out. "Why would you want to hurt Lucy?" David demanded.

With his eyes still closed, the man mumbled, "My wife threw me out because of her. She brought the devil into our house and turned Michelle against me. Evil takes root and poisons everything."

"The devil?" David looked to Wyatt for what that could mean, but Wyatt shrugged helplessly. "What are you talking about?"

Ron shook his head and groaned from the pain of it. "Women like Lucy don't belong in our town, and you don't either. Mustang lover. If you get your way, none of us will be using the public lands, will we? You plan to give it all to those fucking horses." Ron slurred on, "Mr. York will stop you. He's buying up enough grazing land that those who are loyal to him won't need to lease public land. We'll be fine."

Wyatt made at face at Ron. "You think York gives a shit about your drunk ass? You're drinking the Kool-Aid, Ron."

Ron's eyes flew open. "My wife would rather fuck an Easter egg than me." He pointed at David wildly. "Your girlfriend told her it was better than a man. Watch out, or you'll be replaced by the blender."

Wyatt gave David a sidelong look, then bent until he was face-to-face with Ron. "Son, the only thing ruining your marriage is the bottle. Michelle is a saint. If she threw you out, it's because you were drinking again."

Ron covered his bloody face with one hand and started sobbing. "Wan' her back. Wanna be there with her and my babies."

The sheriff entered the barn. "Tell me one of you didn't do this to him."

Wyatt straightened. "He tried to take David's mare, and this is the result of her telling him what she thought of the idea."

The sheriff's eyebrows rose, then fell. "I heard about that horse. I hope you're planning on putting her down after this."

Wyatt countered, "I believe we should focus on the reason Ron is here in the first place."

Ron looked to the sheriff for support. "York says town needs a cleanin' out for things to be right again. Ain't that right?"

The sheriff reached for his handcuffs. "We'll talk about this on the way in, but I'm guessing you'll need a lawyer."

David raised a hand. "I'm not pressing charges."

Wyatt said, "He came here to—"

"People do stupid things when they're drunk. I'm not saying what he did was right, but it looks like he's already received his punishment for it. Let's sober him up and see if we can help out." He nodded at one of the men. "Get the vet out here."

The sheriff looked at David in surprise. "Don't you mean the doctor?"

David shook his head. "No, we'll get Ron medical attention and call his wife, but first I want to follow up on a hunch I have. I think I know what's wrong with the horse."

Chapter Nineteen

On the way back to her ranch, Lucy had decided to talk to David about why he'd looked into the land maps, but when she pulled into the driveway, he and Wyatt walked out of the barn to meet her.

David gave her a quick kiss, but he seemed distracted. Wyatt had the same look about him. "Is everything all right?" Lucy asked.

"Everything's fine," David assured her quickly. "Why don't you go inside and get some work done. This should be over before dinner."

"Over?" Lucy folded up the list she'd carried from the car to show him and stuffed it in her back pocket. Wyatt and David exchanged a look that only served to make Lucy more convinced they were hiding something.

A truck pulled up behind Lucy's. The local vet, Ben Farms, stepped out and headed toward them. He was a good-looking man with sandy-blond hair and dark-brown eyes. Locals joked that half his business came from women who said their animals were sick, but just wanted to see him.

Suddenly, David's reluctance to let her into the barn made sense to Lucy. David didn't want her to witness what was most likely the vet putting down one of the horses. Lucy tucked her hand into David's. She hoped it wasn't the mare he'd spent so much time with. She knew he was emotionally invested in that horse. Even while facing something like that, David was trying to shelter her from seeing it. What David had obviously forgotten was that Lucy had grown up as a rancher's daughter. Her father hadn't hidden the harsher side of raising animals from her. "Which horse is it?" she asked softly.

David looked down at her as if trying to read her expression. "I called him out to look at Tia. That's the mare's original name. It fits her."

Lucy leaned against David's arm in sympathy. There had been chatter among the men at the ranch about how best to deal with the mare. Had David finally agreed with them? Her father would have come to the same conclusion a whole lot sooner. "I'm so sorry."

"I'm not putting her down," David said. "In fact, I have an idea what's wrong with her."

Lucy would have asked more, but the veterinarian joined them, shaking hands with the three of them in turn.

Ben said, "I brought my portable X-ray machine, but I have to tell you, I'm not going near that horse unless we sedate her first. From what I hear, you're lucky she didn't kill Ron."

David looked at Wyatt as if to say he was disappointed he'd told him.

Wyatt shrugged. "Even if Ron deserved what he got, that horse is too dangerous not to warn Dr. Ben about her."

To Ben, David said, "Get the sedative; I'll give it to her. Then we'll take that X-ray."

Ben nodded and went to the back of his covered truck to retrieve his supplies.

Lucy tugged on David's hand until she had his attention. "Are you talking about Michelle's Ron? When was he here?"

David didn't look like he wanted to answer at first, then he said, "He's still here. He's in the bunkhouse sobering up. He tried to move

Tia from one paddock to another this morning, and it didn't work out well for him. Though Doc Erfe says he looks more banged up than he is."

"Did you hire Ron to work here?"

"No."

"Then why would he be here at all?" Lucy didn't like how no one answered her question. "Does Michelle know?"

"We called her," Wyatt said sadly. "She said she couldn't bear to see him like that, so we kept him here instead."

Lucy went over in her head the conversation she'd had with Michelle that morning. "He's staying at Ted's place right now, anyway. Michelle was telling me about it this morning. She was worried for him."

David watched Ben going to his truck while he answered, "She was right to be."

"She said Ted's place is like some kind of dangerous cult."

Wyatt said, "I doubt there's much religion over there, but he definitely knows how to get inside a man's head."

Ben returned with a syringe and metal box he had suspended from a handle, and Lucy temporarily dropped the subject. The four of them turned and walked into the barn. They stopped in front of the stall where Tia was being kept. David said, "I hope I'm right about what's bothering her."

Ben set up his equipment outside the stall, then handed the syringe to David. "You said she was looked at by a vet over in Fort Mavis?"

"Yes, but nothing like this was done." David opened the stall door. Tia's ears flattened. He spoke to her softly and approached her.

Ben said, "We could try an oral sedative if you want. They're not as effective, but a whole lot safer to give."

"I'll be fine," David said.

Lucy wanted to tell David to be careful. Actually, she wanted to tell him that no horse was worth risking his life over, but she knew how important this was to him. She clasped her hands in front of her and held her breath.

David spoke to Tia gently. He ran a hand along her shoulder. His touch seemed to soothe her, and her ears raised as she listened to him. "Tia, I know all about you now. You're a good horse. You need to let us do this. One little pinch, and we can take your pain away."

David took his time until it almost seemed he had hypnotized the horse. Then slowly, gently, he gave the horse the sedative shot. She looked mildly irritated, but she didn't pull away from him.

From the door of the stall, Ben said, "I never put much faith in what I see on TV, but you can work with me any day."

David continued to run his hands gently over Tia's shoulder and back while the sedative slowly began to work. "She knows I don't want to hurt her, and I don't believe she wants to hurt us. Or she won't want to after you remove what I hope you find."

When Tia's head lowered, a sure sign she was getting drowsy, Ben stepped into the stall. "I've seen stranger things, so you could be right." He held part of the machine up and took a digital picture just behind Tia's ears. "Well, I'll be damned." He took several more shots of the horse's neck beneath the mane. He stepped back and showed them what he'd found. "Right there, do you see it? It looks like a bent needle. I bet that's a piece of the barbed wire you said she'd been caught in. I'm surprised it didn't get infected. Or maybe it did and healed over. It's deep, so I can see how someone wouldn't notice it, but being where it is, it must be painful for her whenever someone puts a halter over it."

David continued to speak gently. "Or applies any pressure while trying to lead her. No wonder she doesn't want anyone putting a lead line on her. And that angry shake of her head is probably her way of saying it hurts." He looked across to Ben. "Can it be taken out today?"

Ben nodded. "I don't see why not. I know exactly where it is. I should be able to get it out with a small incision. After that, it's just a matter of keeping it clean."

When David stepped out of the stall, Wyatt gave his shoulder a pat. "You did good, son."

Lucy stepped into David's arms and hugged him tightly. "You really are amazing."

David kissed Lucy on the forehead and chuckled. "That's what I keep trying to tell you."

From beside them, Wyatt said, "I'll stay with Dr. Ben while he works on her."

David shook Ben's hand again, then slid an arm around Lucy's waist. "I'll walk Lucy in."

As they walked out of the barn, Lucy asked, "Why did Ron try to move Tia?"

David didn't answer at first. He walked with Lucy back to her house. Deciding how much to tell her wasn't easy. "He was drunk, and people make poor choices when they hit the bottom of a bottle."

Lucy tensed beneath his touch. "This is my ranch, David. I have a right to know what's going on." She turned and pinned him down with a steady stare. "And everything you're lying to me about."

"Lying?" David felt like a child who'd been caught doing something he'd been told not to. His stalling question sounded as lame to him as it probably did to her.

She put a hand on one of her hips. Her cheeks were flushed with anger, and her eyes flashed with temper. If she didn't look so close to belting him, he would have told her how beautiful she was just then. "I know you went to town hall about property lines. The clerk said you told her you were asking on my behalf. I'd like to know why. I'd also like to know if you're doing anything else on my behalf."

David went to pull her to him, but she stepped back. He sighed. "I know I promised I wouldn't get involved, but . . ."

Lucy shook her head as if wanting to deny what she was hearing. "But you did? What did you do?" She searched his face, and before he had a chance to answer, she said, "No, don't bother. I won't know if you're telling me the truth or not." She wrapped her arms around herself. "I am the worst judge of character; I thought I could trust you. Really trust you."

He stepped closer to her, but she retreated again. "Lucy, I didn't want to lie to you, but—"

"But you did. How many times? Once? A hundred times? How many lies would I have to tell you before you'd start doubting everything I said?"

It was a harsh stance, but one that David could understand. He'd had many opportunities to talk to her about how dangerous he thought York was and how he needed to look into what he was doing even if Lucy didn't want him to. "All I wanted to do was protect you."

With large, hurt eyes, Lucy said, "Even if I believe that, it changes us. Do you see that?" She put her hand on the door handle of the house. "You can sleep in the bunkhouse, David. I don't want you in the house tonight." She gave him another long, sad look. "Why was Ron here?"

This time David didn't evade the question. "He intended to burn the barn down."

Lucy's eyes rounded. "Because?"

"He thinks you broke up his marriage."

"I didn't."

"I know."

Lucy looked down at a spot on the porch between them. "At least, I didn't mean to. I wanted to help Michelle. I should have known it would blow up in my face. I swear I must be cursed or something. You should run back to Fort Mavis, David, before I take you down, too."

David opened his mouth to argue that point, but Lucy slid into her house and closed the door. He realized then he hadn't said he was sorry about not telling her everything. It felt like a lie. He should have felt sorry, but he wasn't, not really.

She'd forgive him for breaking a promise to her, but he'd never forgive himself if anything happened to her—especially if it was something he could have prevented. David turned and strode back to the barn. Half an hour after Lucy had kicked him out of the house, he learned with relief that Tia's surgery had gone easily. He hoped she would now be out of pain and that it would be a fresh start for her.

Later that evening, he stood beside the cot where Ron was sleeping off his hangover. With the heel of his foot, he rolled the man over, sending him to the floor with a thud.

Ron groaned, then raised himself up by his arms and looked around. "What the hell did you do that for?"

David left his booted foot resting on the side of the cot and leaned forward to look Ron in his bloodshot eyes. "It's by the grace of God your ass isn't rotting in jail for arson."

Ron struggled to his feet. He went to push past David. "Leave me the fuck alone."

David was on him in a flash, shoving him back against the wall and holding a hand to his neck. "Don't mistake my even temper for a guarantee that I won't kill you."

Fear flashed in Ron's eyes.

David maintained his hold on the man's neck. "Did York send you?"

Ron looked away. "Not in so many words."

David gave Ron a shake and repeated the question in a snarl, "Did he send you?"

Ron met his eyes. "He wants you gone. He wants Lucy gone, too. He doesn't care how it happens."

"Did he tell you why?"

"He says you don't belong here."

David let Ron go, and the man slumped against the wall. "He's using you, and you're letting him. What kind of man are you, Ron? What kind of daddy will you be for those children of yours?"

Ron sank to the floor and covered his face with his hands. "I don't know anymore. Does it matter? After today, Michelle will never take me back."

David sighed. He'd seen something in Ron's eyes, a spark of a better man. "Do you want your wife back?"

Ron laid his head back against the wall and closed his eyes. "Of course I do."

"What would you do to keep her?"

Ron opened his eyes. "Anything."

David continued, "As I see it, you've got one chance to get your wife back, but I don't know if you've got the balls to make the kind of changes you need to."

"She said she won't take me back. It's too late."

"Not if you stand the fuck back up."

Ron pushed himself back to his feet and shook his head. "Why do you care? And why didn't you press charges for what I did?"

"Because I believe in second chances, and this is yours. You haven't lost everything yet, Ron, but you need to cut certain elements out of your life. Starting with York."

Still looking somewhat beaten, Ron said, "Michelle hates that I work for him, but there's no real choice around here. Not if a man wants a decent wage."

"I'm always looking for good men to help me with the horses."

Ron was quiet for a long moment. "You'd hire me after what I done?"

"If you stay off the booze and work hard."

Ron's face twisted with shame. "I will. Michelle always said the bottle brings out an ugly side of me. I proved her right today. You may not believe it, but I don't hate Lucy. I don't want harm to come to her or her place. I wouldn't have been able to live with myself if I had hurt anyone this morning."

David walked to the door. If Ron knew anything else, it would come out soon enough. David didn't want to hear lies or a cover story. Once Ron found his place with the men at the ranch and realized they weren't the enemy, he'd talk. For now, it was enough to throw Ron a lifeline. "But you didn't. It's kind of ironic. You owe your second chance to a horse who is about to get her second chance. Might be I've just thought of how you can help around here."

Ron's eyes widened. "You want me to break your mare? The one that tried to kill me?"

"No, I want you to gentle her." He briefly explained to him about the shard of metal the vet had taken out of Tia's neck. He also outlined his philosophy of reaching a horse rather than utilizing more force-ful methods of taming it. "Her name is Tia, and she associates being handled with being hurt. It's going to take patience and a whole lot of understanding of what she's been through to win back her trust."

Like Michelle will, David thought but didn't say. He measured men by what they did, not by what they said. Ron said he wanted his wife back. He said he'd do anything. Tia would be the first test of that. If Ron had no sympathy for an animal that had struck out at him through no fault of her own, then Michelle, his daughter, and his unborn child might be better off without him.

It wasn't really a matter of Ron changing; it was a matter of him choosing.

David walked out of the room and went to sit on the steps of the bunkhouse.

Wyatt joined him. "I once had a dog my wife didn't like in the house. He had that same sad expression on his face every evening when he knew he'd be sleeping outside."

David shot Wyatt a glare, but it didn't bother the older man at all. He could have told Wyatt to mind his own damn business, but Wyatt cared about Lucy, and David liked to think he cared about him, too. "She's right to be mad at me. I lied to her. A couple weeks back, she received a nasty anonymous text. She asked me to stay out of it, and I promised her I would."

Wyatt sat down beside David. "And you didn't?"

"No, I didn't. I went around asking questions, hoping I'd find out who'd sent that text. So far I have a whole lot of rumors and possibilities, but nothing worth lying to her about."

Wyatt tipped his Stetson back and stared out into the distance. "I can't say I support lying to anyone, but I know where your heart is. Lucy does, too. Or she will if you give her time. More important, what did you find out?"

David picked up a pebble from the step beside him and tossed it out onto the grass beside the porch. "This area is being assessed for potential oil pockets. That explains why York is trying to buy up property. I don't fully understand how he expects to benefit from trying to drive Lucy away. Until she pays me back, I own the note on this property. Even if he drove me back to Fort Mavis and scared Lucy into leaving, he has to know that neither of us would ever sell to him."

Wyatt rubbed his chin and made a face. "Son, you're looking at this like a business deal, but my guess is that getting this land has become personal to York. He had everything he wanted before you came into the picture. He had Lucy, he had her land, and he had everyone so scared of him, they forgot they didn't have to be. You took all that away from him. Since you've been here, he's not as welcome in town as he used to be. People are starting to stand up to him. I hear rumblings of an investigation over some of the land sales. Families are saying they sold under duress, and they're talking to lawyers about suing York to get their land back."

"Good."

"Maybe, but that'll take a while to prove, and the law can be slow. Meanwhile, there's a powerful man who feels like he's under attack, and he blames you for his misfortune. This ain't over yet." He kicked off the dirt from the back of one of his boots by banging it on the step. "My son and grandbabies leave tomorrow for Dallas. I gave them what money I could. They're renting out a house in the suburbs, and I suggested my wife go with them to set it up."

David snapped his head around to face Wyatt. "You think it'll get that bad?"

Wyatt pressed his lips together for a moment, then said, "When I see a tornado on the horizon, I send my family wherever they'll be safe. I don't care what I have to say to get them there. You need to get Lucy out of this town, David. I tried to talk to her about leaving, but she won't go. I don't know if we can protect her from what's coming. If you've got one more lie left in you, son, I'd use it now."

Wyatt stood, dusted off his jeans, and left without saying another word. David sat and continued to think long past when the sun went down. By morning, he knew what he had to do, and he hoped if Lucy ever found out, she'd forgive him.

Chapter Twenty

After a sleepless night, Lucy forced herself to shower and dress. She made herself breakfast, but didn't eat it. While pouring her coffee, she spilled some and burned her hand. It wasn't bad, but as she ran cold water over her hand, she shed a tear and tried to tell herself it was from the pain of the burn. But it wasn't.

She'd spent the night asking herself the same questions again and again. *Am I a fool for wanting to believe in a man who admits he lies to me? When will I learn that the only one I can trust is myself?*

Wyatt thinks I should leave town. He says it's not safe for me here.

In all my life, I have never doubted a word Wyatt has said, but isn't being too trusting my problem? For all I know, Wyatt and David are plotting together on how they can take my ranch.

Lucy shut off the water, turned around to rest against the sink, and stared blindly down at the rose-colored skin of her burn. *I feel paranoid.*

But is it paranoia when people are actually confessing to misleading you?

Lucy took out the list of properties Ted had purchased. He'd been systematically buying up one specific area. *Why?* Lucy had searched online last night for all the land that had sold in the area in the last few years. If he was interested in increasing his grazing area, he'd missed prime opportunities to the south of him. *Ted thinks something is here, maybe underground.*

Does David know?

Wyatt?

If so, why won't they tell me?

What kind of relationship could she have with David if he had no problem hiding something like that from her? Lucy thought about how kind David had been. How often he'd stepped forward to help her.

Ted had been just as kind when he thought it would gain him access to her land. He'd also helped her out financially when she'd needed it. In fact, Ted had gone further. He'd offered to marry her, claimed he loved her.

In comparison, David was lagging behind . . . if Lucy took good sex with David out of the equation. Flashes of the two of them passionately entangled on her bed surged to mind, but Lucy stomped them back.

She turned to pick up her coffee cup, but missed and sent it crashing to the floor. Coffee flew in all directions, along with pieces of the cup that had smashed on impact. Lucy looked down at the mess with the same twisting emotion she felt about her relationship with David.

I knew it was too good to be true. No man is that kind, that attentive, while being that hot. This is what women get for reading too many fairy tales when they're young. We're all waiting for our prince to come and save us. But the joke is on us because those stories were written to keep us gullible, to make us think we need a man to be happy. And we fall for it. We believe what men tell us, like lambs heading off to slaughter.

Lucy went to her office window and pushed back the curtain. David was near the barn, talking to his men. With a self-deprecating laugh, she let the curtain drop. *I am back where I started. I took back my ranch only to hand it over to someone else.* Sure, David's men were nicer than Ted's had been. And, yes, being with David had felt like heaven while it had lasted. In that way, he didn't compare with Ted at all, but had any of that been real?

Their attraction for each other couldn't be faked, but David could have used it to his advantage. And the feeling that they had also become friends? *That can be faked.*

Lucy thought about how fragile Michelle's marriage had turned out to be. *All it took to collapse was for Michelle to want something for herself.*

All it took for David and me to end was asking if he was lying to me.

How do you forgive the kind of selfishness Ron shows Michelle?

How do I believe anything David says now that I know he'll break a promise and not even feel bad about it?

Lucy looked at the boxes around her office and covered her face with a hand. She couldn't imagine wanting to ever try another one of the toys. How could she without thinking about David? Without picturing how they would have read over the instructions, laughed over the possibilities, and explored them together?

What if I'm wrong and David is a good man whose only mistake is trying to help a stubborn fool of a woman? What if being angry with him is the greatest mistake I've made since coming home? I've never been happier than I've been with David.

What if he's the one I should be growing old with and I've thrown it away without having the sense to fight for it?

Lucy closed her eyes. *Maybe a woman standing in a room full of sex toys has no right to pray for anything, but if anyone is listening, I need some guidance. Some sign. Please. I don't know what to do.*

Lucy's phone rang, and she jumped. She fumbled to answer it and almost started laughing when she saw the caller ID. It wasn't God or her parents, it was just Sarah.

"Lucy, do you have a minute?"

"Sure," Lucy said while sitting down at her desk. "What's up?"

"How are you?"

Lucy laughed without humor. "Honestly? I'm a mess again. Or still. So really, nothing new to share here. How are you?"

Sarah cleared her throat. "I know you have your business that takes up a lot of your time, but you do most of it on the computer, right?"

"All of it," Lucy answered. *Now that I'm not test-driving anything.*

"I need to ask a favor of you. It's a big one."

Lucy clenched her phone and sat forward. "Anything."

"My OB/GYN said I need to stay off my feet for a little while. She said I should stay as calm as possible. Tony wants to hire someone to be in the house with me while he works, but I don't want that. I don't need someone to clean; I just need someone to be with me for a little bit until we get past this rough patch."

"Oh, Sarah, I don't know if I'm a good choice, especially if you need someone to keep you calm. I'm a human train wreck."

Sarah made a sad sound. "I know things are complicated there right now, but I need you. I wouldn't ask if it weren't important."

Lucy felt horrible. It wasn't that she didn't want to help Sarah; it was that she hated the idea of bringing her negative state of mind into Sarah's home. However, Sarah sounded desperate. *I should suck it up and be there for my friend.*

Her chest fluttered as a thought came to her. *Maybe that's my answer. I need to stop worrying about myself and take care of someone who has always been there for me.*

"Sarah, I can be there by tonight if you need me to."

Sarah let out a relieved breath. "I do."

Still gripping the phone tightly, Lucy said, "I'm sorry I hesitated. It had nothing to do with how much I care. I've let myself get all tangled up in my head, and I didn't want to lay that weight on you."

"We're like family, Lucy. Your problems aren't something you need to hide from me. Friends, at least the ones you're meant to have in your life, want the good and the bad. Let me be there for you while you come and be here for me."

Lucy wiped away a happy tear. A part of her kept expecting to lose Sarah as she'd lost her parents and her brother. Sarah kept proving her wrong, and she loved her more for it. "I love you, Sarah. I'll look into flights when I hang up."

"I love you, too, and your flight is already waiting for you at the airport. I asked Charles to send a plane for you. Prepare yourself; it'll be flashy."

"You didn't have to."

Sarah laughed. "What's the fun of having a super-rich brother if I can't enjoy the perks now and then? He was happy to lend it. He and Melanie said they were sorry they'd missed your visit. They said they might come by while you're here."

"I'd love to see them." Lucy stood and squared her shoulders. "Okay, I'm off to pack. I'll see you this afternoon, I guess."

After hanging up, Lucy went back to the window of her office. David was no longer outside. She didn't know what to say to him before she left or what his response would be. Would he beg her to stay? Would he ask to come with her? Or, worst case, would he be happy she was leaving?

He didn't even attempt to apologize last night. Is that it? He's done? We're done?

Stop. Sarah needs me. First, pack.

Her stomach did a nervous, nauseated flip.

Then, David.

David watched Wyatt carry Lucy's bag to her truck and knew the moment of reckoning had come. A part of him wanted to confess everything and beg her to forgive him until she welcomed him back into her bedroom and her life. He didn't judge himself for that weakness. Any man watching the woman he loved walk away from him would have felt the same. He wouldn't give in to that weakness, though. If he told Lucy the truth, she would stay. She wouldn't believe the real danger she was in. Or she'd want to face it head-on, and he couldn't risk her getting hurt—even if it meant he might lose her over that decision.

One certain way to not win back the heart of a woman who was angry because you lied to her was to lie to her again, and this time pull her friends into it. When he'd called Sarah and Tony that morning, he started by explaining the situation to them, then he asked them to come up with a story that would lure Lucy away to stay with them. Sarah had been opposed to the idea. Her suggestion had been to all sit down with Lucy and explain the situation to her.

David had asked, "What if it's not enough to get her to leave? We've already faced attempted arson. What's next? Wyatt sent his family away because he fears for their safety. If you can think of a better way to get Lucy to go there and stay, share it."

"If she's already angry with you for lying to her, this will only upset her more," Sarah had said unhappily.

"If it keeps her safe, I don't care."

It was only then that Tony had spoken up. "If it were you, Sarah, I would do whatever it took to protect you. Even if I knew you'd hate me for it."

"I would do the same for you." Sarah sighed. "But I'm a terrible liar."

Tony then said, "Although I love that about you, this time you need to be a good one."

"What would I even say?"

"Keep it simple," David suggested.

Before hanging up, Sarah said, "I hate to mention the baby. I don't want to jinx anything, but I can't imagine what else would be enough to get her here."

Tony cut in a moment later. "If it's as bad as you say, why stay there?"

David said, "I have to stay. This isn't just about Lucy. There's a whole town that has been terrorized by one man who thought a little money gave him the right to do whatever he wanted. Right now, York's anger is directed at me. If I leave, he wins. I can't walk away and let him choose another target."

"If you stay, you could get yourself killed."

"I'm counting on York being angrier than he is smart. All he has to do is come for me, and I'll make him regret every last thing he's done to this town."

"I'll be there by tomorrow night," Tony said harshly.

Sarah's voice rose with emotion. "No. Please."

Tony said something to his wife out of earshot, then said, "I won't be heading down alone. I'll talk to Dean and some of the men here. Charles might even have ideas on how to take York down. That bastard might rule his town, but he's about to get an ass-kicking—Fort Mavis–style."

It would have been funny, if the situation hadn't been so dire.

Sarah proved to be a better liar than she'd thought, because Lucy had called Wyatt a short time later and asked him to drive her to the airport. Now she was standing beside her truck, looking as if she were telling Wyatt she'd be right back.

David's heart began to pound wildly when Lucy looked up and met his eyes while walking toward him. He walked out of the barn to meet her halfway.

She stopped a few feet from him, and it was all he could do not to close the distance between them and kiss her until all of this faded away. He held his ground instead. "Wyatt said you're going to stay with Sarah and Tony for a while."

Lucy clasped her hands in front of her so hard, her knuckles were white. "I am. Sarah asked me to, and it's probably a good idea for you and me to have some time away from each other."

Her words ripped at David's core. He didn't want that at all, but it was what he knew had to happen. "Tell her I said hello."

A range of emotions passed over Lucy's face—shock, disappointment, disbelief. "I don't know how long I'll be gone."

Keep it simple. "I'll watch over everything here."

Lucy blinked a few times quickly. "When I come back, you should look for another place to train your horses."

"If that's what you want."

Her eyes welled up with tears. "That's all you have to say?"

He wanted to tell her he loved her. He wanted to explain that he wasn't leaving her as she feared, but actually doing this to ensure they had a future together. The words were on the tip of his tongue, but what then? No, this was the only way. He arched an eyebrow as if to say, *What else is there?*

Lucy spun on her heel and stormed to the passenger side of her truck. If the force she used to slam the door behind her after she climbed in was anything to go by, she was wishing him bodily harm. He told himself that was a good thing, at least for now. The angrier she was with him, the easier it would be to keep her away from the ranch.

Ron surprised David by coming to stand beside him. "Where's Lucy going?"

David considered not telling him, but the thing about giving a person a chance to prove themselves was it had to be all or nothing. "To stay with friends until things calm down around here."

"Good idea."

David glanced at Ron's profile, then turned back to watch Lucy's truck pull away. "If York comes looking for trouble, will it be hard for you to choose a side?"

Ron was quiet a moment. "I called Michelle today and told her what I almost done yesterday. She started crying. She told me she didn't want me around her or the babies."

"I'm sorry to hear that."

"Normally, something like that would have sent me to the nearest bar. My wife and kids aren't at a bar, though. I can't drink my way back to them. I told her I'll never work for York again, and that I took a job here. We've got six months before the new baby comes, and I asked her to take that much time to make up her mind. I'm taking her out to dinner on Thursday. It might sound silly to take your own wife on a date, but I want to start over with her." His voice constricted with emotion. "I don't actually care much how it sounds. All I care is that she said yes." Ron cleared his throat. "Now, if you don't mind, I'd like to see how you work with a horse who has tried to kill people. I'm thinking there might be something I can learn there."

David nodded and turned to walk with Ron toward Tia's paddock. He told himself he was in the right place, doing what needed to be done.

Life was all about making choices, though.

He hoped lying to Lucy had been the right one.

Chapter Twenty-One

Three days later, Lucy was helping Sarah clean up the breakfast plates. She kept telling Sarah to let her do everything, but Sarah refused to sit still. Lucy had worried at first, but Sarah looked healthy and maybe moving around was good for her condition.

Whatever that condition was. Sarah hadn't been specific.

Sarah seemed edgy, and that had Lucy concerned. Lucy was keeping up with e-mails at night, but for now she was devoting her days to keeping Sarah happy and relaxed. "There's a new movie playing in town. Looks like a good one. Would you like to go to a matinee?"

Sarah closed the dishwasher door. "I'd rather lie down."

"Are you feeling okay? Should I call Tony?"

Sarah placed her hand over her stomach. "I'm fine. Just missing him, I guess."

Lucy walked over and gave Sarah a hug. She wanted to say she knew exactly how it felt to miss someone, but at least Sarah was missing someone who loved her and who would return. Lucy hadn't gotten over how eager David had seemed to see her go. "He'll be back before you know it. He's training a horse in—what town did you say?"

Sarah tensed. "In Van Horn, I think."

"I thought you said Sanderson."

"Did I? Then that's where he must be."

An awful feeling spread through Lucy. She didn't want to consider the possibility, but as bile threatened to surge upward, she asked slowly, "Sarah, are you lying to me?"

Sarah turned away from her, gripped the edge of the kitchen counter, and said, "Please don't ask me that."

The room spun, and Lucy leaned on the counter for support. "Look at me, Sarah."

Sarah kept her face averted. "I can't."

"Because you can't lie to my face, but you can lie to the window?" Lucy snapped. She hated that she was even accusing Sarah at all, but more than that, she hated how Sarah was looking guiltier by the minute.

Sarah turned around and met Lucy's eyes. Her hands were shaking at her sides. "Why would I lie to you, Lucy? I don't feel well, that's all. I told you, I need to lie down."

With a rush, Lucy felt like an ass. "Oh my God, Sarah, I'm so sorry. I warned you that I'm not myself lately. I'm an idiot."

Sarah looked away. "It's fine, Lucy. I'm not upset, but if it's all right with you, I want to rest awhile."

"Sure," Lucy said quietly. "I'll check in on you later. Tell me if there is anything I can do. Anything at all."

Once alone in the kitchen, Lucy paced back and forth, berating herself for what she'd said to Sarah. *I can't go on thinking everyone is out to get me or to fool me. That's no way to live.*

I was wrong about Ted.

Wrong about David.

Oh God, I can't believe how wrong I was about David. I thought he loved me. I thought he was a man I could give my heart to.

I told myself the ranch was all that mattered, but I don't care about the ranch. If giving it to David would make him love me, I'd sign it over to him in a heartbeat.

What does that say about me?

Lucy had barely slept since she'd arrived in Fort Mavis. She kept going over her relationship with David, looking for a hint that he was the kind of man who would sleep with her just to get her land. She couldn't think of one single time when he'd been anything but kind, generous, or loving with her. It didn't make sense.

How could he let me walk away like that?

Why not fight for what we have?

If he cared about me at all, wouldn't he have said something when I told him to find another place to train his horses?

He hasn't called to see if I'm okay.

Not a text.

Nothing.

Because he doesn't love me.

What will it take for me to understand that? When will my stupid heart stop going wild every time the phone rings? It's not going to be David.

I need to stop running for the door every time the doorbell rings.

He's not coming.

A week had passed. One of the hardest in David's life. There hadn't been any response from York, and David was beginning to question if he'd been right to send Lucy away.

He was unloading a shipment of hay, glad to lose himself in the physical distraction of the task, when Wyatt walked out of the barn with Tony. Wyatt joked, "There's enough men here willing to unload the hay, but David likes to show off those muscles. Ain't no women around to impress, though, David, so you might as well put that shirt back on."

Tony shook his head and looked skyward. "David, Wyatt talks more than you do. I didn't think that was humanly possible."

Despite the sarcasm, Wyatt and Tony had hit it off. David jumped down from the back of the trailer and picked up his shirt, using it to wipe the sweat off his forehead. "I heard from Charles. He said he knows someone who knows Ted's father. He didn't explain how that would help, but he said he'd get back to me about the situation here."

Wyatt hooked his thumbs in his belt loops. "Any word from Lucy?"

Tony answered, "Sarah says they're both fine."

Wyatt looked at David. "You call her yet?"

David slumped his shoulders. "Don't know what I'd say at this point. Unless it's the truth."

Wyatt added, "I enjoyed meeting your friend Mason. Nice of him to drop in considering what a busy man he must be. He's a character, ain't he?"

"He sure is," David said.

Wyatt cackled. "His suggestion for what to do when she finds out was a hoot."

David snapped, "I'm glad this situation is amusing to you."

Wyatt shook his head sadly. "Son, you've got to keep your sense of humor. This will all work out, and one day we can sit around and laugh about it. I do think you need a plan, though. She will find out, and when she does, I hope you've thought of a really good way of apologizing."

Tony looked at Wyatt. "Saving her life won't be enough?"

Wyatt shot them both a toothy grin. "Shoot, you're talking about women here. The workings of their minds are complicated, but certain rules apply in all situations. You lie, you apologize. You lie big, you apologize big. For that, you need a plan. You convinced her best friend to lie to her. Flowers won't cover this."

Tony made a distasteful face. "Mason said you should think about something Lucy really wants and get it for her. I hate that I can hear his voice in my head."

David chuckled at that. Mason's successful career in television wasn't a surprise. He had a memorable presence. "There's nothing Lucy wants that I know of. Except for her brother to answer her calls. It's not like I could do anything about that." David stopped as he considered what he'd said. "Unless you'd know how to find him, Wyatt."

"I might," Wyatt said. "What would you say to him if I did?"

David shrugged his shirt back on. "I'd tell him it doesn't matter what happened between him and Lucy in the past. She needs him now. He could come back, help make sure York doesn't win this fight, and show Lucy he really does care about her."

Tony added, "I'd threaten to kick his ass all the way home, but your way might work, too."

Wyatt cackled again. "David, I knew you'd be good for this town. I gotta say, I like your choice in friends."

Chapter Twenty-Two

One week became two, and Lucy started to worry about things she could no longer keep to herself. She and Sarah were on their way back from a short walk after dinner when she asked, "Did you and Tony have a fight before he left?"

Sarah stopped to pick a wildflower. She twirled it between her fingers. "Of course not."

"Is he coming back? You can tell me if your marriage is in trouble. I won't tell anyone."

"It's not."

"Then where is he, Sarah? And don't tell me again that he's training someone's horse in Sanderson. You look miserable when you say it and, honestly, I don't believe you." *There. I may be an awful person, but I said what I think.*

"You're right. He's not in Sanderson."

"Then where is he?"

"He's in Mavis with David."

That took a moment to sink in. "With David? You mean, at my ranch?"

"That's exactly what I mean."

"I don't understand."

Sarah leaned over and picked up a second flower, then held them both up. "No two flowers are exactly the same. Did you know that? They may look the same, but they're as unique as people are."

With her heart thudding in her chest, Lucy asked, "How does this have anything to do with Tony being in Mavis with David?"

"Lies can be like flowers. Not all of them are bad."

"Sarah, what are you saying?" That sickening feeling returned. *No, not you, too, Sarah. Don't tell me I can't trust you, either. Please don't do that to me.*

"David asked us if we'd help get you out of Mavis for a while, and we agreed."

Lucy swayed on her feet. "So, the baby?"

"It's perfectly healthy."

"You lied to me."

"Yes," Sarah said, wringing her hands in front of her. "But it was a lie to protect you. David said York was preparing to do something awful, and he wanted you to be somewhere safe."

"And you believed him."

Sarah froze. "Completely."

"Then you're a better person than I am, because I'm trying to wrap my head around the fact that I can't believe anything anyone tells me." She glared at Sarah. "Not even those who call themselves my best friends."

Sarah's cheeks reddened, and she advanced on Lucy. "Stop right there. The more you say, the more you'll have to apologize for later. I have been nothing but a good friend to you. David has been in love with you since the first time he met you. Tony is risking his life because he cares about you and that damn ranch I'm not even sure why you want. I have a baby on the way and a husband who might just get himself killed because David thinks the people in your town need protecting as well. If none of us have earned your trust by now, then please do stop talking to all of us. Really, you'd be doing us a favor." She threw the flowers down into the grass and turned away from Lucy.

Lucy grabbed her by the arm. "Wait." Her mind was racing. "I'm sorry."

Sarah stopped but didn't turn back toward her. "You should be. You're wrong about David. You say we're friends, but if you think I would ever do anything to hurt you, then we have different definitions of friendship."

Lucy lowered her hand. "I get so scared sometimes, I stop thinking straight."

Sarah turned. "You're not the only one who's afraid. I haven't slept since Tony left. David doesn't know if he can save your ranch or help the town, but he's willing to try. He doesn't even know if that's enough to get you to forgive him. The only reason we all lied to you is because we knew you wouldn't leave if we told you the truth. Your ex-fiancé is a dangerous man, and he's going to hurt someone. No one knows who, but we're all waiting for it happen. I don't blame David for lying to you, and I'm not sorry I did. I'd do it again because I love you."

"I—I—" Lucy started to speak, then stopped. She was momentarily crushed beneath the profound reality of how little she'd done to deserve the love of the woman who was standing before her. Saying sorry again wouldn't begin to express how remorseful she felt. "What can I do, Sarah? How can I help?"

Sarah's eyes teared up. "I don't know what to do besides wait and pray, but it would be a lot easier to do both if I had a friend at my side."

Lucy linked arms with Sarah and started walking back to the house with her. "You don't think we should head to Mavis? See if there is some way we can stop anyone from getting hurt?"

Sarah paused. "Tony asked me to stay here and wait for him. I promised I would, and I don't lie." She shot Lucy a quick glance. "Well, usually I don't."

It wasn't funny, but Lucy laughed a little at the joke.

"I thought David didn't care, but it was because he didn't think I'd go any other way." *He lied to protect me. He put my safety above his own, let me think the worst of him. My mom always said love was about sacrifice, and David was willing to sacrifice everything . . . for me. He wants me to be happy even if it means not having me.* "He does love me."

Sarah rolled her eyes. "You are smart when it comes to business, but when it comes to love—yeesh. How could you miss how much that man loves you?"

"He's never said it."

She started walking again. "Yes, he did—a thousand times with his actions. Some men say the words easily, and it doesn't mean anything. Cowboys aren't like that. I have a feeling that when David finally says he loves you, he'll be down on one knee."

"If he forgives me for doubting him," Lucy said, voicing her greatest fear.

"If you can say that, you still have a lot to learn about David."

Chapter Twenty-Three

David was on his way back from picking up grain from a local feedstore when he noticed a white truck riding his bumper. A quick look in his rearview mirror confirmed it was York. David took out his phone and dialed Wyatt. "I'm out on Park Road, heading west. It looks like it's about to go down."

"Don't do anything foolish, David," Wyatt warned.

David wasn't completely sure if Sheriff Dodd had been bought out by York. He believed it was unlikely, but to be safe, Wyatt would also make sure there was someone else there to witness whatever happened.

David would have answered, but his vehicle jerked forward as York slammed his truck into the back of David's. He dropped his phone into his shirt pocket and grabbed the steering wheel with both hands to steady the vehicle.

York rammed his truck into the back of David's classic pickup again, then moved off to one side and tried to run the truck off the road. David sped up and moved his truck to the middle of the road, praying no one would come from the other direction. He didn't need to outrun York forever, just long enough for the sheriff to get there. If the plan worked, York would be angry, drunk, or just plain stupid enough to say something in front of the sheriff that would get him arrested. If it went south, the sheriff wouldn't have to wait for David to turn himself in for killing York. He could cuff him while he still stood over the man's bloody body. One way or another, York's reign over Mavis would end that day.

In the distance, David saw a car headed their way and swore. He moved into the right lane, and York quickly took advantage of that opportunity. He swung his truck into the lane beside David's and forced him off the road.

David would have kept driving, but one of his wheels caught in a ditch and his truck rolled. He hit his head several times before the vehicle came to a rest on its side. Dazed, David released his seat belt and wiped blood from one of his eyes. *Shit.*

York pulled up beside David's truck and got out with a gun in his hand. The car that had been coming in the other direction pulled over, and a young man got out. "Is anyone hurt?"

York looked away, and David used the chance to push up the passenger door and haul himself out. There was no time to bring his rifle with him. He tried to wave the man away, but it was too late. The man saw the gun in York's hand and asked, "What's going on?"

York snarled, "If you like your job, Bill, get back in your car and drive away."

Bill looked past York and saw David standing beside his truck waving for him to go. "Put the gun away, Mr. York. Nothing Harmon has done is worth shooting him over."

David stepped away from the truck. If he could get a little closer, he might be able to knock the gun out of York's hand. His vision blurred temporarily from blood dripping down his forehead. He wiped it away, but the move caught York's attention, and he swung back toward David.

"Not such a big man now, are you, Harmon?" York asked snidely. "I hope you beg me not to shoot you. I still will, but hearing you beg would make up for the trouble you've caused this town."

"This town or you, York?" David growled. "You don't have to do this, you know. There is still time to stop before you go too far."

"Too far? I should have killed you the first time I met you. I knew you'd be trouble. But I thought I could scare you off. My mistake."

"Is killing me worth going to prison?" David asked, hoping to stall him enough for the sheriff to arrive.

"Prison? I'm not going to prison. My family owns this town."

David nodded toward the dented truck. "Someone will see the evidence and follow it back to you. You may think the whole town is on your payroll, but it's not."

York let out an evil laugh. "This truck isn't even mine. One of my men left it at my place. It'll be my word against his if they link it to your death."

Behind York, Bill said, "I can't let you do this."

York turned slowly and, before either David or Bill had time to react, he shot him. Bill crumpled to the ground, and David ran to his side. Bill gasped for air, but the shot had gone through his shoulder. Though he was bleeding profusely, he'd live. If York didn't shoot him again.

David stood between the man and York. He regretted not grabbing his rifle. He'd hoped to have time for that once Bill left. It was a mistake they might both pay for with their lives. York was sweaty and nervous. He wasn't an experienced killer, and David intended to take advantage of that. "Tell me, York, how do you intend to drive back to town? You can't use the truck you came in. Not if you want it to look like someone else killed me. You can't take Bill's. Did you think about that?"

York looked at the three vehicles as if that part of the plan hadn't occurred to him. "Shut up. I need to think."

"You won't have time to walk anywhere. Not once the law comes. I called the sheriff already."

York's hand shook with the gun in it. "No, you didn't."

David shrugged. "You'd better be pretty damn sure before you shoot me. Texas has the death penalty, and no one looks kindly on murdering unarmed people." A siren in the distance announced the arrival of the sheriff. "There he is now. You can kill me, but then you'll need to kill Bill and the sheriff, too. That's a whole lot of murders. And I hear there is a fast track to death row when you kill a lawman."

York looked close to pissing himself, but he still had the gun aimed at David. "I'll tell the sheriff you shot Bill. Bill, if you don't want to die, you'll say that's what happened. Do you understand me?"

Bill didn't answer.

The sheriff got out of his vehicle slowly with a gun in his hand. "Ted, put the gun down."

York kept his gun aimed at David. "Thank God you're here, Dodd. I was just about to call you. He shot Bill. I pulled over just in time to see it happen."

"Put the gun down, York."

"You believe me, don't you?" York asked desperately.

An SUV pulled up. Tony jumped out with a shotgun. He aimed it right at York.

The sheriff said, "Carlton, get back in your vehicle. I can handle this."

Tony didn't move. "Don't worry, I won't shoot him unless you miss."

David sank down to check on Bill. He took off his shirt and pressed it to his bleeding wound. "Someone needs to call an ambulance. He's bleeding pretty bad."

The sheriff spoke into his radio and called for an ambulance and backup. All the while he kept his gun aimed on York.

A black Lincoln Town Car pulled up and an older gentleman, still ruddy and muscular from years of manual work, stepped out of his car. He walked right up to York and backhanded him across the face, sending the man to his knees. He kicked the gun away from him and growled, "You stupid bastard. If you kill someone, we lose everything."

The sheriff rushed in and cuffed York. He spoke to the man who had just taken down York in a tone David couldn't hear. The older man's voice boomed back: "You were right to call me, Dan. I needed to see this for myself. Yes, take him in."

Bill stirred, and David told him help was coming. Tony kept his shotgun up and cocked.

York's attention was on the older man. "Dad, it's all Harmon's fault. He—"

The old man straightened, his face ugly with revulsion. "Shut up, Ted. I should let your ass rot in jail, but it would break your mother's heart. You'll get a lawyer, but not the expensive one you're hoping for. That one will be working on the pile of shit lawsuits you brought on us."

"Dad—"

The older man turned away, got in his car, and drove off. The sheriff put York in the back of his car.

An ambulance pulled up. The sheriff spoke to Bill briefly as he was being put on a stretcher and taken away. Bill retold what he'd come across and how York had shot him.

The sheriff looked at David and said, "You might want to see a doctor, too, David."

I might just do that. David touched his forehead and almost went to his knees when dizziness hit him.

Tony was beside him, propping him up with his shoulder. "I'll take him."

Suddenly feeling dazed, David said, "Thanks, Tony." Odd how life came full circle.

Walking him over to his SUV, Tony said, "You saved my life once. I've waited a long time for the chance to save your sorry hide."

A detailed statement would wait until later. As they pulled back onto the road, David rested his head on one hand and said, "I almost feel sorry for York now that I've met his father."

Tony shook his head. "Not even you can save them all, David. Let that one go."

Won't argue that one. "He made his choice; now he has to live with it."

Tony remained quiet for a moment, then said, "You came real close to dying today."

David grunted.

"You and Lucy need to live in Fort Mavis. I'm not impressed with this town."

Something about how Tony had dismissed the town and everything that had happened that day struck David's funny bone. He laughed, which only made his head hurt more.

Tony looked over, then back at the road. "Are we done here? I'm ready to go home."

"Me too," David said with a groan. Home being wherever Lucy was.

Lucy and Sarah were on a plane so fast neither of them took a thing with them. Tony had called and said David was at the hospital being treated for a concussion. They were keeping him one night for observation. Tony gave them an outline of what had happened. Thankfully, Charles's plane was still there or Lucy and Sarah would have stolen the first one they came across.

They rushed to the hospital where Tony met them. He hugged Sarah for a long heartfelt moment, then looked at Lucy. "Go easy on David. He's had a really bad day."

Lucy wiped a tear away from the corner of her eye. Tony was the master of understatement. "I will. I love him. Nothing else matters." She threw her arms around Tony and hugged him so tightly, he laughed. "Thank you for everything."

When she pulled back, Lucy saw someone in a suit that made her look twice. "Steven?" The man turned, and Lucy's heart leaped into her throat. Even though he was thin, he looked exactly the way she'd hoped he would. He was sober, his hair was neatly trimmed, and he met her eyes like a man who had found his footing again. "What are you doing here?"

He walked over and his shoulders slumped a bit. "David asked me to come back. He said having me here would help, but I wasn't with him when York went after him. I'm sorry, Lucy. I failed you again."

Lucy wrapped her arms around her brother and hugged him with all the love in her. This was her chance to tell him what she'd felt for a long time. "You. Never. Failed. Me." She kept hugging him. "Mavis. The ranch. They're not what matters. You and I were never meant for ranch life, Steven. This isn't where our hearts are. Mom and Dad wouldn't have wanted this for us. It's not what they meant when they asked us to try to hold on to it. We matter more than a plot of land. All I care about is you."

Steven wrapped his arms around her and quietly sobbed against her neck. "I'm so sorry, Lucy. I had to get out. I wanted to talk to you so many times, but I was ashamed of how I left. I didn't think you'd want to see me."

Lucy held her brother's face in her hands and said, "You're my brother, Steven. Nothing you do can change that."

Steven nodded and wiped his face. "David told me you'd say that. We need to talk about the ranch, though. I have a job in Nevada. It's a good one. I can help you out now. If you still need me."

"Money isn't necessary, but I will always need you." As she said the words, she realized how much she meant them. So much of what she'd thought mattered didn't. Steven was alive and looking as if he was on a good path. That's all that mattered.

"You found yourself a good man."

Lucy smiled through the tears still pouring down her cheeks. "I know exactly how lucky I am. I want to go see him, but I don't want you to leave."

"I'll be right here when you're done."

Lucy wanted to ask him to promise. She felt a familiar fear nip at her heels, but she kicked it back. No amount of promising would make Steven stay if he wanted to go. She couldn't decide what he would do, but she was in control of who she was and what she did. She had always believed in people, and it was time to start doing that again.

Believing was a choice. It wasn't easy, but without it, life held no magic. She gave her brother a kiss on the cheek and headed in to see David.

He was sitting up in his hospital bed with a bandage on his head, looking miserable until he saw her. His face lit up, and she had no doubt how he felt about her. He looked down at his hospital gown. "Not exactly how I hoped to look when I saw you next."

Lucy ran across the room and threw herself into his arms. They kissed long and deeply, like the reunited lovers they were. When they finally broke the kiss, Lucy said, "I love you, David Harmon. I love you so much, I'll beat your ass if you ever do anything that foolish again. I want to marry you, raise a family, and live happily ever after with you. We can live in Mavis or Fort Mavis or on the moon. I don't care as long as we're together."

David chuckled and hugged her tightly to his chest. "You stole my speech."

"You stole my heart."

They kissed again deeply. "I have missed you so much. I'm sorry about lying to you."

Lucy hugged him tightly. "I understand why you did it. I'm sorry I doubted you. I never will again."

"I love you."

"I love you, too. Now shut up and kiss me again."

"Gladly." And he did. A lot. She started smiling even through their kisses.

He raised his head, sporting a huge smile of his own. "Now that we have that settled, can you get me out of here? I want to go home."

"Which one?"

"Whichever one you're at will be just fine."

Chapter Twenty-Four

On a beautiful sunny afternoon two months later, Lucy stood with her arm linked with Steven's, waiting for the music to begin. The flurry of getting primped and made up was done. All she had to do now was walk down the aisle, not trip over the hem of the most beautiful dress she'd ever worn, and say, "I do."

Lined up in front of her were Chelle, Melanie, and Sarah in classic navy bridesmaid dresses. David had said he wanted Lucy to have the wedding of her dreams; his only request was that they marry soon. He was impatient for her to be Mrs. Harmon.

Lucy had chosen to have their ceremony on the lawn of Ribblan Ranch, their new home in Fort Mavis. It would be a celebration not only of their wedding, but of the new life they were starting together. It was a simple setting: just white chairs in rows facing a makeshift altar beneath a large tree near the house. The view of the valley below was spectacular, though.

She couldn't look out at the people waiting for the ceremony to start and not reflect on how grateful she was for how her life had changed. David was a large part of it, but even though they were marrying, she'd paid him back the full amount he'd loaned her for her ranch. Saving her ranch, knowing that she'd done what her mother had asked her to, had freed her.

She and David had talked about the future of her partnership with TAP. Although David loved trying out the toys and reading her blog, he asked her if it was her dream job. When Lucy had admitted that marketing was her dream, but not necessarily marketing for one business, he encouraged her to look into helping other companies, also. Lucy had been afraid it would take her away from David and their new home, but he assured her they could make it work. And she believed him—because David didn't say anything he didn't mean. She trusted him in a way she never thought she would trust anyone again.

The open setting allowed Lucy to see David as he stood with the minister, waiting for her. Their eyes met, and even across the distance, she saw his love for her shining in his eyes. She blew him a kiss and hugged Steven's arm to her side.

Steven bent toward her and said, "Mom and Dad are looking down, and they're proud of you."

Lucy glanced up at him. "You too, Steven. Your suggestion that we give the ranch to Wyatt, but keep the mineral rights would have made both of them happy. He has been family to us, and he loves that place."

"Think they'll ever find oil there?" Steven asked, glancing across at Wyatt.

Lucy shrugged. "I don't honestly care. I have everything I want." She smiled up at her brother. "There would have been a huge hole in my heart today without you here."

Steven ducked his head in a show of shame. "I'm back, and I'm not going anywhere. Well, I am going back to my job in Reno, but I'll visit often."

Sarah turned around and said, "David asked me to read over the vows he wrote. He is so romantic. How did yours come out?"

Lucy gulped in surprise. "He wrote his own vows?"

Sarah's eyes rounded, and she smacked her forehead with one hand. "Did he say it was a surprise? I wouldn't forget something like that, would I?" She turned forward again. "Pretend I said nothing."

The music began, and Chelle slowly walked down the aisle. Melanie followed her. Sarah went last.

The music changed to the wedding march, and Lucy started down the aisle, holding Steven's arm. At the altar, the minister asked, "Who gives this woman?"

"My brother," Lucy said before Steven had a chance to answer. She couldn't help it. She was simply that happy to have him by her side.

Steven blinked back a tear and kissed Lucy's cheek. "I do," he said, then shook David's hand. "If my father were here, he would have said that he couldn't have found a better man for his daughter."

David's smile widened. He took Lucy's hand, and they both moved to stand in front of the minister. In all of Lucy's life, she'd never seen anything more beautiful than the man she loved looking across at her, waiting for the minister to speak. She hadn't written her own vows, but she wasn't worried. It was hard to be afraid of anything with David at her side.

The minister welcomed everyone. At Lucy and David's request, he kept the opening short and simple. He asked for the rings. Jace, who was almost seven, walked up the aisle with two rings on a white pillow. He handed them to the minister, then turned to David.

"David, do we get to eat after this?"

Everyone laughed.

David nodded.

Melanie, Jace's mother, called him over. Jace ignored her, his focus remaining on David. "Mom said getting married means you might have a baby soon, but she said that won't change how much you love me. Do you make the baby at the wedding or after?"

David ruffled Jace's hair and winked. "After. But you should ask Charles about that."

Satisfied, Jace went to stand beside Charles and took him by the hand with an expression that implied he would do just that the first chance he got.

A roar of laughter erupted, and Lucy joined in. If the wedding was any indicator, a life with David would be filled with love and joy.

The minister asked, "David, you said you wrote something you wanted to read?"

David nodded and took a piece of paper out of his pocket. A slight shake in his hand was the only indicator that he might be nervous. He cleared his throat. "My parents would say I've always been a bit stubborn. I get something in my head, and there's no shaking it out. Until you, Lucy, I didn't know my heart was the same. I knew you were the one for me from the very first time we met. The road here was bumpy, but I don't regret a moment of it because it brought you to me. I promise to love you, to cherish you, to challenge you for the rest of our lives. I promise to be faithful, loving, and supportive of anything you choose to do. Give me your forever, Lucy, and I'll give you mine."

"Yes," Lucy said as David slid a ring onto her finger.

Smiling, Lucy gently teased David. "I was not told we were writing our own vows, but it's not hard to know what to say. David, your faith in me, your belief that I could get to this place, is probably what I first loved about you. I don't know, though, because I could go on and on if I tried to list what I love about you. You have a heart the size of Texas. You are kind when others would judge. You are strong when others would run. I was lost when you found me, and you led me back not only to myself but also to my family. I promise to love you, to cherish you, to challenge you, too, for the rest of our lives. I promise to be faithful, loving, and supportive of anything you choose to do. Give me your forever, David, because you sure as hell have mine."

The minister made a tsk sound.

"Yes," David said.

She slid the other ring on his finger.

The minister looked out at the crowd. "Is there anyone here who knows a reason why these two should not wed?"

With preplanned synchronization, the wedding party turned to look at Chelle, who had accidentally spoken up at Sarah and Tony's wedding.

Chelle blushed, but took the ribbing with a smile and proclaimed, "Not this time."

Laughter echoed through those gathered, leaving a few whispering questions about why.

"Then I now pronounce you husband and wife. You may now kiss the bride."

David didn't need to be told twice.

After the ceremony, David and Lucy made their way through the crowd, toward his parents. When he'd called them and announced his engagement, he expected them to express some sort of disappointment. He hadn't known if it would be because they thought it would keep him farther from them, or because she wasn't working in a profession they approved of. He hadn't given them a chance. He'd immediately informed them that Lucy was the love of his life, and he expected them to respect his choice.

His father had taken his time answering and eventually said, "David, we will love her if for no other reason than you do. All we ever wanted was the best for you."

"You mean what you thought was the best for me."

In a sad voice, his mother had said, "When you have your own children, David, you'll see that it's not easy. Yes, we pushed you, but look at the man you've become."

"A horse trainer," David said, echoing the disgust they'd once shown toward his career choice.

His father had sighed. "A fine man. That's all we ever wanted for you. No, we didn't approve of all of your choices, but you've made a good life for yourself. What we want now is to be part of it. We don't see you nearly enough. Bring this Lucy home for us to meet. She might be just what we all need."

Lucy had been. It might have been because she'd lost her own parents, but she took to his like a long-lost daughter. She even seemed to enjoy his father's long-winded stories and his mother's questionable cooking.

Lucy said he brought her family back to her, but she'd done the same for him.

After giving Lucy a long emotional hug, David's mother asked, "Lucy, I didn't realize you were an author, too. Sarah was just telling us that you also write stories. Are any of them published? I'd love to read one."

Lucy blushed and shook her head. "Sarah has a wild imagination." David heard her mutter under her breath, "And a potentially short life."

To save her, he asked, "Wasn't Jace a hoot?"

His parents agreed, and the conversation turned to how soon David and Lucy thought they might be having a child of their own. Normally, it would have been an awkward conversation, but it was a whole heck of a lot less awkward than explaining to his mother why he enjoyed helping Lucy find new material for her blog.

Mason joined them with Chelle at his side. David introduced them to his parents. Another couple came by to meet David's family, and Mason used the opportunity to pull Lucy and him aside. He took out an envelope and waved it in the air. "I don't want to say that I'm the reason the two of you are together, but—"

David laughed. "But you will."

Mason smiled widely. "I didn't mind helping out. When it comes to knowing how to win a woman's heart, I'm gifted."

Chelle slapped her hand on his chest and rolled her eyes. "It's his humility that I fell in love with first."

Mason looked down at Chelle and arched an eyebrow. "Humility. Is that your nickname for it this week?"

Chelle gave him a playful shove. "You will pay for that one."

"Bring it on," Mason said with a laugh.

David groaned.

All smiles, Lucy hugged him while watching Chelle and Mason. "Our friends are crazy, but I love them."

David kissed the top of Lucy's head. "Me too."

Mason handed the envelope over to David and said, "I heard you didn't have plans for your honeymoon yet. I have a yacht ready and waiting in Galveston with instructions to tour the Caribbean for two weeks."

"Really?" Lucy squealed happily. "Mason, that is too generous. David, we're going away on a yacht!" She rushed over and hugged Chelle, then Mason. "I can't believe you would do this for us."

Mason made a face. "There's only one thing you should know. I meant to change the name of it, but haven't had a chance to yet. It's called *Little Fucker*. It was a joke from when I was younger. I could see if I can have something done fast if it'll be a problem."

"*Little Fucker?*" David repeated, remembering the toy that Lucy had affectionately, officially given that nickname to the second time they'd used it. He winked at Lucy. Life had a way of circling back, and this time with a wicked sense of humor. He liked it. "Sounds like our kind of yacht."

Lucy blushed, but she agreed with a naughty smile that meant she knew what he was thinking and completely agreed.

Acknowledgments

I am so grateful to everyone who was part of the process of creating *Taking Charge*. Special thanks to the following:

My very patient beta readers. You know who you are. Thank you for kicking my butt when I need it.

My editors: Karen Lawson, Janet Hitchcock, Marion Archer, and Krista Stroever.

My Roadies for making me smile each day when I log on to my computer. So many of you have become friends. Was there life before the Roadies? I'm sure there was, but it wasn't as much fun.

My husband, Tony, who is a saint—simple as that. I don't know how I'd meet a deadline without him.

About the Author

Ruth Cardello was born the youngest of eleven children in a small city in northern Rhode Island. She lived in Boston, Paris, Orlando, and New York before coming full circle and moving back to Rhode Island. She now lives in Massachusetts. Before turning her attention to writing, Ruth was an educator for twenty years, eleven of which she spent as a kindergarten teacher. She is the author of over twenty novels, including *Bedding the Billionaire*, which was a *New York Times* and *USA Today* bestseller. *Taking Charge* follows *Tycoon Takedown*; *Taken, Not Spurred*; and *Taken Home* as the fourth book in the Lone Star Burn series. Learn about Ruth's new releases and sales by signing up for her newsletter at www.RuthCardello.com/Signup.

Printed in Great Britain
by Amazon